Helen McCloy and

>>> This title is part of T[...] [...]d to making available out-[...] ic crime writers.

Crime fiction has always held up a mirror to society. The Victorians were fascinated by sensational murder and the emerging science of detection; now we are obsessed with the forensic detail of violent death. And no other genre has so captivated and enthralled readers.

Vast troves of classic crime writing have for a long time been unavailable to all but the most dedicated frequenters of second-hand bookshops. The advent of digital publishing means that we are now able to bring you the backlists of a huge range of titles by classic and contemporary crime writers, some of which have been out of print for decades.

From the genteel amateur private eyes of the Golden Age and the femmes fatales of pulp fiction, to the morally ambiguous hard-boiled detectives of mid twentieth-century America and their descendants who walk our twenty-first century streets, The Murder Room has it all. >>>

The Murder Room
Where Criminal Minds Meet

themurderroom.com

Helen Worrell Clarkson McCloy (1904–1994)

Born in New York City, Helen McCloy was educated in Brooklyn, at the Quaker Friends' school, and later studied at the Sorbonne in Paris. From 1927–1932 she worked for Hearst's Universal News Service after which she freelanced as an art critic and contributor to various publications, including the *London Morning Post*. Shortly after her return to the US she published her first novel, *Dance of Death*, in 1933, featuring her popular series detective-psychologist Basil Willing. The novel *Through a Glass Darkly*, a puzzle in the supernatural tradition of John Dickson Carr, is the eighth in the Basil Willing series and is generally acknowledged to be her masterpiece. In 1946 McCloy married fellow author Davis Dresser, famed for his Mike Shayne novels. Together they founded Halliday & McCloy literary agency as well as the Torquil Publishing Company. The couple had one daughter, Chloe, and their marriage ended in 1961. In 1950 Helen McCloy became the first woman president of the Mystery Writers of America and in 1953 she was awarded an Edgar by the same organisation for her criticism. In 1987, critic and mystery writer H.R.F. Keating included her Basil Willing title *Mr Splitfoot* in a list of the 100 best crime and mystery books ever published.

By Helen McCloy

Dr Basil Willing

Dance of Death (1938)
The Man in the Moonlight (1940)
The Deadly Truth (1941)
Who's Calling? (1942)
Cue for Murder (1942)
The Goblin Market (1943)
The One That Got Away (1945)
Through a Glass, Darkly (1950)
Alias Basil Willing (1951)
The Long Body (1955)
Two-Thirds of a Ghost (1956)
Mr Splitfoot (1968)
Burn This (1980)
The Pleasant Assassin and Other Cases of Dr Basil Willing (short stories) (2003)

Standalone novels

Do Not Disturb (1943)
Panic (1944)
She Walks Alone (1948)
Better Off Dead (1951)
Unfinished Crime (1954)
The Slayer and the Slain (1957)
Before I Die (1963)
The Singing Diamonds and Other Stories (short stories) (1965)
The Further Side of Fear (1967)
A Question of Time (1971)
A Change of Heart (1973)
The Sleepwalker (1974)
Minotaur Country (1975)
The Changeling Conspiracy (1976)
The Impostor (1977)
The Smoking Mirror (1979)

Two-thirds of a Ghost

Helen McCloy

An Orion book

Copyright © Pollinger Ltd as Literary Executor of the Estate of Helen McCloy 1956

The right of Helen McCloy to be identified as the author of this work has been asserted in accordance with the Copyright, Designs and Patents Act 1988.

This edition published by
The Orion Publishing Group Ltd
Orion House
5 Upper St Martin's Lane
London WC2H 9EA

An Hachette UK company
A CIP catalogue record for this book is available from the British Library

ISBN 978 1 4719 1254 2

All characters and events in this publication are fictitious and any resemblance to real people, living or dead, is purely coincidental.

No part of this publication may be reproduced, stored in a retrieval system or transmitted in any form or by any means without the prior permission in writing of the publisher, nor be otherwise circulated in any form of binding or cover other than that in which it is published without a similar condition, including this condition, being imposed on the subsequent purchaser.

www.orionbooks.co.uk

Printed and bound by CPI Group (UK) Ltd, Croydon, CR0 4YY

one

More than one glance followed Meg Vesey through the dusk as she stepped across Madison Avenue. Tall heels foreshortened her feet like little hoofs and made her tread delicately as a doe. Flakes from the light snow flurry frosted her furs and the Christmas packages in her arms. Her chin was firmly rounded in profile and luscious as ripe fruit. Her mouth was a little wide, but it seemed to smile even in repose. Her eyes were her real beauty—a clear, sparkling hazel-brown, large and well set, darkened by long, black lashes. Her make-up was light. You could see the petal-pink freshness the cold wind brought to her cheeks.

At 58th Street she passed under a brightly lighted marquee into a dim, hushed lobby. "Good evening, Mrs. Vesey!" The doorman had a smile for her and she didn't have to give the elevator man her floor.

Her glance strayed to a tabloid someone had left on the elevator bench. Something moved behind her eyes. Her face congealed, losing color.

"Charles, is this your paper?"

"Yes, ma'am."

"May I borrow it?"

"You can keep it, Mrs. Vesey, I'm through with it."

"Thank you, Charles."

Even her voice had changed. It was dull and withdrawn now.

She left the elevator and rested her packages on a hall table while she took a latchkey out of her bag. The door opened into a vestibule glowing softly with shaded lamps. Voices and laughter came through another door, but she turned in the opposite direction.

The room she entered was a study. Against a background of dove-gray walls and olive-green upholstery, there stood a desk, a typewriter, filing cabinets and bookcases, all new, bright and efficient-looking. But any functional grace the room might have had was spoiled by its wild disorder. It had the same effect on the beholder as a pretty, young girl in sluttish disarray.

Newspapers and cigarette ashes were a drift across the floor. A doll, its wig half torn from its head, sprawled nude and abandoned on the sofa. A box of crayons had spilled on the window sill. A puppy's tooth marks scarred the leg of a charming little footstool and a cat's claws had ripped dangling threads from the silk brocade of an armchair. A cigarette had burned out on the mantelpiece, leaving a brown oval under its cylinder of ash. The open dropleaf of the desk was an inchoate mass of typescripts, recording tapes, letters and cardboard folders stamped AUGUSTUS VESEY, INC., AUTHORS' AGENTS. Beside the telephone, a sheet of handsome, engraved writing paper was scrawled with doodles and cryptic messages in some private shorthand: "Call Tony? NY op 2 for West Coast after 8 London will call back." Evidently Gus had been home for lunch.

Meg sighed. She knew from long experience that it would take just about thirty minutes to make the room anywhere near presentable again. At this moment she didn't have thirty minutes.

She tossed her packages on the sofa, cast aside hat, coat and gloves. She swept the carbon script of a TV show off the nearest chair and dropped into it. She took tortoise-shell spectacles out of her bag and looked at the tabloid.

There was a photograph, but it was impossible to tell if Vera had changed greatly in the last four years. The smudged print showed only a faint blur of pale hair and a sharply pointed chin.

The news was in the printed matter.

STARLET FIGHTS STUDIO
Beverly Hills, Calif., Dec. 12. *Special*
Beauteous Vera Vane, fabulously successful starlet on the Catamount lot, threw aside the glittering promise of stardom in pictures today for love's sweet sake when she broke with the studio over a clause in her new contract requiring that she remain in Hollywood for the next three years.

"My place is with my husband," said gorgeous Vera, at a press conference this morning, with tears in the great blue eyes that have won the hearts of millions of movie fans throughout the civilized world. "Hollywood's glitter is just that—glitter and nothing more. Movie people are a bunch of phonies. I'm taking the plane east on Sunday and, in future, I'm just going to be a homebody and cook for my husband in a little farmhouse in Connecticut. Any of you boys know a good recipe for corned beef and cabbage?"

When asked if she intended to have a family, Miss Vane answered promptly: "Of course I'd like to. Who wouldn't?"

Miss Vane's husband is Amos Cottle, author, who skyrocketed to fame four years ago with his best-selling war novel, *Never Call Retreat*. His latest book, *Passionate Pilgrim*, has a religious theme. The couple separated three years ago, but neither has remarried.

A representative of Catamount Studios told newsmen today that Miss Vane's option had been dropped because she and the studio were unable to come to an agreement on salary.

Meg let the paper fall from her hands. After a moment, she crossed the room to the desk. Her address book was not in the proper pigeonhole. Polly, who was just learning to print capital letters, had doubtless appropriated it as an exercise book. Maddelena, who functioned as both cook and nurse, wouldn't think of objecting to anything Polly did. So Meg had to ask Information for Amos's number.

After a few minutes, she heard his phone ringing in icebound Connecticut, but there was no answer. She put the phone back in its cradle.

She found her box of notepaper on the floor, but there was no sign of a pen anywhere. She sat down at the typewriter and began to type furiously, words tumbling off the keys almost as fast as the thoughts whirling through her mind.

Dear Amos,
I saw the evening paper. I'm so terribly concerned about you. Gus will be, too. We both know how you feel about that dreadful woman. I can't understand how she has the face to tell reporters that she's coming back to you after you told her so explicitly three years ago that you never wanted to see her again under any circumstances. A talent like yours should not be subjected to this sort of persecution. Just when you've really got going on the new book, too! You know a vicious woman like Vera could ruin you utterly.

Please let me know if there's anything Gus or I can do. Would it be a good idea if she stayed with us when she reached New York? I can't imagine a more difficult house guest, but I'd gladly take her in if that would leave you free to go on with your work unmolested. Perhaps Tony Kane can help. As your publisher, he ought to. He knows lots of people. Perhaps he could get her a part in some Broadway play. That would keep her away from you, though I pity the producer—she's such an embarrassingly incompetent actress. Anyway, let us hear from you as soon as possible and don't despair. We'll do something.
  Best wishes from both of us,
  As ever.

She signed herself "Meg" with Polly's red crayon. She found a stray envelope in the stamp drawer and typed the address.

> AMOS COTTLE, ESQ.
> ROGUE'S RIDGE
> WESTON, CONNECTICUT

She sat still a moment, frowning. Then she put another sheet of writing paper in the typewriter and began to type more slowly.

My dear Vera,
  I learned from this evening's paper that you are planning to return to the East. After all that has happened, I'm sure you won't care to see Amos, but Gus and I should be glad to help you get settled here. We have a large apartment now with a pleasant guest room. Would you care to stay with us for a few days while you look about for a place of your own? Do say yes.
  We both look forward to seeing you soon and hearing all the latest Hollywood gossip.
                                  Yours sincerely,
                                  Meg Vesey

The *sincerely* cost her a grimace, but a more intimate ending would have been even more repugnant. She didn't use a crayon for a scrawled signature this time. She found a fountain pen in her handbag and wrote her name carefully, wondering why antagonism should be more polite than affection.

After another search, she turned up an air-mail envelope and typed rapidly:

> MISS VERA VANE
> CATAMOUNT STUDIOS
> HOLLYWOOD, CALIFORNIA

As she licked the air-mail stamp, she wondered if the letter could reach Vera before she left the West Coast. Surely she would stop at the studio to collect her mail before she boarded the plane on Sunday.

Did the letter sound too friendly to be real? Vera must know how everyone who cared for Amos felt about her. Or did she? Probably not. Her vanity was a thick shell, lined with mother-of-pearl illusions which she secreted from her own press releases. Every irritating foreign substance—like lukewarm praise of her acting—was soon turned into a pearl.

"Mommy!" The door burst open and Hugh catapulted into the room. "I didn't even know you were home till I went in the hall and heard the typing." A touch of surprise and reproach in this, then forgivingly: "Joe Devlin wants me to spend the night with him. They live in a penthouse. They have a dog and a pet turtle. They don't know his sex—the turtle's—so they call it He-she, and . . ."

"Just a minute, Hugh. Let me get these letters off."

"But, Mommy, I want to wear my blue suit and Maddelena can't find a white shirt and . . ."

They found the last clean, white shirt in the toy chest in Polly's room.

"Now how did it get in there?" mused Maddelena, with Sicilian indolence in every line of her ample body.

"You should know. If only . . ." Meg checked herself.

"If only Daddy and Maddelena and Polly and I would be neater," put in Hugh. "You've said that a million times, too. And when you were a little girl, your mother's house was five times as big as this apartment and everything was always in apple-pie order and nobody ever lost anything and . . ."

"All right, Hugh. I see I have the makings of an old bore. Don't rub it in."

"Mom-mee!" Polly's talent for tragedy at the age of five almost equaled Mrs. Siddons's who could bring tears to a shopkeeper's eyes when she asked for a spool of thread. "Mom-mee, nobody ever asks me to spend the night. What shall I do now?"

"Would you like to color?"

"I've been coloring all afternoon."

A whoop from Hugh, who had wandered back to the study. "Christmas presents! Oh, Mommy, who are they for?"

"I can't imagine, can you?"

Polly was at the desk. "Why has this envelope got pretty little red-and-blue stripes on it? And why is there an airplane on the stamp?"

"Oh, Polly, darling, please don't ever touch anything on Mother's desk. That's an air-mail letter and I must get it off right away." Meg grabbed the envelope from Polly, put the letter inside and sealed the flap. "Hugh, are the Devlins calling for you?"

"Yes, in half an hour."

"Then let's pack your bag. You may drop this letter in the mail chute for me on your way out."

Packing Hugh's bag in half an hour was an exhausting ordeal for everyone concerned. In the children's rooms, hairbrushes and combs, toothbrushes and toothpaste all had wings and vanished the moment you turned your back. "It's *The Borrowers*," said Polly.

Gus arrived in the middle of the riot and watched them with affable unconcern in his handsome, dark eyes. Gus hailed from Louisiana originally and he had enough Mediterranean blood to believe that Maddelena's light hand with a soufflé more than made up for her impressionistic housekeeping. An earlier, bachelor existence in shabby, furnished rooms had left him as indifferent to disorder as a gypsy. "Buy why shouldn't I keep that TV script in the kitchen salad bowl? If it's there, I'm sure to see it when I want it."

Meg loved him and made a great effort to conquer her Northern yearning for a well-run household, but it was a partial conquest that made her sometimes irritable and often confused and distracted. Like that time they were sailing for South America and couldn't find their passports at the last moment . . .

Mrs. Devlin and Joe arrived just as the hasps of the suitcase were snapped shut. After a five minutes' search for Hugh's rubber snow boots, that should have been in the hall closet and were, strangely, under the dining table, Hugh departed with the Devlins, clutching the air-mail letter in one hand, and Meg was left to cope with Polly's disconsolate wail: "But what shall I do-o-o?"

Maddelena took Polly into the kitchen to help make some cookies for dinner.

"Alone at last!" Gus took Meg in his arms and kissed her in the way that made her realize Mediterranean blood had its advantages. "What's on your mind?"

"What makes you think there's something on my mind?"

"I know you very well, darling. To me your face is just like a sparkling clean window. I can see into every mood."

"Oh!" It all came back to Meg in a rush. "I haven't mailed that other letter yet."

"What letter?"

"I'll get it."

Meg hurried into the study. The envelope addressed to Amos Cottle was lying on the desk, just as she had left it. She picked up the letter beside it and glanced at her own typing. The words seemed to dance on the page.

"My dear Vera, I learned from this evening's paper . . ."

What had she done?

The untidied room—the frantic search for pen and paper—Hugh's sudden interruption—Polly's persistent wail, "But what shall I do?" —the mad chaos of getting Hugh off with the Devlins . . . It had been one long series of distractions and, in the general confusion, she had put the letter addressed to Amos in the envelope air-mailed to Vera.

Tomorrow morning Vera would be reading the letter to Amos that described Vera herself as a difficult house guest, an embarrassingly incompetent actress and a vicious woman.

two

When Christmas shopping brought Philippa Kane to town, she usually arranged to meet her husband at the Commodore Bar close by Grand Central, so they could go home on the train together. Tonight she found their favorite table empty and established herself with a champagne cocktail, where she could watch both the clock and the revolving door.

Philippa was an aristocrat in the antique sense of the word. She always obtained the best for herself in every phase of life, great or small. She was wrapped in a voluminous cloak of the rare, sea otter fur, so dense that the finger cannot be forced down through the pelt to the skin. An enormous black alligator bag matched tiny alligator shoes. An unbelted dress of black jersey sculptured her torso to the new, Grecian line, and a speckled pheasant's breast gave her turban the new width. Her gloves were soft, natural doeskin; her jewels, jade set with diamonds. Even her little coin purse was a limp, elegant affair of gold mesh with a diamond clasp, and her cigarette case was polished olive wood with an ivory intaglio of Apollo and the Three Muses, cunningly carved in miniature after a design taken from an Attic vase.

A russet lipstick brought out the faint, reddish glints in her pale chestnut hair and the faintest touch of emerald eye shadow gave her gray eyes an olive cast. Her face echoed portraits of the Empress Eugénie—a pallid, perfect oval with fastidiously arched brows, long, narrow eyes, an arrogant nose and a disillusioned mouth. Her smile twisted sardonically when she saw Tony struggling through the revolving door with two typescript boxes under one arm and an evening newspaper stuck in his overcoat pocket. He didn't look at all the way Philippa thought the President of Sutton, Kane and Company should look.

Philippa had come into the world of writers and publishers through marriage. She was born into a different world of gilt-edged bond portfolios and real estate holdings in the heart of Manhattan, apartments on upper Fifth Avenue and palatial cottages in the Hamptons. Like most third-generation heiresses, she took little interest in the unromantic industries that built her grandparents' fortune. Her Europeanized education made her ideal of luxury the life of the Victorian leisure class. It was inevitable that she should shape her life around one of the three classic amusements of that class—politics, sport or the arts. But today all three are highly competitive professions where the amateur has small chance of success. Philippa wanted to write and couldn't, but, through her attempts to write she met Tony Kane, then a young assistant editor with a publishing firm called Daniel Sutton and Company.

Her widowed mother tried everything short of corporal punishment to break off what she called a mésalliance. Time had its usual revenge. The 1929 crash swallowed the substantial residue of a once great fortune. Tony and Philippa were married in 1931 and, for several years before her death, Philippa's mother was wholly dependent on Tony as Philippa herself was now.

Like many literary amateurs, she had soon discovered that professional writers are more attractive in books than in real life. Some of the most talented, and therefore the most profitable to Tony, had the most outrageous personalities and no manners at all. In fact it seemed almost as if the more successful a writer was the more eccentric he became—exactly the reverse of the situation in her father's cosmos where the most successful were the most conventional.

Philippa today had just one word for writers—impossible. You never knew where they came from or what their parents had been. Some got drunk at parties, some tried to borrow money, some got involved in tortuous love affairs and all talked openly about things that were never mentioned in other circles. The fact that they sometimes talked brilliantly was no mitigation to Philippa now. Writers were economically unstable, broke one day and living like princes the next. Even a publisher as prosperous as Tony seemed like a tramp to Philippa. For one thing, he had no capital; he had to spend all he earned after taxes in order to maintain what she considered a normal standard of living. For another thing, he was constantly in touch with writers, and their influence corrupted his sense of decorum.

Of all her youthful ideals, Philippa had kept only one—her worship of the really great writer. She could forgive any eccentricity or even vulgarity in a man she believed to be a genius. What she found intolerable was the eccentricity without the genius that was so common in Tony's world today.

Tony finally extricated himself from the revolving door and threaded his way between other tables to hers.

"Hi, Phil!" He dropped his bundles on a vacant chair, added his hat and overcoat to the pile and slumped into a seat opposite her. "Whew! What a day! Double Gibson for me."

He lit a cigarette and eyed her warily through the smoke. His eyes had not faded with middle age. They were still a deliberate blue, without a hint of gray or hazel, and his rather full, round face was unlined. But his figure had lost its lean look and there was gray in the blond hair like a sprinkling of ashes.

"What's wrong, Tony?"

"Wrong? Nothing's wrong. It's just that I've had a hard day and . . ."

"Tony, dear, you really can't fool me after all these years. That wary look means you want me to do something for you that I won't want to do. What is it this time? Not one of those dreadful creatures from behind the Iron Curtain who has written another *Twenty Years in a Slave State?* The last one broke Grandmother's Dresden teapot and I'm sure he has those missing salt spoons unless he's pawned them by now."

"Nothing like that." Tony reached eagerly for his Gibson. "Amos is in trouble."

"Amos? Oh, dear, what are we supposed to do for him now?" Petulance poisoned her voice. "He even has to live near us in the country so you can spend all your spare time holding his hand. And he's such a dull, common little man."

"But you do like his books," protested Tony.

"The last one wasn't as good as the others. I think he's slipping."

"Don't say that." Tony frowned and took another swallow of his cocktail. "Don't even think it. Amos means a lot to us. More than you realize. Not many men can turn out four books in four years and win the approval of both critics and public. Amos is quite a phenomenon. He made Sutton, Kane what it is today."

"Couldn't we do without him now?"

"Frankly we couldn't." Tony's voice was unusually hard. "What's more, we're not going to. Amos is loyal. He'll stick with us through thick and thin."

"No matter what Doubleday offers?"

"Don't be silly. Amos knows he can't go to another publisher."

"Why not?"

Tony sighed. "I just told you—Amos is loyal. We can trust Amos. He's perfectly well aware of all the things I've done for him. What's worrying me is that wife of his."

"Vera?" Philippa dropped her eyes as she lit a cigarette. "I thought they were divorced."

"Only separated. And now she's flopped in Hollywood, she wants to come back to him. It's in the evening paper."

"What am I supposed to do? Reason with her?"

"Worse than that." Tony's sudden grin was as engaging as he could make it before he took the plunge. "I phoned her in Hollywood this afternoon and invited her to stay with us until she's settled in New York. You see, I've got to have her where I can watch her and keep her from bothering Amos. She accepted and I want you to be nice to her."

Philippa stubbed out her newly lighted cigarette so vehemently that it broke in half. "Really, Tony! There are limits. In the first place, the invitation should have come from me. In the second place, do you think I can live in the same house with that smarmy little adventuress for any length of time? I shall go mad—stark, staring mad."

"Oh, Vera's no picnic, but she's not as bad as all that. For one thing, she's not loud. You ought to like her nice, low voice. You're always complaining about women who squeal and shriek. What is it you call it? Unmodulated?"

"I detest her soft, sly, insinuating voice. I detest everything about her."

"So does Amos. So you ought to be on his side. If she stays with us, he'll only have to see her once—Sunday when he meets her at the airport. He feels he has to do that much. But he's going to drive her straight to our house and we'll have a supper party so he won't be stuck with her for the rest of the evening."

"A party at two days' notice? You're insane, Tony. Why can't Vera stay with Gus and Meg in New York?"

"Gus is too soft-hearted to handle a wildcat like Vera. He couldn't keep her from bothering Amos. And it's particularly important that Amos isn't bothered on the eve of the Bookbinders' Dinner."

"Does Amos have to go?"

"Didn't I tell you? Amos is getting the Award. The Most American Author of the Decade. Ten thousand bucks and fifty thousand worth of prestige and publicity. We've got the layouts of the ads all ready to be released the day after the dinner. He'll have to make a speech and it better be good."

"There are a lot of things you don't tell me, Tony," said Philippa thoughtfully. "Just what do you really mean when you speak of Vera 'bothering' Amos? She can't keep him from writing. Lots of writers do their best work when they're unhappy."

Tony sighed. "I suppose I'll have to tell you now. But keep it under your hat. No one has ever known except me and Gus."

"Known what?"

"When Amos wrote his first book he was a recently reformed alcoholic. Didn't you ever suspect?"

"No. I thought he just didn't like to drink."

"He likes it too well," said Tony grimly. "When I first met Amos he still had to take Antabuse. He's shown a lot of character holding himself in line without the help of a drug for the last four years, but he had one bad relapse. That was during the three months he lived with Vera."

"So that was why you got Vera a job in Hollywood!"

"Precisely. She kept liquor in the house, she drank in front of him and she taunted him with his weakness. It was just too much for him. It mustn't happen again. Think what it would do to his TV program. And, in the end, it would kill him."

Philippa was moved. "Even Amos doesn't deserve a woman like Vera. . . . Or maybe he does." Her smile twisted. "Maybe men get the women they deserve."

A few years ago Tony would have answered: "How did I ever deserve anyone as wonderful as you?" Now he merely said: "Do women get the men they deserve?"

"I'm sure they do." Her smile teased him as she, too, avoided the obvious gallantry. "All right, Tony." She capitulated suddenly. "I'll do what I can with Vera, but don't except me to like it. Are you sure Amos hates Vera now?"

Tony hesitated. "I hope so. He has to live alone to accomplish the immense amount of work he does. The monastic life—bad for the writer, but good for the writing."

"And the publisher," murmured Philippa. "I still think he may be slipping. *Passionate Pilgrim* bored me in galleys."

"You're nuts!" Tony's protest was a little too loud. "We've sold out a first printing of forty thousand copies before publication and it's the July choice of the Book-of-the-Week Club. Catamount Pictures is bidding against . . ."

"Oh, he's still a commercial success. That's momentum. But artistically . . ."

"That's not what Maurice Lepton says."

Tony dragged the newspaper from his overcoat pocket. It proved to be an advance copy of next Sunday's *New York Times Book Review* section. "Look at that!"

The first page was headed A LANDMARK IN AMERICAN LETTERS. A photograph showed a thin, mild face with a short beard, gazing at some remote object outside the picture. The shirt collar was open, the shoulders were tweedy and the frail fingers held loosely onto the bowl of an old, charred pipe.

"Where's the dog?" said Philippa. "Authors with tweed jackets and pipes always have a dog lying at their feet."

"There was a dog," admitted Tony. "The *Times* cut out the feet to get a better enlargement of the face."

"Amos doesn't own a dog."

"I know, but Red Nicholas, our bright new publicity man, rented one for the picture."

"Mr. Nicholas may be bright, but he is scarcely original. Amos doesn't smoke either. You should have had a little box of Antabuse in his hand and Vera lying at his feet."

"That isn't very funny, Phil."

She ignored him and began to read aloud: "PASSIONATE PILGRIM. By Amos Cottle. 450 pp. New York: Sutton, Kane and Co., $3.75. By Maurice Lepton."

Her eye ran down the column to a passage Tony had marked with a red pencil. "Amos Cottle surveys our tawdry, TV society with the clinical eye of a social anthropologist annotating the mores of African pygmies. . . . His mystique is rooted in classical humanism, detached, witty, skeptical but always urbane and not incapable of compassion and even reverence. His ear for the cadences of contemporary idiom is accurate as a tape recorder, but he does what no machine can do—he selects the meaningful and allows it to stand as a symbol suggesting the rest. This is life itself in all its squalor and glory. Cottle spares us nothing—the dirt, the sweat, the blood, the ugliness and lust and cruelty of existence. It is all there under the velvet texture of his intricately organized prose, transmuted by Cottle's art into a richly rewarding experience. What other writer today could have written this stark, lean sentence: 'As I bent his arm behind his back with all my strength, I heard the dry crack of his tibia'?"

Tony explained the marking of his passage. "A fine quote for the jacket of Amos's next book. Good old Leppy! What would we do without him?"

"I believe Lepton really does like Amos's work," said Philippa. She read the note at the bottom of the review. "Mr. Lepton is best known for his monumental work, *The Green Corn,* a definitive study of American belles-lettres from 1900 to 1950. He is a regular contributor to various critical journals."

"Of course he does!" rejoined Tony. "Amos's stuff isn't bad at all. I rather enjoy reading some of it myself and you used to like it. There's no question about it—the guy can write."

"So Lepton remarked in his review of Amos's first book."

"Not quite in those words." Tony's eyes narrowed, remembering. " 'I put down this volume with a sense of exhilaration all too rare in a reviewer today. Here, I told myself, is a discovery. Make no mistake about it—the man can write. He may be young, he may make technical mistakes in his first few novels, but he has that indefinable quality that sets the born writer apart from the hacks and amateurs who clutter the literary scene today and stifle the flowering of true talent by their very multiplicity, like weeds in a garden.' "

"Lepton always seems to see himself now as a gardener slaying the misfits with weed killer so there'll be room for Amos," reflected Philippa. "Isn't Amos the only writer he's ever really praised?"

"Every critic has his pet writer," returned Tony. "Luckily for us, Amos is Leppy's pet. They're so identified in the public mind by this time that Leppy can't let Amos down, no matter what Amos writes."

Philippa glanced at the clock. "We'd better be going if we want a seat on that 4:39."

Once they were settled in the train, her mind went back to the projected supper party. "Who on earth can we invite at such short notice?"

"The Veseys, of course. I have a feeling that Vera is really fond of Meg and Gus. If they have another date already, they'll break it. After all, Gus is Amos's agent."

"But who else? All our friends are dated weeks ahead."

Tony frowned. "Amos is a lion now. Must be somebody who'd like to meet him. How about that widow down the road who says she always wanted to write?"

"A woman alone?"

"She has a son at college. He must be home on Christmas vacation now. Ask him. Then we'll get a couple of other novelists and . . ."

"Oh, no, we won't!" cried Philippa fiercely. "They're all madly jealous of Amos and he despises them. Haven't you any non-fiction writers on your list who live in Connecticut?"

"Yes, but Amos is hardly their cup of tea. They're all scientists and such."

"We can still ask them. They can hardly refuse their publisher, can they? What about the Willings? Didn't you publish a book of his years ago?"

"The Psychopathology of Politics," muttered Tony, "That was way back in the forties when Dan Sutton was still alive. Not what you'd call a best seller, but it still brings in some royalties. Some of the medical schools use it as supplementary reading in their advanced psychology courses."

"Good. Then I'll ask the Willings and that will have to be it. Amos and Vera, the Veseys and the Willings and that little woman down the road and her son."

Tony took a typescript out of its box and began to read, but Philippa went on, thinking aloud: "We'll have a simple buffet supper. Ham and turkey, potatoes au gratin and salad, fresh fruit and Stilton. Let's have Scotch and soda first. I'm sick of sweet, messy cocktails. And it'll make Amos less conspicuous drinking his iced tea in a tall glass, too. If only I had time to get that cushion recovered. The one the mystery writer burned a cigarette hole in and . . ."

"Why, Tony!"

The masculine voice brought Tony's head up from his script with a jerk and cut off Philippa's hostess chatter.

The man who stood in the aisle was small and slender with a sickly, pallid face and burning, black eyes. His straight, dark hair lay lank and glossy against his well-shaped skull. The mouth was thrusting, a little simian and mischievous, but there was intelligence in the eyes and the speaking voice was beautiful—a thing of light and shade and color expressed in terms of sound. He faced them, smiling with an easy self-possession that seemed to announce: here is an individual of unique importance.

"Why, Leppy!" Tony shouted. "It's been a coon's age. Where did you come from?"

"Got on at 125th. I've been lecturing at Columbia. I was prowling the train looking for a smoking car and . . ."

"Sit down." Tony was on his feet. Luckily the seat in front of them was empty. Tony pushed the back over so that the two seats now faced each other. "You've met my wife, Philippa, haven't you?"

"I don't believe I've had that pleasure." It said a great deal for Lepton's grace that his bow did not seem grotesque in such a small, ugly man. He slid into the opposite seat that Tony had provided and Philippa smiled at him pleasantly. "I remember you at our wedding, but that was a long time ago. Do you live in Connecticut now?"

"No, I'm on my way to the Shadbolts for the week end. You know Shad, don't you, Tony? He wrote that South Windish thing laid in Taos last year."

"I've just been reading your review of Amos Cottle's latest," put in Philippa, determined not to be left out of the shop talk.

"Ah!" Lepton's eyelids drooped but the slitted eyes were more brilliant than ever. "Now there's a man who really can write. He doesn't imitate anybody. He's just himself. An original. That's what American letters needs so desperately today."

"I think he's good myself," said Philippa, loyally.

"Good? Dear lady, he's magnificent. If the word hadn't been so brutally abused, I'd say he was a genius. There's nothing else in contemporary literature quite like the Cottle touch. You're to be congratulated, Tony."

"Thanks." Tony composed his features to a suitably reverential gravity, but Philippa had always suspected that Tony was far more interested in Amos's sales figures than his literary qualities.

"Cottle must be a very lonely man," went on Lepton, in a musing tone. "A talent like that is like great wealth—it cuts you off from the rest of humanity. I think of him as a monkish figure, withdrawn and abstracted, submerged in his own—er—ah . . ."

"Mystique," suggested Philippa, like a bright child trying to join a grown-up conversation.

The brilliant gaze shifted to her. "I see you really have been reading my review."

"It's a nice word. I like it spelled that French way," she prattled on, while Tony winced. "I like all the words you use—words like *meaningful*. If I were writing a review, I'd just say *significant*, but I suppose there must be an opposite of meaningless in the dictionary and it sounds a lot more *Thursday Review*. . . . You know Amos really isn't monkish at all. He's quite a lot of fun sometimes."

Lepton looked thoughtfully at Tony. "I'd really like to meet him sometime. He must be as fascinating as one of his own characters."

"Why, haven't you ever met him at all?" Philippa was astonished.

"Leppy is not the kind of critic who frequents publication-day cocktail parties at Toots Shor's," said Tony.

"Haven't you ever seen Amos on TV?" demanded Philippa.

"I do not own a TV set," answered Lepton firmly. "I avoid TV whenever I can."

"Amos has had his own weekly program for the last six months," explained Tony. "He interviews other authors about their books. He doesn't criticize. Just draws the other guy out and gets him to talk about what he was trying to do when he wrote the book in question."

"I'm sure he doesn't criticize," said Lepton a little bitterly. "I've been told many times that there is no place for real criticism on TV."

Philippa had an inspiration. "If you really want to meet Amos, we could arrange it for this week end. We were just planning a small supper party for Amos when you came by. Sunday at our house at six o'clock. We'd love to have you come and bring the Shadbolts."

"That's very kind of you indeed." Lepton made another graceful little bow and Philippa wondered: why did critics always have much more charming manners than the wild, rough lot who called themselves creative writers?

"I'm sure the Shadbolts would appreciate it, too," went on Lepton. "But I've already told them I would have to leave Sunday afternoon, and they may have made other arrangements for the evening. Why don't I just get a taxi to run me over to your place around six?"

"I can run over to the Shadbolts in the Austin and pick you up," said Philippa. "If you're really coming."

"Of course I'm coming." He smiled. "I've never been able to live up to the standard of that English critic who made a point of never meeting a writer in the flesh throughout his long and acidulous career."

The smile transmuted his monkey face into something Philippa found fascinating. She was reminded of an old story—an Edwardian rake who boasted: "I am considered the ugliest man in Europe, but give me half an hour alone with any woman and I can win her away from the handsomest man in the world." What would half an hour alone with Maurice Lepton be like?

The thought was pleasantly disturbing. She began to plan what she would wear tomorrow when she went over to the Shadbolts. Of course Maurice Lepton wasn't really her type. Indeed she wasn't sure she even liked him, but . . .

Something feline in her nature enjoyed hunting for the sake of the hunt itself, without feeling either desire or hostility toward the quarry. Like a domestic cat, she managed her life so that she could enjoy both the civilized satisfactions of peaceful luxury at home and the savage excitements of the chase abroad. It was an ideal life, she thought—a life where all the prizes of a policed society were enjoyed without the repression of a single feral impulse. Philippa might have her faults, but she was entirely free of repressions. Sometimes she wondered if Tony had ever suspected the fact.

When Lepton left the train at Norwalk, Philippa allowed her ungloved hand to linger a moment in his. Their eyes met and for an instant that feeling of sweet disturbance swept over her again more strongly than before. She was a little frightened. Pleasure she understood, but she had always avoided passion. She had always been mistress of herself.

"Well, what do you think of Leppy?" asked Tony as the train rumbled on toward Westport.

"I don't know." Philippa was as puzzled as she was fascinated by the unplumbed depths in those eyes. Out of sheer intuition she plucked a curious phrase. "I think he's unscrupulous and dangerous."

"Dangerous? That poor little bookworm who hasn't seen the sun for twenty years?" Tony laughed.

three

Sunlight woke Amos Cottle Sunday at noon. It streamed through the uncurtained picture window onto the vast double bed where he sprawled in a sweaty tangle of sheets and blankets. He rubbed his gummy eyelids and lay passive, half-awake, listening to the stillness of the empty house. A general uneasiness possessed him. For a few moments he could not particularize its source. Then he remembered: Vera. He had to meet her at the airport this afternoon.

He rose wearily and groped for slippers and dressing gown. His eye caught his own movement in the wall mirror. He paused to survey his face coldly as if it were the mask of a stranger.

The eyes were wide and lost. The eyes of a stray cur, he thought bitterly. The morbid mouth was a mute expression of pain. The weakly tapered jaw was mercifully veiled by the thin straggle of brindled beard. No wonder Meg Vesey mothered him. She was the sort who would mother any forlorn creature. But would a stranger, who didn't know his name, ever suspect that he was considered one of the three or four most distinguished novelists of his period? Were his fans disappointed when they discovered that the author whose virile characters took rape, incest and torture in their stride looked as if he couldn't say boo to a goose? A sudden inspiration consoled him: Van Gogh. The self-portrait. That was how he looked. Genius housed in a frail vessel. The idea of genius brought a wry smile to his lips.

With a sigh he ambled into the kitchen, got out a can of frozen orange juice, and made coffee. He sipped the cold drink and the hot one alone at the kitchen table. I'm always alone. I'll be more alone than ever if Vera comes to live here. But she shan't. I won't let her.

Abruptly he was overwhelmed by a great distaste for his whole situation in life. What am I doing here? How did I ever get into all this? His feeling of being trapped had grown with the success of each new book. What would Gus and Tony say if he told them this evening that he had decided to retire? What could they do to stop him?

Still in gown and slippers he retrieved the Sunday *Times* and *Tribune* from the front door mat. No neighbors could see him. The house stood in its own five acres of woodland. In summer he took his sun bath naked beside the swimming pool.

The house itself was modern, all on one floor, with many glass walls. Tony had chosen it for him. The fireplace, without a mantel, was set flush in a wall of whitewashed brick. The invisible chimney was divided into two branches so that an apparently impossible window could be set directly above the grate. This illogical window had always bothered him as something too surrealistic for comfort, and the glass walls made him feel exposed and unprotected. But Tony had insisted that it was the sort of house that people expected a man like Amos Cottle to live in and it was going cheap just at the time Amos got the money from his first movie sale, so—here he was, a prisoner in a house he didn't like, close to Tony's beautiful estate, where Tony could keep an eye on him.

His own face greeted him from the first page of the *Times Book Review* section. A cleverly composed portrait. That guy really did look like an author. Amos relaxed as he read the Lepton review. The stuff must be pretty good after all or an egghead like Lepton wouldn't take it so seriously. What was more, other people took Lepton seriously. This lush praise should be good for a second printing of forty thousand.

He dropped the *Times* and picked up the *Tribune*. They had put that sickeningly romantic bilge of Shadbolt's on the first page of their *Book Review* section with a photo of Shad that must have been taken at least twenty years ago.

Amos turned the pages, but it was not until he came to the fourth inside page that he saw a woefully smudged and diminished cut of his own picture, flanking a single column review.

> PASSIONATE PILGRIM. By Amos Cottle. 450 pp. New York: Sutton, Kane and Co. $3.75. Reviewed by Emmett Avery.

And, farther down the column: "Mr. Avery is best known for his recent book, *A Mess of Pottage,* a provocative attack on current trends in the contemporary novel."

That was warning enough. The rattlesnake's rattle. Amos didn't want to read further, but he couldn't help it. His gaze was glued to the page hypnotically.

A conscientious reviewer hardly knows what to say when he is confronted with another book by the industrious, nay, indefatigable Mr. Cottle. All that is jejune and meretricious in contemporary letters is embodied in the verbose, pretentious prose of this incredibly popular novelist, overlaid with a slick-magazine varnish sticky enough to act as flypaper for book club subscribers. The appalling thing is that Cottle gets away with it. People actually buy and read these books. Yet Cottle's characters are merely types, his principles are prejudices in fancy dress and his whole narrative creaks woodenly from the first contrived scene to the last musty artifice—a thing of lath and plaster made to look like steel.

The only amusing thing about this sorry performance is the number of gross typographical errors, some as hilarious as "these United States." The house of Sutton, Kane and Company needs some new proofreaders and, in the opinion of at least one reviewer, some new authors as well. . . .

Amos angrily threw the paper across the floor. It was absurd to care. Let Gus and Tony do the worrying. They never worried much about things like this. Gus always said that book club subscribers didn't pay any attention to reviews. Besides, Amos had never had the slightest sense of personal identification with these books, and yet —and yet . . .

He could not rid himself of the unpleasant feeling that his livelihood was being threatened. He was astonished at the strength of his own rage. At that moment he would have liked to get his hands around Emmett Avery's throat and . . .

A faint sound from the terrace startled him. That aloneness that was so important to his inner sense of security was about to be disturbed. He waited uncomfortably, listening.

A light step came across the flagstones to the glass door. Through the glass he saw a lissome figure in gray slacks and a green sweater with green shoes. The pale, oval face smiled and the russet lips moved, but he couldn't hear anything through the soundproof glass. Reluctantly he went to the door and pulled it open.

"Amos!" She threw her arms around his neck. He had to hold her. Their lips met. After a decent interval, he drew back.

"Phil, does Tony know you're here?"

"Of course not. I'm supposed to be walking his boxer. I left the brute tied up outside."

"Gosh, you've used that dodge for the last two years—almost every time you come over here. Doesn't Tony have any idea what's going on?"

"I'm sure he hasn't. . . . Oh, Mos, what are we going to do about Vera?"

"I don't know." He sat down heavily on the edge of the sofa. The affair with Philippa had bothered him from the beginning. He had been afraid to refuse her. There was no knowing what tale she might have carried to Tony if he had. Now he was afraid to break with her. But his sense of guilt was intensified every time he saw Tony and as he saw Tony a great deal, the whole thing was becoming intolerable, for guilt bred fear.

"Tell me, Phil. Are you quite sure Tony doesn't suspect us?"

"Of course not. Every time he mentions you now I tell him I think you're an awful little man and I hate your writing. He believes it. He's actually afraid you'll find out I don't like you. He just begs me to be nice to you."

Amos sighed. "Not very subtle, are we?"

Philippa laughed. "Subtlety is wasted on Tony. He's as bothered about Vera as we are. He's afraid she'll drive you to drink."

"If anyone could, it's Vera."

She sat beside him, leaning her shoulder against his. "Amos, is it true you used to be an alcoholic?"

"That was a long time ago."

"Tony told me Friday night. Why didn't you ever tell me?"

"Why should I?"

"Most men like to confide in their women. It's another form of intimacy." She turned her head toward him and their eyes met within a few inches of each other. "Why is Vera coming back? Have you any idea what she wants?"

He drew back, and looked away.

"I think she's broke, and I'm a lot more successful now than I was when she left me. Maybe she got wind of Lepton's review at the studio before it was published and decided that I was worth cultivating. If that's it, Avery's review in the *Tribune* this morning should scare her off again."

"If not, what are you going to do?"

Amos shrugged. "What can I do? I'll meet her at the airport this afternoon and drive her to your house. I owe her that much. When the party's over, I'll come back here and leave her there. No need to see her again. Tony and Gus, between them, should be able to keep her out of my hair."

Philippa eyed him curiously. "Why are you so passive, Amos? Already you're letting Vera push you around. Why do you have to meet her at the airport? Why not let Tony do it?"

"He wanted to, but I said no. I want her to see me once so she can see for herself how utterly indifferent I am to her now."

"If I were you, I'd hate her."

"You probably would. I—well, as the young people say, I couldn't care less."

"Maybe that's the best attitude. Hate is a compliment, like love, but indifference is devastating. If you can really make Vera believe you don't care, she may leave you alone. I'm beginning to feel almost sorry for her."

"Sorry? For Vera?"

"I feel sorry for any woman who has to do with you, Amos." A sudden recklessness came into her eyes. "You don't really care for me, do you?"

"I enjoy being with you," he answered cautiously.

"But you don't love me, do you?"

Their eyes met again. His were honestly puzzled. "Phil, what in God's name does a woman like you see in a man like me? I'm not young or strong or gay or gallant. I'm not even good-humored and lovable. Sometimes I think you're more in love with my writing than you are with me. There are a few clever women who unconsciously seek greatness of mind in their men just as the dull majority unconsciously seek greatness of fortune or strength of body. Is that what you're looking for? The extra kick of being loved by a man with a great intellect? It would explain why your conscience doesn't bother you."

Amos sighed again.

"I believe that's it. You're in love with the idea of loving a man of genius, the way some women are in love with the idea of loving a man of great wealth or power. Would you care for Amos Cottle if he were a garage mechanic? I doubt it.

"You don't care about money or ordinary power because you've been familiar with those things all your life in one form or another. But you do care about intellectual power. It's an unfamiliar mystery that inspires wonderment. Women always love the thing that overawes them. Isn't that the real clue to your feeling for me?"

"Does it matter?" Her voice was husky. She leaned toward him, the green sweater molding the firm lines of her bosom, her lips parted, her eyelids drooping.

"Tony might walk in at any moment!"

Philippa was amused. "You do feel guilty about Tony, don't you?"

"He's done a lot for me."

"Just because he published your first book? He didn't lose anything by that."

"But he's so unsuspecting. It would be such a shock to him if he ever found out. No knowing what he'd do. That bothers me and it ought to bother you."

"It doesn't, but then I'm not analytical. Most writers analyze their own emotions too much, but now and then they forget they are writers and remember they are human beings. You never do. You're always the observer, never the participant. Always the audience, never the actor. Even in your own love scenes part of you is detached —damnably detached. It's as if—as if you weren't all here. As if some part of you were missing. Why don't you ever tell me anything about your early life? Your mother and father and things you did at school and the first girl you ever kissed. Most men like to talk about themselves. You don't. Tell me something: has Vera any hold over you? Could she blackmail you, if she wanted to? That would explain why you don't talk about your past and why Vera seemed so sure in that newspaper interview that she could come back to you."

"No. Vera couldn't blackmail me." His voice was even, but she saw a sudden uneasiness in his eyes. Somehow the shot had gone home and he was trying to conceal it. He got up and walked over to the window.

"Is there anyone else who could blackmail you?" she probed. "Come to think of it, you never talk about your early life."

"It's all on the jacket of my latest book." He picked up a copy and tossed it at her. She caught it deftly and laughed.

"Tony writes all those jacket notes."

"But I gave him the material," retorted Amos. "Do you know it's nearly three? Mix yourself a drink while I take a shower. Then I must be off to the airport."

But Philippa didn't walk over to the bar. When water gushed in the bathroom beyond, she sat on the bed reading the jacket note on the back flap of *Passionate Pilgrim*.

> Amos Cottle was born in China in 1918 where his father was a Methodist missionary. He attended mission schools and was graduated from the University of Peking. Then began a rolling-stone existence that gathered moss—a rich treasure house of varied experience for his future writing career. Cottle has been a sailor, a bartender, a Hollywood press agent, a cattle rancher, a chemist, a construction engineer and a barker for a carnival show. During World War II he served with the Seabees in the Pacific. Out of that interlude came his memorable first novel *Never Call Retreat*. He is married to Vera Vane, Hollywood actress, but he spends most of his time in a modern house in Connecticut where the walls are either all window or all bookcase.

Philippa put the book down thoughtfully. Tony's glib, hackneyed phrases really told very little about Amos as a man, and Amos had never talked about his childhood in China or his rolling-stone period. She was not a sensitive woman but now she was overwhelmed with desolation as she realized how purely physical their bond had always been. Amos was inaccessible. She didn't really know him at all. Now that Vera was precipitating a crisis in their lives, Amos's responses would be utterly unpredictable.

Suddenly she was aware of a tiny seed of distaste for Amos. His remoteness, his fatalism, his fear of Tony's suspicions, his indifference to Vera's onslaught—was this really the sort of man for her to love? She knew the seed would grow. Once again she was on the verge of falling out of love, as she had fallen out of love with Tony himself, long ago. . . .

She wandered into the living room and saw the *Tribune Book Review* section crumpled into a ball. She smoothed it out and reread the article by Emmett Avery which she had glanced at this morning. She recalled Tony's rage. "That little pipsqueak Avery! To think that I introduced him to his first publisher because I thought his stuff wasn't quite good enough for us. I suppose he's never got over our rejection."

The water had ceased to run. In the silence, she called softly: "I must go, Amos. See you later."

"We'll be there around five," he called back cheerfully.

"Good-bye." She went across the terrace slowly to the tree where she had tied the dog. An unwelcome thought invaded her mind. Suppose—just suppose—that Maurice Lepton was wrong for the first time in his long and distinguished career as a critic. Suppose that this Emmett Avery was right in all his nasty sarcasms about *Passionate Pilgrim*. Suppose Amos Cottle's mystique was pure sham, a pose to enhance the prestige of mediocre books.

Philippa did not trust her own judgment entirely in intellectual matters. She was intelligent enough to know her own limitations. She had taken the word of people like Maurice Lepton for Amos's writing ability and Amos was right about one thing—that was the secret of her desire for him. If she couldn't write great books herself, she could at least serve those who did as primitive priestesses served male worshippers of their goddesses.

But if the worshipper were insincere and his gifts unworthy of the goddess? Then the priestess must find a worshipper with greater gifts.

Maurice Lepton's disturbing smile came back to her mind's eye. No one had ever questioned his intellectual power. He himself seemed to radiate a superb confidence in his own power as Amos never had.

The boxer rose to greet her. Before she bent to untie his leash, she looked back at the house. Why did she suddenly feel that she had said good-bye to Amos Cottle forever? Could it be that she was already seriously in love with Lepton, a man she had seen only twice in her whole life?

four

That same Sunday Meg Vesey, like Amos, woke late to full daylight. Friday's snow had turned to muddy slush in a temperature just above freezing. The bleak December day painted the city scene in the hushed, faintly ominous palette of Utrillo. To Meg the world seemed like an empty stage where something dreadful was just about to happen.

She hadn't told Gus yet. She had shown him the news story in the tabloid Friday evening and the letter that should have gone to Vera. "Don't send it," he told her. "Vera's going to stay with the Kanes, thank God! And we're going out there to dinner Sunday. Tony's got it all fixed."

It was then that Meg opened her mouth to tell Gus about the other letter that had gone to Vera by mistake, but the words wouldn't come. They had just settled down for a cosy evening alone together with Hugh away at the Devlins and Polly soon to be asleep. Why spoil it? She'd wait and tell him Saturday. Or Sunday at the latest. She'd have to tell him then.

But when she found Polly running a slight temperature with a sore throat that Sunday morning, she forgot everything else for a while. The doctor came and prescribed the latest antibiotic. Aspirin, too, if the temperature went over 100 that afternoon.

"I'll have to stay with her," cried Meg. "You can go to the Kanes without me."

"It would be better for you to come with me," insisted Gus. "Better for Polly and better for you. The doctor's been here, so we know it isn't polio or anything horrible, and anyway we'll be home early. If you stayed here, there's nothing you could do but watch her temperature and give her pills. Maddelena can do that and Polly's just as happy playing with Maddelena as she would be with you, maybe happier. Maddelena is much nearer a child's level than you are."

Meg yielded reluctantly. "A party should be fun," she moaned. "But driving fifty miles on a winter day and leaving Polly ill . . ."

"This isn't fun, this is business," said Gus firmly. "We must hold Amos's hand while Vera is around."

"Don't worry, Mommy, I'll be here," said Hugh, relishing melodrama. "I'll call you at once if anything goes wrong, so you can dash back."

Gus quelled him with a glare. "Nothing is going wrong. How could it? We'll only be gone a few hours."

Meg knew that Gus hated to leave Polly ill almost as much as she did herself. They had never left Hugh with a fever when he was Polly's age. But by the time Polly came along they had learned that a slight temperature in childhood rarely meant serious illness. A sore throat was something that would bear watching because so many serious illnesses began that way, but, thank God, nine times out of ten it wasn't serious at all.

She dragged herself into her room and put on the old black velvet. A tortoise-shell locket and chain matched the high comb in her hair, and she wore the big ruby Gus had bought for her with his commission on Amos's first movie sale. Even the glitter of its great red eye did not raise her spirits today. Even the soft, thick folds of her fur coat could not warm the chill in her bowels.

I must tell Gus now. I must. I've waited too long already. But still she was silent.

She tried to imagine how Vera's face had looked when she read that letter. Had the dulcet voice lost its saccharine smoothness for once?

Imagination boggled. This just wasn't one of those annoying mishaps that could be straightened out by a frank apology. "So sorry I called you an incompetent actress and a vicious woman. I didn't really mean it, you know." This was a colossal blunder, an irrevocable declaration of war. And how was it going to affect the fortunes of Augustus Vesey, Inc., member of the Society of Authors' Representatives?

Meg knew all about the literary side of the agency. An editor's daughter, herself an author of short stories, she was useful to Gus as a first reader, winnowing the slush pile of unsolicited scripts that came into the office and selecting the few that might stand a chance after revision. It was she who had discovered Amos Cottle when she found the script of his first book in a mass of trash that Gus had handed over to her without bothering to read himself one week end five years ago. But Meg had never been able to understand the financial side of the agency. She had no idea just how important Amos Cottle was to them.

Maybe Vera would never get the letter. Maybe she hadn't stopped at the studio on Saturday to pick up her last mail. Maybe Catamount secretaries were careless with letters for actresses who left the studio in a huff and it would never be forwarded. Maybe the postman would break a leg, or maybe Vera's plane would crash.

Meg tried to drag her mind away from such a wicked thought. But the image persisted balefully. Fog, a great transcontinental plane crashing in flame against a peak in the Rockies, and a soft voice that suddenly began to scream like a slaughtered animal.

When they ran into fog on the parkway, the coincidence seemed like a materialization of her evil thought. The world was a mass of dirty, damp cotton wool pressing in on every side, clogging speed and blurring vision. Other cars were glaring yellow headlights with no form or substance, going much too fast for comfort. In her morbid frame of mind she found herself running through the terms of her will and wondering whom Gus would marry if he survived and she didn't. All the while, gnawing underneath the surface of her thought, was a little maggot of guilt. She couldn't stand it any longer. She must tell Gus now, before the party.

"Gus."

"Yes?"

Again the words wouldn't come. Not right away. She must lead up to this confession somehow. "Gus, how does Amos himself really feel about Vera?"

Gus hesitated. "It's hard to tell about Amos. He was damn glad to see her go. We both know that. He told us all about it. But he's reticent about her now, and of course she must have some attraction for him or he wouldn't have married her in the first place. Just how strong that attraction will be when he sees her again, I don't know. Sometimes he seems to miss her, but perhaps he's just lonely."

"Poor Amos!" Meg was touched. "I never thought of it before but he must be lonely. No family, no friends, just business associates like you and Tony and living all alone in that big, isolated house. Yet he hardly ever goes to parties."

"In our world it's hard for a reformed alcoholic to lead a normal social life," said Gus. "There are so few parties without drinks, and it's awkward to demand ginger ale when everyone else is mopping up gin and tonic. As it is, nobody knows about his weakness except you and me and Tony. You never told anyone, did you?"

"Of course not. Not even Philippa."

"I think Amos is wise to lead a hermit's life," went on Gus. "He works hard at his writing, he reads a lot, he plays a little golf with Tony and he goes to town once a week for the TV show. He has no financial worries or family problems. It's an ideal life for a writer of talent."

Meg glanced at him sideways. "Do you really believe Amos has a great talent? Just between you and me and the lamppost?"

"You should know. You discovered him yourself."

"That was his first book and it was so much better than those other scripts I was reading. But these later books . . ."

"Meg, how often have I told you that you aren't really capable of appreciating anything written since 1910? Amos is extremely representative of his period and it's a period you hate. His output is prodigious and yet it has never fallen below the standard he set himself in that first book. That is always a sign of superior talent. His success was immediate with his first book. All the critics hailed him as a rising star. That wasn't accident, you know. Amos has something. Just what it is, I can't say, but, whether you like his later stuff or not, his writing has that mysterious something that makes people want to read his books."

"The Cottle touch." Meg sighed. "That man in today's *Tribune* doesn't like it at all."

"Do you mean to tell me you're allowing yourself to be influenced by a review?" Gus poured scorn into the word *review*. "Emmett Avery is an old rival of Maurice Lepton's. Avery's review was probably written to take Leppy down a peg because he's gone all out for Amos every time."

"What a mean thing to do!"

"Don't worry about that review of Avery's. It's the first adverse criticism Amos has ever had in a literary journal of major importance, and that's a sign of his final success. A writer hasn't arrived until one important critic has said publicly that his work stinks. Then all his admirers leap to his defense, and the controversy stirs up more excitement about him than ever before."

"You'll be making me think that Tony planted Avery's review in the *Tribune*."

"You can't plant things in the *Trib*, but if you could, Tony is perfectly capable of it."

Silence held the fog-choked car for the next twenty miles. Then Meg screwed her courage to the sticking point again.

"Gus." Her voice was small, almost a whisper.

His eyes were on the murky red taillights of the car ahead. "Yes?" He sounded impatient.

Once again Meg's nerve failed at the jump. "Why do you care so much about what happens to Amos? We have other clients."

"Yes, but there's only one Amos." Gus took a chance and swung around the car ahead at higher speed while Meg held her breath.

"I don't suppose you ever have really understood what an important part Amos plays in our economy," went on Gus as they came back safely into the right-hand lane. "A small literary agency like ours is in the same position as a small publishing house like Tony's. One really successful author who produces regularly and hits the best-seller list every time can make or break us. Amos is exceptionally prolific for a writer of such prestige. One book a year for the last four years. With each new book, I'm scared to death that he'll slip, but he hasn't yet, and as long as he doesn't, he's a big slice of our bread and butter as well as all our cake and jam. When Amos gets a movie sale, that ain't hay. It's the cornerstone of our economy. Amos pays for the apartment, the car, clothes, entertaining, everything. Without Amos, my agency would just be one of a dozen little outfits that struggle along with a gross profit of ten or fifteen or twenty thousand a year. After taxes and overhead, our income would be even less. We've got all our eggs in one basket, Meg, and that basket is named Amos Cottle."

"Ten or twenty thousand." Meg's smile was haggard. "In 1933 I would have considered that a nice income, but . . ."

"You wouldn't now with prices what they are and two children to support. You've got used to spending a lot more, and spending is one of the habit-forming drugs, you know. We're both addicts." Gus frowned. "So—we've got to head off Vera somehow."

"Gus."

"Yes?"

"I— There's something I have to tell you."

But Gus was hardly listening. His mind was still fixed on Vera. "Telling her flatly to leave Amos alone would probably be the worst thing we could do. Remember when Polly was two and we got her to eat by telling her positively not to touch her food? Vera has all the perversity of a child of two. Maybe that's it. Maybe we should tell her that we all want her to come back to Amos. That he needs her and that it's her duty to do so, no matter how hard it is on her. Maybe she'd have nothing to do with him if she thought he wanted her back and we approved the idea."

"Would she believe that?"

"Why shouldn't she? There's only one really good thing about this whole situation. If it weren't for that, we'd be sunk."

"And that is?"

"That Vera herself has not the slightest idea of how all the rest of us feel about her."

Meg choked.

"Something wrong?"

She managed to swallow. "No."

"What was it you wanted to tell me, darling?"

"I . . ." Meg hesitated. Then, "It seems to have slipped my mind."

"Then it can't have been very important."

Through the swirling fog, they saw the signpost that marked the Weston exit. Gus pulled farther to the right and slowed down for the turn. Meg sighed with relief. Once they were off the parkway, on winding country roads, there would be less traffic and speed would be reduced automatically.

Ten minutes later they left a highway and turned into a wooded drive. When they came out of the trees, they saw Tony's house at the top of a hill, its lights glowing golden through the mist. It was that rare thing in New England, an old farmhouse built of stone with a large, stone barn. Tony, who had lived and worked in Manhattan, was aggressively bucolic now that he could afford that greatest of all modern luxuries—a farm. There were saddle horses in the stable, Jersey cows in the barn, hens in the hen house, pigs in the sty, and even doves in the dovecote—all screened from the house by distance and a twelve-foot hedge of juniper and hemlock. On Tony's writing paper the place was described as Hilltop Farm, and when Tony filled out forms he always put under Occupation the words *farmer and publisher* in that order, though even Tony knew he could never have been a farmer if he hadn't been a publisher first. At Christmas his office staff received presents of home-grown turkeys and homemade fruit cake. At Easter they all got baskets of fresh eggs from Hilltop.

The house itself stood at the highest point of the hill overlooking a brook with a lily pond. Beyond, lawn and meadows sloped down to the treetops of the woods on the hillside below. In summer these trees formed a leafy screen that hid the nearest houses from view. In winter their shapes, scattered at random like a child's blocks, could be seen dimly through the branches. Tonight, with snow on the ground and lights at all the windows, the view looked like a giant Christmas card derived from Currier and Ives.

There was only one other car in the half moon of gravel—Philippa's little Austin. Gus parked his car and rang the bell. Meg shivered nervously inside her warm coat as they waited.

A Negro in a white jacket opened the door. Gus surrendered his wraps while Meg made her way up the familiar stairs to the guest room. When she came down again, Gus was waiting for her in the hall. Together they entered the great drawing room that made even an apartment as large as theirs seem cramped and cluttered.

Philippa, in gray velvet and emeralds, stood with her back to a blazing fire in the grate. At her elbow, in an attitude of gallantry, was Maurice Lepton, the critic. An ugly, fascinating man, thought Meg, a perverse compound of grace and malice.

There was no sign of Tony.

"He's gone to call Amos's house again." Philippa's voice was strained. "They should have been here by this time."

"There's fog on the parkway," said Gus. "Everyone will be late."

Philippa sighed and rested one slender arm on the mantelpiece, trailing a chiffon stole of pale green. "What a responsibility Amos is! I hate to think of his driving out from Idlewild in a fog. I know just how the owner of a winning racehorse must feel."

Maurice nodded. "A good analogy. Each book is a new race that he may not win. Between races, there's always the possibility of illness or accident or . . ." His eyes twinkled. "Somebody slipping into the stable with a hypo."

"It's a little like being a mother, too." Meg's mind went back to Polly with a sudden pang of anguish. "The more people you care about, the more vulnerable you are to every kind of disaster."

"Amos has solved that problem," said Philippa tartly. "He doesn't care about anybody but Amos."

"Oh, really, Phil!" protested Meg. "How can you say such a thing?" In her mind she added, especially in front of Maurice Lepton, whose good opinion is so important to Amos.

"Well, who does Amos love?" demanded Philippa. "Not Vera, I'm sure."

She halted as Tony came into the room. His worry was obvious. "No answer. I let the phone ring ten times. Of course they were supposed to come directly here from the airport, but . . ."

"Just so Vera doesn't stop off for a drink somewhere," murmured Philippa.

"Even Vera wouldn't do that on a night like this!" said Tony, loudly and firmly.

"Who else is coming?" asked Meg.

Philippa sighed again. "At such short notice I had to scrape the bottom of the barrel. I've got a widow from down the road who is writing her first novel at the age of sixty-seven, and her son, home from school for the Christmas holidays. The name is Pusey. And then I've got the Willings from Westport. He is, or was, one of Tony's authors."

"Willing?" repeated Maurice. "Not Basil Willing?"

"You know him?"

"I know of him. They call him a forensic psychiatrist but he seems to me more like a criminologist. He solved a number of rather curious murder cases when he was with the district attorney's office in New York."

"You mean he's really a sort of detective?" put in Philippa. "If I'd known that, I would never have dared invite him. There's no knowing what he may find out about us!"

Everyone laughed and Tony said, "I told you not to bury that last body in the dahlia bed! The next time you murder someone, use the incinerator."

Just then the doorbell rang.

In the sudden silence, they could hear the Negro man's step as he crossed the hall to the door.

"It must be Amos!" Gus's voice sounded as if he were praying.

"And Vera." Meg discovered that her hands were ice. Her heart was racing jerkily. Her gaze went through the archway to the hall and she saw lamplight shining on Vera's brassy hair.

Amos stumbled as he came into the room. Gus and Tony looked incredulously at Amos's flushed face and muddied eyes.

It was Tony who whispered to Gus, "God almighty, the b - - - - - - is drunk!"

"Submerged in his mystique," murmured Philippa. "Cottle spares us nothing."

five

Amos had reached the airport when the sun was a blurred halo in a low ceiling of gray cloud, formless and faintly silver as a light seen through a frosted windowpane.

The plane was due in ten minutes. Information said that it was on time and directed him to Gate 14 near the Orville Wright Cocktail Bar. Even on Sunday at four in the afternoon there were a few limp, masculine figures draped over the mahogany bar, and other men with women sitting at little tables. Amos eyed them with contemptuous tolerance. To think that he had once been like that!

It was cold waiting. He stood with his hands in his pockets, his shoulders hunched and his bearded chin snuggled inside his coat collar, a sullen figure who seemed bored with the whole business of airports. Through a vast wall of glass he could see the landing field. It had been snowplowed, but here and there a patch of greasy slush caught the light like a slick of oil on water.

He remembered the wheels of his car spinning uselessly on his driveway this afternoon. Landing speeds were close to the edge of the margin of safety. Suppose, just suppose, there was a spot of half-melted ice slippery as oil on the runway beyond Gate 14. And suppose the great transcontinental plane skidded and lost traction at landing speed. It would spin in a circle and overturn and there would be a flaming explosion and—all the problems created by Vera's arrival would be ended decorously without his lifting a finger. Then, he'd be free, really free, for the first time in his life. After he made a little more, he'd retire to Majorca. . . .

He sighed and shrank deeper into the warmth of his overcoat. A man should not allow such thoughts to invade his mind. Where did they come from? This unseen, unproved, unknown subconscious the psychiatrists prated about? Or some force outside his own being that medievalists personified as the devil? Perhaps the subconscious was just a pipe line to forces outside the individual. Had the psychiatrists ever thought of that? Probably not. The pontifical posture of medical research had always irritated him. Whoever decided to name primitive tribal magicians "medicine men" must have felt the same way. . . .

Lost in his musings, he did not see the plane land, but he saw Vera before she saw him. He had a moment to observe her when she did not know she was being observed. Her face had changed little. There were no lines, hardly any sagging, yet it had a curiously used look that did make her seem older than he remembered her.

She was using the latest Parisian cosmetic tricks, the so-called Chinese style—two shades of white powder, supposed to produce a lucent, porcelain effect, eyes and brows tilted as well as darkened, and a deep, ruby lipstick that followed the natural line of the lips. It was not a good style for Vera. It accentuated the smallness and petulance of the mouth and the mean, narrow point of the chin. The eyes that should have been languorous, as well as slanting, in such a mask were shrewd and alert, darting here and there with a look of restless greed. The hair, under the wide, fur turban, was a slightly paler shade of brass than when she left New York. Her furs were opulent and ample. You couldn't see her figure at all, only the delicate, prehensile hands gloved in black suede and the tiny, brittle feet perched on tall heels. She clutched a luxurious-looking jewel case in one hand. The other hand lifted in a sudden signal: "Amos!"

He slouched forward, unsmiling.

"Dearest, take this!" She pushed the jewel case at him and pouted. "Aren't you going to kiss me?"

"No." The ungallant word lay between them for a moment.

"Darling, please don't be tiresome!" It was a silky smooth voice, so light and gentle it was almost inaudible without a microphone. It was a voice that said: *I am a lady. Really I am. There is no doubt about it whatever.* The sharp, blond face, with its heavy cosmetic mask, looked shrewish and hard. But when she opened her mouth you thought of velvet and vintage Burgundy and everything else that was soft and delicate. Amos had often wondered if it was artifice or accident.

She went on, still more gently: "Where are the reporters?"

"There are no reporters. This isn't Hollywood."

"Oh . . ." She looked around the vast, impersonal waiting room and shivered in her nest of furs. "Such a brute of a day. Cold as death.

And you're as cold as the day. Do you know sometimes, Amos, I think you're not completely human?"

"Inhuman? Or subhuman?" They had fallen into step. He shortened his stride to keep pace with her Chinese tottering. Her feet weren't bound, but her heels were five inches high.

"Neither." The painted brows met in a frown. "Just, somehow, incomplete. You lack something everybody else has."

"What?"

"I don't know. Just something. A dimension maybe. As if you were cut out of paper and had no depth."

He pretended to take her literally. "I weigh 147 pounds. I have volume so I must have depth."

Her glance flew past him and alighted on the neon sign: Bar. "Oh, Amos, I feel so miserable. I could use a drink, but I suppose you wouldn't . . ."

"I won't drink, but I'll go in with you," he answered calmly.

"Thank goodness!" She swerved and quickened her pace with a sly glance at him over her shoulder. "You're not afraid of bars any more?"

"Good lord, no! I don't even want to drink these days."

"Antabuse?"

"I gave that up long ago. I don't need it. After all, a man has to be pretty weak if he can't say no to a drink."

They passed through glass doors and found a table. She threw back her furs and he saw the new torso dressed in fluid, black crepe. Art had slimmed her waist, widened her pelvis and made her breasts, once rather full, just what Monsieur Dior said they should be—"little apples."

A waiter hovered. She didn't wait for Amos to give the order, just as she had never waited for him to give the address to a taxi driver or the floor to an elevator man. She said promptly and clearly: "A double Scotch on the rocks."

The waiter glanced at Amos. "Just ginger ale, please."

Amos wondered uncomfortably just what the waiter was thinking of a man who let his woman order for herself and then took ginger ale while she was taking whiskey. Why were all vices considered proofs of masculinity? Did most people secretly believe that it was impossible to be a man and be good? Perhaps women had invented the idea of decorum in prehistory and men had never accepted it wholeheartedly. Perhaps everyone realized this subconsciously.

He studied Vera across the table. She still had many of the mannerisms of an irresistible siren, but there was a fatal flaw in her performance—she was bossy. A bossy siren: it was a contradiction in terms. She couldn't be a really good actress or she would have learned by now to play her off-stage role with more art and intelligence.

"Amos, why do you look at me like that?"

He dropped his eyes.

"You know I really meant what I said to the newspaper men about coming back to you. Is it too late?"

He looked away from her. "It's impossible, Vera. I like the life I have now. I don't want to change. Why should I?"

His gaze came back to her and he saw her eyes had narrowed to calculating slits. "It's those awful people!"

"What awful people?"

"The Veseys and the Kanes. They treat you as if you were their property—a robot or a slave—and they don't like me."

"But they do like you," protested Amos. "Tony and Philippa are throwing a party for you this afternoon and you're going to stay with them, aren't you?"

"Maybe. I haven't decided yet."

"But Tony said you'd accepted their invitation."

"I can change my mind, can't I?"

Amos tried another tack. "Tony and Philippa will do everything they can to help you with your stage career in New York."

"So I'll be too busy to be with you. I don't want a stage career. I want you. Acting is hard work. I want to sit back and enjoy being the wife of a really successful author."

The softly implacable voice brought Amos to the verge of panic. "You're—you're unreasonable, Vera. Why don't you want to stay with Tony and Philippa? They . . ."

"Look at this." She lifted her jewel case onto the table and snapped open the locks. On top of the jewel boxes lay her wallet and a few papers. She picked out a letter and slid it across the table. "Read that."

He looked at it, puzzled. "The envelope's addressed to you but the letter begins: 'Dear Amos.' "

"Exactly. Your charming Meg Vesey was so flustered when she heard I was coming east that she put the wrong letter in my envelope

—a letter meant for you. That's how I found out exactly what your precious friends really think of me, and I am telling you, Amos, whether we live together or not, I want you to get another publisher and another agent—people who will treat me with respect and consideration. I think you owe me that much courtesy. After all, I am your wife."

Amos glanced swiftly through Meg's letter and pushed it back across the table. "I'm sorry, Vera. What you suggest is impossible. I cannot go to another publisher or another agent."

"Why on earth not?"

Amos sighed. "For one thing, I don't want to. For another, no other publisher or agent could do for me what these two are doing."

"I never heard such utter nonsense in my life!" The voice that still sounded like pigeons cooing emphasized the force in the words themselves. "Amos, I'm thinking of your interests as well as my self-respect. You know I have a copy of your contract with Sutton, Kane. I showed it to my Hollywood agent when I was out there. He said you could get much better terms from any other publisher in the business. Better publishers than Sutton, Kane, people like Random House or Dodd, Mead. And do you realize that Gus Vesey gets a great, big hunk of everything you earn? Why is that? Most literary agents get less. Have you ever stopped to think that Sutton, Kane is getting a large slice of all your subsidiary rights? Why? Even the royalty rate on the trade edition of your books is much less than any other publisher would pay an author as successful as you.

"Jim Karp—he's my agent—says that Sutton, Kane must be crooks and you should have your head examined. That's one reason I decided to come east when the studio dropped my option. Sam says you could just about double your income if you had somebody like him to look after you. He has a New York office run by his brother Sam and I'm going to take you up there tomorrow."

Amos's eyes hardened and he spoke between stiff lips. "Vera, this happens to be my business and not yours. I'll help you get a start on the stage here. I'll give you a divorce and pay you alimony. But I don't want you messing up my relations with Gus and Tony. For the love of . . ."

"What is the matter with you, Amos? Some insane idea of personal loyalty? Sentimentality just because Sutton, Kane published your first book? Have you ever tried asking either Gus or Tony for better terms? They can't shoot you for asking, can they?"

Amos looked as if he were going to weep. "Vera," he croaked hoarsely, "I want you to mind your own business. I want you to . . ."

He hadn't seen the stranger approach. He was warned by the sudden change in Vera's face. The petulance vanished in a warm, bright smile that matched the dove voice. She was all siren now. "Why, Tom Archer! Do you know my husband, Amos Cottle?"

Amos rose, clumsy and disconcerted. The other man was tall and thin and rather untidy. Youth and credulity met happily in his long, plain face. "How do you do, Mr. Cottle? I'm a great admirer of your work. I left my drink at the bar. May I bring it over and join you?"

"Of course!" Vera answered for Amos and he hated her for doing so. He stood awkwardly watching the tall, gangling figure stride back to the bar.

Still Vera did not raise her voice but there was deadly menace under the restraint now. "Tom writes for the *Times*." It was almost a whisper. "Second-string theatrical and movie stuff. Either you let me tell him that we are reconciled and going to live together or I'm going to tell him about the sort of contract you have with Sutton, Kane. You'll have to change publishers when he prints that."

"He can't print it," said Amos. "There are laws of libel."

"How can it be libel when it's true? Anyway he can always print it as a rumor: 'It is alleged that Amos Cottle is dissatisfied with his contract with . . .' "

"That wouldn't be theatrical news."

"Your wife's an actress—that will make it theatrical news. I'm going to tell him that you're thinking of writing a play for me because you're disgusted with Sutton, Kane's handling of your books and . . ."

"Be quiet, Vera. He might hear you now."

"What of it? You can't silence me. I hate those Kanes and Veseys and I'd love to let the cat out of the bag about the way they're exploiting your genius."

"Vera! If you will keep your mouth shut about my affairs, you may tell Archer that . . ." He gagged a little. "That we are reconciled."

Her eyes widened. His sudden surrender had surprised her so much that she was silenced for a moment, completely off balance.

He saw calculation replace surprise and he knew what she was thinking: *Once we're living together again I'll work on him day in and day out until I get him away from Tony and Gus.* She believed every word Jim Karp had told her about the contracts with Gus and Tony and she would never forgive Meg for that letter. Vera didn't know how to forgive.

It was many years since Amos had felt quite so trapped as he did now. He was no longer ashamed of wishing that Vera's plane would crash on landing. If he could have killed Vera at this moment without immediate consequences to himself he would have done so.

Tom Archer was smiling as he came back from the bar. He looked at the empty ginger ale glass in front of Amos. "Oh, I didn't realize you needed another. What will it be?"

Amos hesitated. It was years since he had felt any craving for alcohol. The old habit was broken. Of course the pompous doctors didn't think so. They warned him not to be too sure of his cure. They claimed that it was the first drink that counted in cases like his. Once he had taken that first drink, his defenses would crumble, they said, and he would be unable to stop.

It wasn't true, of course. The fool doctors had no idea how he had learned to discipline himself, how strong his will had become. He'd been a good boy for a long time. He'd gone to literary cocktail parties and stuck to ginger ale or iced tea for nearly four years now. It was no longer an effort to do so. He didn't mind the sly jokes or the feeling that his abstinence was a silent reproach to others that made them uncomfortable. He had gone through many trying times —headache and disappointment and fatigue—without resorting to the lift of alcohol, and he had resisted the even more subtle temptation to celebrate his success when the TV show first won a high rating.

"Just this once—champagne, not hard liquor," the sponsor had said and, even at the risk of offending the sponsor, Amos had shaken his head. The physiological craving that had been so strong in his days of poverty and insecurity was entirely gone. He never had liked the taste of the stuff. Now he had no desire for its effect either. He had the thing licked. He could take it or leave it alone.

He had actually done what so many doctors said no man could do. *The true alcoholic is never cured, for a single drink will always start him on his way again.* That was nonsense and he could prove it.

It was years since he had had to rely on the pathetic crutch of Antabuse. He had cured himself entirely by his understanding of that great psychological mystery, the will, one of the very few things that really did distinguish man from other animals. What had Jung said: *Will is domesticated instinct.* The impulsive force that drove animals to instinctual acts as predetermined as post-hypnotic suggestion harnessed by man in the service of free, reasonable choice. A neat conception, possibly a true one.

He was his own master now. He knew better than the doctors and suddenly he saw this moment as a great opportunity to prove it.

Of course there was that speech he had to make at the Bookbinders' Award Dinner. Gus had warned him to be especially circumspect until that was over, but . . . One little drink this afternoon wouldn't affect his condition Wednesday night. After all, wasn't the award for the Most American Author of the Decade? Wouldn't it be distinctly un-American never to take a drink at all, at any time?

How could he demonstrate his strength of will to himself or others if he never dared to take one single drink again as long as he lived? But if he took one drink now and then stopped for the rest of the day and the rest of the year and all the years to come—that would show them. His first drink in three years would be his last drink for all the rest of his life.

The phrase lingered in his mind: his last drink for all the rest of his life. . . . Better make it a good one.

Amos smiled up at Tom Archer. "I'll have a double Scotch on the rocks like my wife."

Vera was startled. "Amos, do you think . . . ?"

"Don't worry." He was furious. "I can handle it now."

"But you're driving and there's slush and I . . ."

"Look here, Vera, there's something you'll have to understand: I am going to be my own master in every way from now on."

Vera, aware of Tom Archer's gaze across the room, managed a sweet smile. "Of course, you are darling, but . . ."

"But what?"

"I never thought—when we came in here . . ."

"You never think. Period."

Tom Archer came back with the drinks. Genial, smiling, he lifted his own glass. "Here's to your reconciliation—or shouldn't I believe all I see in the papers?"

Vera managed to look shy. "It's true, isn't it, Amos?"
"Yes, it's true."
"May I print that?"
"Sure. Why not?"
Amos took a deep draught of whiskey. The taste was acrid and hateful to him as it had always been, but in a moment he felt the singing in his blood, the curious, luxurious loosening in his brain tissue, the lift, the glow, the blessed release, blessed ecstasy. I go out. Out of what? Out of myself, of course. Out of my wretched, little, finite self into the painless infinite where anything and everything is possible.

He smiled across the table at Vera and Tom Archer and muttered his favorite quotation at such moments:

> *Drinking this, I shall see*
> *Far Chaos talk with me.*
> *Kings unborn shall walk with me*
> *And hear the poor grass plot and plan*
> *What it will do when it is Man. . . .*

Vera tittered in a ladylike way. "You can print that, too."
Tom said: "If I can get permission from the copyright holder . . ."
Amos laughed. "Don't those modern schools teach you brats anything that was published before 1914? That's been in the public domain a long time." He drained his glass, muttered something about "the belly of the grape" and then shouted: "How about one more for the road? And this round is on me!"

six

Gisela Willing looked through her big bedroom window at four o'clock and saw that the leaden sky was darkening. Beyond the grape arbor, sentinel ranks of leafless willows stood beside the brook, hunched under mantles of snow. They looked desperate and forsaken and chilled to the marrow, like pictures of Napoleon's soldiers retreating from Moscow. It was a night to stay at home, relaxing around a brisk fire with a glass of mulled wine, and here they were committed to adventure on dark, rough roads, coated with ice, for the sake of a silly supper party. She thought longingly of Manhattan, its paved, level streets, brightly lighted and snowplowed, its buses and taxis, even its subways. Why did sensible people, like Basil and herself, ever decide to live in the country in winter?

But she knew her husband's old-fashioned Baltimorean sense of obligation where hospitality was concerned. Nothing short of serious illness was a valid excuse for repudiating an accepted invitation. To renege at the last moment, because the weather was bad or you were tired or you had just got a more interesting invitation was something he never inflicted on a host and found hard to forgive in a guest. . . .

Basil Willing stood in the lower hall listening to the keening of the icy wind as it swept around the corners of the house. Sunday evening should be a time for slacks and sweaters and comfortable old shoes, a light supper and an early bedtime to store up energy for the week ahead. But somehow, in a moment of inattention, he had said yes to the invitation from the Kanes relayed through Gisela and now they would have to take the long, hilly road to Weston on one of the bitterest nights of the year and spend an evening among strangers who would probably be deadly bores.

He was sorely tempted to ask Gisela to telephone their hostess at this last moment and plead a diplomatic illness, but he knew what Gisela would think of such rudeness. Austrian-born, she had a European's sense of the sanctity of social duties. He admired this trait and, tired as he was after a day of tedious, hospital paper work in his study, he was not going to let her down.

He lifted his eyes as he heard her step on the stair. Her dark hair was a black cloud shadowing her pale face and brilliant eyes. Her dress, long and straight, was the odd shade of off-black with a bluish cast that they called gunmetal, cut low to show off the whiteness of her shoulders and arms. The high heels of her gunmetal slippers were paved with smoky mother-of-pearl and around her throat was a strand of dusky, black pearls. She wore no other ornament but her wedding ring, a band of small diamonds. She was smiling as she came down the stairs, the long skirt moving fluidly around her ankles, and she seemed the very essence of the romantic feminine—a gentle swish of silk, the faintest fragrance of violets—or was it mignonette?—dignity in her step, grace in her carriage and sweetness in her smile. Why did the mature American woman strive so often today to dress and look like a hoydenish, high school girl? Gisela was something much more subtle and interesting—a woman—and he silently thanked the gods for it.

Little Gisela ran downstairs after her, already wearing pyjamas and robe and furry bedroom slippers. She leapt from the bottom step into her father's arms. "Do you *have* to go out tonight?"

"I'm afraid we do. And right away. We're late already."

"Wait till I give Emma the telephone number." Gisela hurried into the kitchen. "We're going to be at a Mr. Anthony Kane's," she told the motherly Negro cook. "A Weston number. I've written it down. But we should be home early. Ten at the very latest."

Basil's old factotum, Juniper, had long since retired to his family in Baltimore and his granddaughter, Emma, had taken over the household when it moved to Connecticut.

"Don't you worry about us, ma'am," said Emma. "We'll have a nice chicken and waffle supper and be in bed by seven-thirty."

Gisela slipped on carriage boots, shrugged her shoulders into a fur cape, snatched up gloves and a black lace scarf and caught a last kiss from small warm lips; then hurried out to the car where Basil was already scraping ice off the windshield.

He eyed her in the light of the lamp on the gatepost. "You look just like the popular idea of a young Russian princess, vintage 1914."

She laughed. "And, of course, the real young Russian princess of that vintage dressed most of the time just like her English governess."

The car wheels spun for a moment on the ice that lay treacherously hidden under a thin coating of snow. Then the snow tires found traction and Basil eased the car gingerly into the road. The heater hummed and they sat in snug warmth while their headlights bored a tunnel of light through the darkness. No other cars on this road tonight. They might have been alone in some Alaskan or Siberian waste. But it was intimate and pleasant in the car, and the bitter night gave them just a little spice of adventure.

"What sort of party will this be?" asked Gisela. "Everyone talking about Art and Letters in capitals?"

"The publishers will talk about Art and Letters," returned Basil. "But the artists and writers will talk about subsidiary rights and the termination clause in somebody's contract, and did you know that Tom Jones, who used to be with Lippincott's, has gone to Simon and Schuster, and Mary Jones is getting a divorce in Las Vegas so she can marry Bill Smith who used to be Tom's agent?"

"Unconventional?"

"Not at all. No one is more conventional than your well-heeled Bohemian—a new species produced by the twentieth century."

The road dipped into a valley and now the headlights showed only fog, gray, churning, impenetrable as heavy smoke. The light was trapped and diffused in its various thicknesses. Impossible to see anything more than four or five feet ahead. The car slowed to a crawl.

She didn't distract him with further talk. She sat in companionable silence and counted her blessings: Basil himself and little Gisela, Emma and the nice house and even the party ahead of her. It might not be as boring as they feared.

Twenty minutes later they were in Weston scanning the names on letter boxes. "I called Tony for directions while you were dressing," remarked Basil. "He said the third box after the second traffic light after you leave the Wilton road."

"Tony? I didn't know you knew him that well."

"I saw quite a lot of him when my book was in galleys. Even if I hadn't, the theatre habit of first names has spread to all the other arts."

"What do I call his wife?"

"Gosh, what was her name? That's the worst part of this artificial intimacy. It's easy to remember 'Mrs. Kane' but—Isobel? No. Francesca? I think not. . . . We'll have to listen to what the others say and play it by ear."

"There's the box—A. F. Kane, Jr."

"Anthony Francis." The car swerved between fieldstone gateposts. "Uphill. I hope it's sanded."

It was. They stopped in front of a stone house with mullioned windows, all bright with interior light. In the misty night it seemed unreal—a play house cut out of cardboard with a candle flame behind waxed-paper windows. Basil rang the bell and they waited, shivering in the open after the warmth of the car.

The door was opened by Washington Lincoln, the county's most popular caterer who provided service as well as food on such occasions. He greeted them with that perfect blend of natural dignity and deference that only a Negro butler seems able to achieve. Disposal of wraps was a faultless ceremony, a ritual dance—hadn't Lincoln been doing this almost every day for the last thirty years?

A few moments later they found themselves in a large modern

drawing room, sixty feet of polished oak under foot, a beamed ceiling twenty feet high, white walls on three sides, glass on the garden side. A goldfish pool was sunk in the center of the floor with trailing green vines planted around it in a circular copper trough. Chairs and sofas were covered with perverse shades of mauve and magenta that echoed the violet undertones in a collection of antique lustre, ranging from lavender to the roseate brown of certain pigeons. Ornament was used sparingly. The general effect was one of airy spaces and immaculate housekeeping. Gisela thought: if only there were just one thing out of place—a book on the arm of a chair, a child's toy on the white hearth rug or an open pack of cigarettes on one of the low tables. But there were no books and no sign of children and all the cigarettes were in a large handsome silver box lined with cedar and initialed AFK.

Tony Kane and two other men stood near the goldfish pool, oddly aloof from the others as if they were huddled together in conspiracy. Three women and a fourth man were scattered at the other end of the room in rather loose juxtaposition as if some awkwardness had inhibited their sociability. One of these women came forward now, followed by the solitary man. Her chin was high, her step firm, but her very rigidity suggested hysteria, hardly controlled.

"You must be Gisela Willing. So glad you could come. I'm Philippa Kane." She stood several inches taller than Gisela and her eyes seemed as green as her emeralds. "Basil, it's been ages. Much too long. Do you know Maurice Lepton?"

The man beside Philippa was small and swarthy with a pleasant smile.

"I know your writing," said Basil. "Or rather my wife does. She reads the *Thursday Review* every week."

"Especially the essays by Maurice Lepton," said Gisela.

"My dear Mrs. Willing, I'm all in a pretty confusion," said Lepton. "For one thing, you said 'essays,' not 'reviews.' For another . . ."

Basil, seeing that his wife as usual could take care of herself, drifted toward his host. Tony was a little stouter, a little grayer, but he still had the comely face and candid smile that had once helped him to become the boy prodigy of the publishing world. "Now you're settled in the country, you must have more time for writing," he told Basil. "How about another book? How about the *Psychopathology of Trea-*

son? You know, a rehash of Famous Spy Cases with a lot of stuff about the subconscious thrown in."

When Basil shook his head, Tony introduced the other two. "I think you've met Gus Vesey before. And this is Amos Cottle."

Gus Vesey was obviously younger than Tony, in years and in spirit. There was a simplicity about him that engaged Basil's sympathy immediately. More slowly, Basil turned toward Amos Cottle and suddenly saw the reason for the conspiratorial grouping around the pool. The celebrated novelist was royally drunk. His agent and publisher had formed a little bodyguard around him with the obvious intention of seeing that he didn't make a fool of himself if they could prevent it.

Amos was doing his best. Though his bloodshot eyes looked quite without focus, he stood erect and spoke with unnatural precision. "I am delighted to make your acquaintance, Dr. Willing. I read your book years ago when it first came out. I am one of your—admirers." The last word slurred a little sluggishly. Amos closed his eyes for a moment and swayed on his feet.

The doorbell rang. A little woman in white lace with a froth of white hair came into the room, followed by a youth and an older man. The youth could have been an undergraduate at Yale or Harvard. The older man had a long, hard, wooden-looking face, and frosty gray eyes. He might have been one of the boy's professors. Certainly there was nothing about him or the other two to explain the sudden look of horror in Tony's eyes.

Philippa advanced again with that strained rigidity. "Mrs. Pusey, so good of you to come on such a night."

"My dear Mrs. Kane, I wouldn't have missed meeting Amos Cottle for anything!" Mrs. Pusey's voice was high and metallic. It penetrated to every corner of the large room. "This is my son, Sidney and . . . Well, dear Mrs. Kane, I hope you won't mind, but, after all, it is only a buffet supper, so I took the liberty of bringing a neighbor. Mr. Avery. Emmett Avery. He writes, too."

There was unheard thunder in the abrupt silence. It was like the hush after an explosion. Basil and Gisela exchanged bewildered glances across the width of the room. What had Mrs. Pusey said or done to create such a charged stillness? It was obvious that everyone else in the room was aware of catastrophe.

Philippa Kane threw back her shoulders and took a deep breath.

"That's perfectly all right, Mrs. Pusey." Her voice was colorless and hard as stone.

"He writes, too," repeated Mrs. Pusey, floundering a little. "I thought as long as it was a gathering of writers and publishers and so on . . ." Her voice trailed uncertainly.

Maurice Lepton sprang into the breach. "A very happy thought on your part, Mrs. Pusey. As a matter of fact, I believe most of the people in this room know Emmett Avery already, including myself. How are you, Emmett?"

"Very well, thank you, Leppy." The two men eyed each other without shaking hands, but there seemed to be a curious sort of understanding between them, along with the hostility, as if they shared a common secret that gave them knowledge of each other without affection. Basil recalled how some Latin writer had claimed that when two augurs met by chance in the streets of Rome they winked at one another.

Mrs. Pusey had recovered her volubility. "And now I want to meet Mr. Cottle!" she announced, in the tone of a child saying "And now I want that candy you promised me after dinner."

Maurice Lepton detained Avery in conversation, while Philippa, moving like a sleepwalker, brought Mrs. Pusey over to the little group of refugees by the goldfish pool.

Mrs. Pusey beamed. "Mr. Cottle, I just want to tell you how tremendously I enjoyed *Never Call Retreat*. My niece was a WAC in the Quartermaster's Corps at Fort Monmouth in 1941, so I know all about war and I think you handled it beautifully. Just like *War and Peace*, only better, of course. And I do think the love story was touching. That's the only word for it. Touching. I liked Sandra and I didn't like Ida. I was so glad Sandra got him in the end, even though they couldn't get married, but of course that's realism. You know, Mr. Cottle, I thought Sandra was just a little bit like me—I mean the way I was a few years ago. There's just one question I should like to ask you now, dear Mr. Cottle. Just how do you get your ideas? I mean, how do you begin to write a story? That's the part I find so hard—the beginning. All my friends tell me that I write the most beautiful letters. They all say I ought to write for publication. But I just don't seem to find the time and then I don't know how to begin. I have lots to write about. I have had the most extraordinary experiences all my life. If you could hear about the way my stepmother tried to cheat me out of my inheritance—well, people like Proust and Faulkner would just give their eyeteeth to have a story like that to write."

Amos had purred under the first part of her oration, but as soon as she shifted to her own ambitions, his eyes glazed.

"How do I get my ideas?" There was an uncomfortable note of ribaldry in his voice. "I'll tell you, madam. I just . . ."

Gus intervened swiftly. "Amos, I'm sure that Tony has an extra copy of *Never Call Retreat* around the house. Wouldn't it be a nice gesture if you autographed if for anyone who admires you as much as Mrs. Pusey?"

"Oh, Mr. Cottle, would you? You have no idea what that would mean to a poor little country woman like me! Why if you would actually write your own name in a copy of one of your books with a little inscription—best wishes to one of my most adoring fans, Peggy Pusey, why I—I really . . ."

Amos uttered an unprintable word and everyone pretended to be deaf. This time it was Sidney who tried to save the situation.

"Really, Mother, how can you bother a serious artist like Amos Cottle with this sort of bobby-socks hero worship?"

"Sidney, darling, don't be so rude!" Mrs. Pusey looked helplessly at Basil. "Sometimes I wonder if I should have sent him to that progressive school."

Sidney was addressing Amos on a lofty plane, as man to man. "I must apologize for my mother, Mr. Cottle," he said with desperate honesty. "She is not poor and she is scarcely a country woman. She was born in Nashville and my father was a stockbroker who commuted to Wall Street all his life."

"But, Sidney, dear, I only meant . . ."

"Mr. Cottle," went on Sidney solemnly. "I should like to say that I regard you as the most fearless and original novelist this country has produced in this generation. You have left Faulkner far behind you, sir, far behind. Where his style is involved, yours is lapidary and your thinking has an ethos peculiarly its own. But the thing I admire most about your art is your feeling for the shape of the narrative form. Galsworthy speaking as a critic, once said: 'Form is Life.' I may add that Form is Literature. Your organic feeling for contour reminds me of a principle in biology . . ."

Amos looked at Tony owlishly, and enunciated distinctly, "When am I going to get a drink?"

Sidney was stopped in midstream, mouth open. He looked as if Amos had slapped his face.

Tony answered Amos soothingly, "Right away, old man, right away."

He took Basil's arm and drew him away from the group. "I could use one myself. How about you?"

"After seeing such an awful example . . ."

Tony groaned. "This is the most fabulous situation. Amos has been a reformed alcoholic for years, ever since he began to write. This afternoon he slipped a cog and—God knows what will happen now. Hey! You're a psychiatrist. Could you do anything to get him back on the wagon?"

"Not until he's slept this off. What made him relapse?"

"That's the worst of it—I don't know exactly. But it has something to do with that woman, Vera, his wife. You know my father's story about the old apple woman who said, 'I don't wish her no harm—oh, no!—I just wish to God she'd fall down and break her damned neck!' "

Basil had heard this story of Tony's several times before. He smiled dutifully as his gaze followed Tony's to a small, fat, blond head on a long, slender neck. There was something unpleasantly serpentine about its supple, forward pose.

"That's Meg Vesey with her. I wonder what she's saying to Meg now? Meg doesn't look a bit happy."

Basil's glance shifted to a brown-haired woman, pleasantly plump and alert as a little hen pheasant. Tony was right: she did not look happy at all, yet her face was made for smiles.

The bar was at the other end of the room. Lincoln had just brought in a tray of glasses. Everyone was moving in that direction now.

"What are you going to give Cottle?" asked Basil.

"He'll get what he always gets here: iced tea. It saves face because it looks just like Scotch and soda. I'd better take over. Lincoln might give me the iced tea and hand the Scotch to Amos." Tony went behind the bar. "Will you serve canapés now, Lincoln?"

Lincoln had already filled the tall glasses with ice cubes. Tony added Scotch from a decanter, Gus added soda, then Lepton, Avery and Basil served the women. Tony filled the next glass with dark fluid from a cut glass pitcher. "Here you are, Amos." It was done so smoothly that no one could notice the difference in Amos's drink—not even Amos himself who took his glass eagerly.

Tony was already filling six more glasses from the decanter. Gus added soda. Basil handed one to Lepton and one to Avery. The others helped themselves.

Amos took one sip of his drink and made a hideous grimace. For a moment he looked as if he were going to dash the glass in Tony's face. But he didn't. Without a word he quietly emptied his glass on the floor, walked over to the bar and filled it again with neat whiskey from the decanter.

Gus took a step toward Amos, but Tony said softly: "Hold it, Gus. There's nothing we can do now."

Avery laughed aloud. "How about the Bookbinders' Award Dinner? Amos going to that Wednesday night?"

Maurice Lepton's usually pale face reddened and he looked at Avery with unmistakable hatred in his eyes. "Why don't you ask Amos? If it's any business of yours. While you're about it, you might ask him what he thought of your review in the *Tribune* this morning. He's in a condition to give you a really honest answer."

"He's in a condition to give me a punch on the jaw," answered Avery. "You'd rather enjoy that, wouldn't you, Leppy? Something you've always wanted to do, but you're not quite big enough."

Philippa was standing beside Basil. "Oh, Basil, how are we going to get through this dreadful evening?" she whispered. "Why did that stupid woman have to bring Emmett Avery of all people? I don't think Amos knows who he is yet. We've got to do something to keep Amos from finding out before he passes out. Some parlor game would do it."

"Charades?"

"No, something we can play sitting down until Amos goes to sleep in his chair. I have it! Two-Thirds of a Ghost."

Philippa started briskly down the room. The others were regrouped around the goldfish pool where Lincoln was passing a tray of his famous hot canapés.

Philippa's voice commanded attention. "Do you all know how to play Two-Thirds of a Ghost?"

"What a marvelous idea!" cried Peggy Pusey. "Mrs Kane, I haven't heard of that game since I was a little girl in Tennessee."

"You never told me about it," remarked Sidney.

"It's awfully simple, really." Tony was quick to pick up Philippa's cue. "The one who's It asks trick questions of each player in turn. If you can't answer a question the first time, you're a third of a ghost. If you miss a second time, you're two-thirds of a ghost. If you miss the third time, you're three-thirds of a ghost—that is, a whole ghost. In other words, you're dead—out of the game. Whoever stays alive the longest wins the game and gets to be It next time."

"It sounds dreadfully juvenile," drawled Sidney Pusey. "I should much rather discuss the significance of aesthetic experience in an industrial society with Mr. Cottle."

"But Amos would rather play this game with us." Tony sounded a little desperate. "It's not a juvenile game if you ask the right sort of questions, and Amos is especially good at this sort of thing with his quick wits and enormous fund of information."

"Okay, I'll give you all a treat," mumbled Amos. He was obviously bored with young Mr. Pusey. Tony had intervened just in time to prevent another alcoholic explosion.

"All right, here goes." Tony assumed the suavely dictatorial tone of an M.C. on television. "I'll be It first to get the ball rolling. Who wrote *English Bards and Scotch Reviewers?*"

Amos peered at Tony over his glass. "Damned if I know!"

Emmett Avery stared at Amos as if he couldn't believe his ears.

"Wrong," said Tony. "You're a third of a ghost, Amos."

The fractional ghost comforted himself with whiskey. Maurice Lepton got the ice bucket from the bar and began replenishing glasses.

Meg Vesey got the last question in the first round.

"Where are the Islets of Langerhans, Meg?" demanded Tony.

Her eyelids fluttered. "Er—Dutch Indonesia?"

"Wrong. You're a third of a ghost now, darling. Miss the next two and you'll be dead. Amos, we're back to you again. Where are the Islets of Langerhans?"

"In the human body, of course. Langerhans was a physician."

But Amos was not so fortunate on the third round. He missed an absurdly easy question: "Who wrote *Of Human Bondage?*"

Basil could see that Tony was troubled. He didn't want Amos out of the game altogether. Amos might use his leisure to find himself another drink. When the question came to Amos once more at the start of the fourth round, Tony was obviously trying to find something simple enough for the most befuddled wits. "What are galley proofs?"

Amos blinked. "Slaves rowed in them. Sat chained to benches. Publishers and agents stood over them with great, long whips until they died. So they were called galley slaves."

"Amusing but I can't pass it as correct," said Tony as gently as possible. "You're three-thirds of ghost now, Amos. You're dead."

Amos spared him a glance of sluggish defiance. "I r'sent that." His empty glass slid out of his fingers to the floor and he slumped in his deep chair, his chin on his breast.

Basil won the first game and so became the inquisitor. He was not enjoying himself. Privately he agreed with poor Sidney Pusey that the game was juvenile and the sight of a celebrated author stupefying his brain with neat whiskey was depressing to anyone with so much knowledge of the brain's precariously delicate balance of sanity. He couldn't help wondering if this incident would affect Maurice Lepton's appreciation of Amos's next book. He suspected that Tony was wondering the same thing.

"Well, Basil?"

It was Tony, prompting him.

Amos was first in the circle. Now a second game was starting the first question should be addressed to him. But Amos had closed his eyes.

"Mr. Cottle," said Basil quietly.

Amos did not stir.

Basil made his voice more incisive. "What war is considered a defeat for this country in most foreign textbooks on history?"

Still Amos did not stir.

Tony was on his feet. "Passed out, I guess. I'll get him up to bed."

Before Tony could reach Amos, Vera had darted to his side. Her long, thin, grasping fingers held his shoulder and shook him roughly. "Amos, don't be a clown! Tony was only joking . . ."

Amos's head rolled to one side, eyes shut, mouth open.

Vera gasped and swung around toward Tony.

"You said he was a ghost." Her soft voice cracked. "You said he was dead. And—he is."

seven

A diamond day, thought Meg as she stood by the window in the Kanes' breakfast room, dry and cold and bright. The della Robbia blue of the sky and the lemon cast of the sunshine were incidental in the general whiteness of snow and ice, like the prismatic flashes of blue and yellow when a diamond catches the light. White paint made the houses in the valley below an integral part of the winter landscape. Dark shutters gave each house accent and style, like the black tip of the ermine's tail.

The telephone rang and Meg hurried into the hall. "Your New York call is through."

"Maddelena? I'm calling from the Kanes. There was—an accident last night. Mr. Cottle is dead and the police want us to stay here another day. I didn't call last night because I didn't want to wake you or Polly. How is she?"

"Just fine," said Maddelena. "She had a good breakfast. Her temperature is just a little above normal, less than one degree."

Did Maddelena really know how to read a thermometer? Was she minimizing Polly's symptoms to keep her mother from worrying? Meg kept these doubts to herself. "Call the doctor and have him see her again today. Just to make sure she's all right. I think they'll let us come back this evening."

"She'd like to talk to you."

"Oh, I don't want her to get out of bed."

"She's in your bed right beside the telephone."

"Mommy!" Even when Polly was well, the telephone distorted her voice, making it sound small and forlorn. "Did you get me a present?"

Polly always tried to extract a present as conscience money when both parents left her overnight. Meg knew she should be firm and correct this growing talent for extortion, but—discipline could wait until Polly was entirely well. "Not yet, darling."

"But you will?"

"I probably shall, Capone."

"What do you mean by 'Capone'?"

Hugh came on the wire. "Mommy, I've just seen the morning paper and it says . . ."

"Hugh! Not in front of Maddelena and Polly, please! You're big enough to understand that I don't want either of them to worry about us. I told Maddelena that Amos Cottle was dead, but that's all."

"Oh, I see. But what shall I do if she sees the paper?"

"Try to keep her from telling Polly anything about it."

Hugh sighed, then went on gleefully, "The other fellows at school are going to ask me a lot of questions this morning!"

"Maybe you'd better not go." Meg frowned, thinking how bad all this was going to be for Hugh, with his delight in melodrama.

"Oh, Mommy, not go this morning of all mornings! That would be running away."

"I suppose it would." Meg's frown deepened in greater perplexity. "Very well, Hugh. You may go. But remember—you knew Amos very slightly. I don't want you to gossip about him at school or to give anyone an impression that you knew him better than you really did. Indeed, the less you say the better for all of us."

"Okay, I'll clam up. I'll just say: 'No comment!' Like a senator. Then they'll be more curious than ever. Boy, what a day I'm going to have! Even the teachers will be bursting with questions. Only I suppose they won't ask me anything."

Meg returned to the breakfast room and poured herself a cup of coffee. Breakfast at the Kanes' house parties was always *à l'Anglais* —chafing dishes and hot coffee on the sideboard, each guest at liberty to wake when he pleased and help himself, any time up to noon.

She was turning away from the sideboard when Philippa came into the room, trim and fresh in navy blue slacks and sweater. Meg was suddenly conscious of the silk pyjamas and robe that Philippa had lent her, all a little too large for her figure and too bland a shade of green for her coloring.

"Meg, you must eat!"

"I can't." Meg stirred her coffee. "Is—Vera still asleep?"

"I hope so. I told Nora to take a tray up if she heard any sounds from that room. I'm hungry." Philippa helped herself to scrambled eggs with chives and toast. "Shock always affects me that way. But I'd lose my appetite if I had to have breakfast with Vera."

Tony and Gus were talking as they came downstairs together, but their voices were indistinct at that distance and they fell silent as they came into the room. Both men looked exhausted, but while Gus was merely haggard, Tony seemed grim.

"Good morning!" Philippa was resolutely brisk and cheerful.

"Why don't you ask us if we slept well?" said Gus.

"Did you?"

"Like a top, of course! This country air . . ."

Everyone grinned but Tony.

"I've been wondering about the Bookbinders' Award," said Philippa. "What happens now that . . . ?"

Tony looked at her with level eyes. "We have two other guests who may appear at any moment—Vera and Leppy. We have to put on a show for them—shock and grief. No thought of anything practical."

"Show?" Meg looked at him, bewildered. "It was a shock and I do grieve for Amos. Don't you?"

"Of course. But someone has to pick up the pieces. And there are an awful lot of them."

"Poor Amos!" Philippa produced a sigh. "Even in death, he's just a pawn in the game to you two, isn't he?"

Gus looked startled and Tony said, "I don't know what you mean. I . . ." He stopped as he heard a footfall.

Maurice Lepton came in carrying the morning newspaper. He ignored the sideboard and spread the paper on the breakfast table. "Nice photo of Amos. I wonder what will happen to that poor dog now?"

"Dog?" Gus craned his neck for a side view of the paper. "Oh, I see," he muttered as he recognized the publicity still. "Is it a good obituary?"

"As good as it could be with Fred Newell writing it. He does all their literary obits from stuff in the morgue. The news story is short and sweet."

Leppy began to read aloud, weighing each word with professional interest.

> Weston, Conn. Dec. 16th. Amos Cottle, best-selling author, was the victim of a fatal poisoning last night when he was attending a supper party at the Weston home of his publisher, Anthony Kane, President of Sutton, Kane and Company. Captain James Drew of the Connecticut State

Police, who made a preliminary investigation of the circumstances, was still considering the probability of accident at a late hour tonight though he admitted to reporters that he had not altogether ruled out the possibility of foul play.

Mrs. Cottle, better known as Vera Vane, the actress, who had attended the supper party with Mr. Cottle, could not be reached for comment. It was understood that she was prostrated with grief. Others who attended the party included Maurice Lepton and Emmett Avery, both well-known critics, and Augustus Vesey, Mr. Cottle's agent.

Amos Cottle was best known for his war book, *Never Call Retreat*. His fourth novel, *Passionate Pilgrim*, was published a few weeks ago by Sutton, Kane and Company. The *New York Times* Sunday book review section hailed it at the time as 'a landmark in American letters.' Mr. Cottle also conducted a weekly TV program known as the 'Amos Cottle Show.' Obituary on page 12.

Newsprint rustled as loudly as taffeta in the silence while Leppy turned to page 12 and continued to read aloud:

"Amos Cottle's sudden death under mysterious circumstances came as a great shock to the literary world. Born in China on March 1, 1918, the only child of Martin and Amanda Cottle, Methodist missionaries originally from Akron, Ohio, he was educated at the University of Peking. After graduation, he returned to the United States where he experimented with various vocations and temporary jobs for a period of several years. Old residents of Miami still recall the time when he was a bartender at the Blue Grotto Night Club there and it was known to regular customers that he had ambitions as a writer.

"This roving life came to an end with Pearl Harbor, when Mr. Cottle enlisted in the Seabees, with whom he served throughout the war in the Pacific. On being released from the Navy, he used his severance pay to retire to a small cabin in the Adirondacks where he wrote his first best-selling novel, a war story entitled *Never Call Retreat*, published in the spring of 1953. This spare, taut, intensely realistic study of twelve marines marooned on a tropical island, surrounded by hostile Japanese, was an instant success. The action took place in twenty-four hours and ended with the death of the last marine, just as a rescue party arrived to take over the beachhead. The grimness of the actual story was relieved by flashbacks showing the previous civilian life of each man.

"The book was criticized by some few for its candid use of military profanity and its outspoken treatment of physiological detail, but it was generally admired as a fearless picture of modern warfare. Hollywood turned it into a memorable film starring Spencer Tracy as a chaplain and Rita Hayworth as a Japanese geisha, characters who did not appear in the original story.

"The success of this first book was followed by three others in the next three years, the latest being *Passionate Pilgrim*, a Book-of-the-Week Club choice for next July. Maurice Lepton, reviewing it last Sunday in the *New York Times*, remarked . . ."

"I won't bother to read that," said Leppy, modestly. "But I have something else here I would like to read to you."

Out of his pocket came a sheaf of Philippa's best, guest room writing paper, covered with a fine, spidery longhand. "Lew phoned me last night after you'd all gone to bed and asked me to rush him a personal appreciation of Amos, the man, for the next issue of the *Thursday Review*. I want to make sure I got all my facts straight."

Leppy cleared his throat and began reading again.

AMOS COTTLE AS I KNEW HIM
An Appreciation
By
Maurice Lepton

"Mos Cottle, as he was known to his intimates, was a simple, unassuming little man, quite without vanity or 'side.' Nothing about his personal appearance suggested the keen, incisive mind or the powerful creative urge that informed his least work. Mos was slender and frail with the gentle eyes of a dreamer and a sensitive mouth and chin, half hidden by the straggling beard he affected. There was a certain resemblance to Van Gogh's self-portrait—the same hollow cheeks, the same lonely, patient, enduring look of a man dedicated to an artistic ideal.

"I shall not say too much about Mos's tragic addiction to alcohol. It was well-known to all his friends that for six long years he had fought a hard battle against temptation. How successful he was may be realized from the fact that he produced no less than four books in the last four of those years, books that will be remembered when most contemporary writing is forgotten.

"If I were asked to describe Mos Cottle in one word, I should say the word for him was 'modest.' The one time I met him he seemed to shy away from any discussion of his own work and he was equally reticent about his early life. When I asked him how many of these youthful experiences had gone into his books, he smiled a little sadly and quoted: 'I am a part of all that I have met.' He was almost pathetically eager for you to think of him as a fellow man, with all the weaknesses of an ordinary human being, rather than as a writer whose great gifts set him apart from the rest of his generation.

"Like many men of talent, he was quite innocent and childlike in his pleasures. He hated formal parties. He preferred small gatherings of intimate friends. He delighted in simple parlor games and entered into the spirit of such games with a zest rare in a mature man. His responses were always direct and uninhibited, sometimes tinged with the eccentricity of genius. Once when he found a drink was not entirely to his taste, he quietly emptied his glass out on his host's floor and helped himself to something more palatable. In a lesser man this would have seemed intolerably churlish, but not in Amos Cottle. It was just a part of his disarming simplicity.

"It was a rare thing for him to attend any parties. He lived quietly in the country surrounded by his books, his only exercise an occasional round of golf with his publisher, who was also his neighbor. His wife was the beautiful Vera Vane, famous Hollywood actress. Though the exigencies of two careers often separated them and there was some estrangement, they were fundamentally devoted to one another and all his friends find consolation in the thought that Vera Cottle was with Mos when he died, and they were completely and happily reconciled. He had no children and I suspect that this was one of the real regrets of his life. He would have made a tender and devoted father.

"His older friends tell me that they never saw Mos Cottle angry or irritable. An inner serenity sustained him through all the vicissitudes of a harsh life. 'He was the least self-centered author I ever knew,' said Tony Kane of Sutton, Kane and Company, his publishers. Mos hardly bothered to read reviews of his own books. He just sat down and wrote another book, no matter what the critics said. Of course, favorable reviews did please him, much as a child is pleased with candy. But unfavorable reviews only left him hurt and baffled rather than angry. 'I guess that guy just didn't understand what I was trying to say,' he would remark mildly. 'I must try harder next time. I want to communicate with everyone.'

"To Mos, communication was the writer's most important function. 'I want to make the little guy see the world from the big guy's point of view,' he would say. 'And I want the big guy to understand the little guy. If I can help them to find each other, my work has not been in vain.'

"He had a scorn for all panaceas and isms. 'The answer to man's tragic predicament in an unknowable universe lies in man himself,' he would say. 'Not in creeds and codes.'

"He was invariably helpful to young writers. No script was so bad that Amos Cottle would not read it, if it were sent to him, and return it with a long, detailed criticism. His generous financial assistance to struggling, young writers was well-known to everyone in the literary world.

"Is it too early to assess the place of his *oeuvre* in American letters? A warm heart, a strong mind that could reflect as well as observe, a quick eye, a keen ear—Mos Cottle had all these, plus an unique gift for the matchless music of our language. He wrote prose that sings in every line. A stern sense of the self-discipline essential to good writing pared his style to the bone. He had an almost clairvoyant understanding of the dark and secret places of the human heart. He was close to true greatness and certainly we shall not look upon his like again in this generation."

Leppy ceased reading. The silence lengthened. Meg, genuinely moved, felt salt sting her eyelids. Philippa, more composed, poured another cup of coffee and lit a cigarette.

Leppy looked at Tony and Gus. "Well? Anything wrong with it?"

"Seems all right to me." Tony exchanged glances with Gus. "Perfectly accurate and a very touching tribute to Amos."

Gus hesitated, his eyes serious as they considered, first, Tony, and then, Lepton. "It's Maurice Lepton at his most characteristic," said Gus, finally. "I have only one question: do you have to say anything about Amos's drinking?"

"Oh, yes." Leppy was firm. "It's bound to come out with the full story of last night. I've done my best to prepare the ground—make it sound human and pathetic. But if I left that part out altogether, my article would be dishonest. I can't have that."

"I think Leppy is right," said Tony. "Once a man's dead, he's allowed a few vices. If he's a famous author, they're rather expected."

Gus looked unconvinced, but he shut his lips and said no more.

"Well!" No one had heard Vera's step. Startled, they all looked up to see her in the doorway. As she had brought her own luggage from the airport, the ice-blue satin gown with the silver mink collar must have been her own. She had brushed her hair and taken pains with her make-up. There was no trace of fatigue or shock in her face. The cold eyes were sharp and the mean little mouth was set in a tight line.

"Coffee, Vera?" Tony was on his feet.

"No, thanks. Your maid brought me breakfast upstairs." She took out a cigarette and Gus lighted it for her. "I came down because I thought it was time we had a little talk about Amos's affairs."

Tony frowned. "Then we'd better go into my study. I'm sure Mr. Lepton isn't interested . . ."

"I'd rather talk here, where there are witnesses," said Vera.

Slowly Tony's blond skin turned a light red.

"I have a lot to say, but, first, I want to know about Amos's will."

Tony fought for self-control and achieved it with an effort that deepened the redness in his cheeks. "I can tell you one thing. Amos appointed Gus and myself as his literary executors."

Before Tony could go on, a maid appeared in the doorway. Her light blue uniform and white apron brought out the look of freshness and inexperience in her face. She spoke with an Irish cadence. "Mr. Willing to see you, sir."

"I'll see him in the study," said Tony precipitately.

"Oh!" The little maid gasped. "And to think that I told him to come right in here and have a cup of coffee with yez!"

Tony looked at Philippa as if it were her fault the maid had not been trained more carefully. It was too late to do anything. Basil Willing was standing in the doorway.

As his eyes took in the six people around the table, his interest quickened visibly. "Am I interrupting something?"

"Not at all!" Vera answered promptly. "I'm glad you're here. I'm trying to find out what I can expect from Amos's will."

"Bring us some fresh coffee, Nora," said Philippa to the maid. "Do sit down, Dr. Willing. Vera, can't you postpone your discussion of Amos's affairs until later?"

"No. I want to know right now what's going to happen to me. The TV program will stop, so that's out. Amos can't write any more books, so there won't be any more income from that. Is there anything left?"

Gus intervened. "As a matter of fact, there will be considerable income from books for some time to come. There are three reprints of old books on the stands now and the latest book has only just been published in hard covers. I can't see how Amos's death could harm its sales. It may even increase interest."

Tony nodded. "I've been thinking this morning that now Amos is dead I might issue a library edition of his complete works. Gold-tooled leather binding and a foreword by Maurice Lepton and . . ."

"Okay," interrupted Vera. "But, as there can't be many more new books, this won't last long."

"As a matter of fact, there may be one or two new books." Tony turned to Gus. "Didn't you tell me that Amos left a mass of unpublished material?"

Gus agreed. "He had already completed the script of the next book that was to follow *Passionate Pilgrim*. There's a rough draft of another book, a group of short stories he never tried to publish, and two or three book-length scripts he wrote before he was in the Seabees. I advised him not to publish them when he was alive, but they might be publishable now—with a little editing, of course. Then there's a mass of notes I haven't gone through."

"And you're sure his being dead won't make any difference to sales?"

"It shouldn't," said Tony.

"Death is fatal on the screen," said Vera with entire seriousness. "Audiences just don't like to see the shadow of a dead actor moving and talking."

"It's quite different with books," put in Lepton. "Tony, could you possibly let me see some of this unpublished material? I'd be glad to help you get it organized for publication in any way I can."

"Thanks, Leppy," said Tony. "Gus and I will probably take you up on that. We have great faith in your critical judgment."

"It wouldn't do to publish anything that wasn't quite up to the standard of Amos's mature work," began Lepton. "If . . ."

But Vera cut him short. "I say, publish anything that will pay off. Do I have any say in the matter?"

"No, you simply get Amos's royalty checks on everything published," returned Tony.

"Oh, is that all?" Suddenly Vera unleashed her anger. "Think again, Mr. Kane! You'll have to have a little talk with my New York agent, Sam Karp. I'm not a dedicated dreamer like Amos. I don't want a contract that gives you a big cut of my subsidiary rights. And—" she whirled on Gus—"I don't want any agency clause in my contract at all. You're fired as of now."

"I'm afraid you can't fire Gus," said Tony wearily. "The agency clause in each of Amos's contracts with me is still operative. It states in plain English that all monies payable under this contract are to be paid to the author through the agency of Augustus Vesey, Incorporated."

Vera pounced like a playful tigress. "That would only apply to books already contracted for. It can't apply to the new, posthumous books. Sam Karp is going to act for me in future," she informed Gus. "Whether you're a literary executor or not, you're not going to be my agent."

"Please, that's enough for now, Vera," said Gus. "We all know Dr. Willing isn't interested in . . ."

"Don't mind me," said Basil quietly, accepting the fresh coffee Philippa had just poured him.

Another idea had come to Vera. "Tony, Amos told me he was getting this Bookbinders' Award. That's ten thousand dollars, isn't it?"

"Yes, but now . . ."

"Why should his being dead make any difference? Aren't there such things as posthumous awards as well as posthumous books?"

"That's an idea," admitted Tony. "I'll call Sloan Severing, President of the Bookbinders' Association, some time this morning and see if he'll let Amos's publisher accept the award for Amos. We have ads set up and . . ."

"Amos's publisher?" Vera forced an unnatural laugh. "Why not Amos's widow? I could use a little publicity in New York myself."

"Then you'd lose the Award money," said Tony. "Sloan would never agree to that. You're supposed to be in mourning."

Meg looked at Vera indignantly. "Didn't you care for anything about Amos except his money?"

Before Vera could respond, Tony answered Meg. "An unnecessary question, my dear. We all know that Amos, like many men of talent, made an unfortunate marriage. If he had lived, he would have divorced Vera."

"He would not!" cried Vera. "How dare you . . ."

Lepton looked at Tony curiously. "I understood from this morning's paper that Amos and Vera were completely and happily reconciled."

"Translation," said Tony. "Catamount had dropped Vera's option, so she insisted on returning to Amos. He was too generous—or perhaps I should say too weak—to say no."

This seemed to satisfy Lepton. "Great artists are notoriously weak and indiscriminate where women are concerned," he murmured.

But it didn't satisfy Vera.

"Tony Kane, I can go back to Catamount whenever I feel like it!"

Tony turned to Basil. "I hardly know how to apologize for inflicting all this on you."

"It's I who should apologize," returned Basil. "I was so fascinated I didn't interrupt to tell you that I am investigating the death of Amos Cottle. Not telling you makes me a sort of eavesdropper, but the temptation was just too much for me. An investigator rarely has a chance to hear witnesses talk so frankly among themselves."

"Investigating . . . ?" Tony, like everyone else, was taken completely off balance.

Basil explained. "You all know that for many years I have been attached to the district attorney's office in New York as a psychiatric assistant. I still am. I've kept my office and apartment in New York and technically I'm still a resident there. This murder occurred in Connecticut, but most of the people involved live in New York or have offices there. There will have to be close coöperation between Connecticut State Police and New York city police. Many answers to questions raised by the murder will be found only in New York. Captain Drew has asked me to act as a sort of liaison officer between the two police forces. I am here this morning to ask you some questions. They are questions of a quite different sort from those the State Police asked you last night."

Meg looked at him aghast. "You said—murder. The morning paper was still talking about the probability of accidental poisoning."

"We had very few facts at the time the morning papers went to press," said Basil. "We know more now. Sometimes I think it's helpful to everyone concerned to let those involved in a case know some of the things the police have discovered. Captain Drew has given me permission to tell you a good deal abut his findings. Amos Cottle was poisoned with cyanide. The alcohol he had taken masked the usual symptoms—heavy breathing and spasmodic movements."

The stillness in the room was heavy, almost tangible.

Basil went on. "I need hardly point out that cyanide is not likely to find its way into a glass of Scotch by accident. It's too quick and far too unpleasant for the taste of most suicides. Such a poison automatically suggests murder and more—premeditation."

Lepton's monkey-grin was more malicious than usual. "I think we'll all agree that no one but a murderer would attend a supper party equipped with cyanide."

"Was I belaboring the obvious?" said Basil. "Fortunately there was a critic present to correct me."

"How could any ordinary person get hold of a thing like cyanide?" demanded Gus.

Meg looked at Basil incredulously. "Do you mean that there was cyanide in the iced tea? That was the only thing prepared for Amos and not for the rest of us."

"But Cottle didn't drink his iced tea last night," Basil reminded her. "He poured it out on the floor and helped himself to whiskey. I'm in a unique position for an investigator of crime. I was present at the scene of the crime when it took place and I'm my own witness for all the physical details of what actually happened. I suspect that the murderer had planned originally to poison the pitcher of iced tea, but as soon as he saw Cottle was drunk he knew that Cottle was in no mood for tea. The murderer had to change his plan at the last minute and put poison in Cottle's glass after Cottle had filled it with whiskey."

"Without Cottle's noticing?" protested Gus.

"Cottle was really too drunk to notice anything," retorted Basil. "And it must have been that way because there was no trace of cyanide at all in the iced tea pitcher, or the whiskey decanter or the soda siphon—only in Cottle's own glass."

"But how could the murderer plan to poison the iced tea?" cried Tony. "The only people who knew that Cottle was supposed to drink iced tea were Philippa and myself and the Veseys."

"And Vera," added Philippa. "She saw Amos drink iced tea at our parties when they were living together."

"But I couldn't know beforehand that he was going to drink it last night," said Vera. "And, as a matter of fact, he didn't."

"Let's face it squarely," cried Gus. "Dr. Willing is implying that one of us—the five who knew about the iced tea—poisoned Amos."

"Not necessarily," remarked Basil. "The fact that Amos Cottle usually drank iced tea at parties might have been noticed and talked about. Anyone could have known it, even someone who didn't know the reason for it. But the poisoner does have to be someone who was near Cottle after he picked up that glass of whiskey."

"And that includes everyone at the party," added Gus.

Meg shuddered. "You said cyanide was—quick. How quick?"

Basil answered gravely. "A matter of seconds."

"But I'm sure there was no one near Amos in the last few minutes before he died. We were all sitting down playing that silly game. Don't you remember?"

Basil nodded. "The police are considering the possibility that the poison was in some sort of capsule. For one thing, that would explain why there was only the slightest trace of cyanide in Amos Cottle's glass, though there was a large dose in his body."

"A dissolving capsule?" Lepton was curious. "If the murderer planned to poison the iced tea, he'd have to have a capsule that was soluble in water. How could he be sure that such a capsule would also be soluble in alcohol? Remember there was only whiskey in Amos's glass. No soda or water except for the water content of whiskey itself."

Basil smiled his appreciation of Lepton's alertness. "That's a curious and interesting point that bothers the police chemists. How could the murderer take a chance on a capsule designed for tea dissolving in whiskey? Unless we find a reasonable answer, we'll never know exactly how Cottle was murdered. But we're pretty sure there was a capsule of some kind. Cottle had swallowed more than half that drink before he was affected by a poison that takes effect in a few seconds and, as Meg pointed out, no one else had been near his glass from the time we started playing Two-Thirds of a Ghost until he died. That was an interval of ten or twelve minutes."

"This is all fantastic!" exploded Tony. "It must have been suicide. You have to have a motive for murder. No one in the world had a motive for killing Amos, least of all those at the party last night. As Vera has just told you, Gus and I were both making a lot of money out of Amos. What conceivable motive would we or our wives have for . . ."

"Killing the goose that laid the golden eggs?" suggested Philippa sweetly.

Tony ignored her. "Mr. Lepton is a critic and one of Amos's most ardent admirers. You can read his review of *Passionate Pilgrim* in last Sunday's *Times*."

"I read it when I got home last night," said Basil. "No motive there. But I also read Mr. Avery's article in the *Tribune*."

"Oh, Emmett didn't care much for Amos's work," admitted Tony, putting it rather mildly. "But you're hardly suggesting that a critic would murder an author because he didn't like the author's work?"

"It would have been kinder than the review," put in Lepton, speaking as a connoisseur. " 'The kindest use a knife, because the dead so soon grow cold. . . .' "

"How did Emmett Avery happen to attend a party for Amos Cottle so soon after that review?" asked Basil.

"The unspeakable Mrs. Pusey brought him, uninvited," said Philippa acidly. "For all her literary airs, Peggy Pusey doesn't read book reviews. Her son slept so late he missed the papers that morning. She was sorry. She told me last night that she thought *all* writers were *bound* to be friends."

"My God!" murmured Gus.

"The Puseys had never met Amos before," went on Tony. "Neither had Emmett or Leppy—Mr. Lepton."

"Leppy?" Basil looked up. "You've known each other a long time?"

Philippa laughed. "My dear Basil, the writing and publishing world is a very small one. Everybody has known everybody else for a long time. A lot of them have inherited their jobs in one way or another and when it come to second- and third-generation marriages it gets positively incestuous like medieval dynasties."

"Yet Cottle had never met Avery or Lepton before?"

"Amos was a really dedicated artist who lived alone as much as he could and devoted himself to his work," explained Tony. "And he wasn't born into this world as the rest of us were. He'd had no contact with publishers or writers before he began writing himself and he'd only been writing for the last four years. Now Meg's father was editor of the old *Anybody's*. Emmett Avery's father was a certified accountant who specialized in publishers' and authors' accounts and knew more about contracts than any man in the business. Emmett worked in that office for several years before he became a critic. Leppy's father ran a small bookbinding firm in Chicago. The Lepton de luxe editions are collectors' items today. Unfortunately he was too much of an artist to make any money and bookbinding is just a hobby with Leppy now. My own father was a contract book salesman who represented various New York houses on the West Coast. Gus's father was an editor at Scribner's for years. We're all lice in the locks of literature except Philippa."

"And Vera," added Philippa. "And the Puseys."

"Wasn't there anything in the least literary about Amos Cottle's family?" inquired Basil.

"No. You can tell that from the biographical note on the jacket flap of *Retreat*."

"Retreat?"

"His first book, *Never Call Retreat*. You can't say all those words every time. We call it N.C.R., or *Retreat*. All that stuff is copied in his obit in the papers this morning. It often happens that way. We who edit and publish and sell books may produce critics sometimes, but rarely creative writers. There's no accounting for their origin."

" 'The wind bloweth where it listeth,' " added Leppy. "Taste is inherited and even talent, but not genius."

"You consider Cottle a genius?"

Leppy shrugged. "I thought so. Emmett didn't. Time will tell. That's what makes publishing a speculative business. There's no yardstick."

"But Amos had a knack of writing books that sold," added Tony. "What more can a publisher ask?"

Basil waited until the two had run down, then he spoke gently. "I read the biographical note on the jacket of *Retreat* this morning. You had told me last night that Amos Cottle was not a pen name. So this morning I pointed out to Captain Drew that the jacket note was a convenient thumbnail sketch of Cottle's personal history and that we could get more facts about him if we followed the leads it offered. He and I agreed that the University of Peking was a little remote both geographically and politically at the present time, but we got in touch with the police in Akron, Ohio, the press relations offices of the Protestant churches, the Navy Department in Washington and the staff of the Blue Grotto Night Club in Miami."

No one took advantage of Basil's pause. He went on more slowly. "The city of Akron has no record of residents named Cottle, the birth of a Martin Cottle or his marriage to a woman named Amanda. The Methodist Church has no record of two missionaries in China in the thirties named Martin and Amanda Cottle and parents of a child named Amos. The Blue Grotto in Miami opened in 1935 and it has no record of a bartender employed there at any time named Amos Cottle. The Navy Department has no record of an enlisted man in the Seabees named Amos Cottle. There is no record in Washington of a draft card or a social security card or a ration card being issued during the last war to anyone named Amos Cottle. According to all available records, Amos Cottle never existed at all."

Basil looked directly at Gus and Tony. "Who was the man who called himself Amos Cottle? What was he?"

eight

Tony's face was a hard blank, a true poker face. Gus, more responsive by temperament, allowed a look of ironical resignation to flit across his face swiftly and silently as a cloud-shadow racing before the wind on a hillside. Maurice Lepton's eyes were extraordinarily bright as they shifted from Tony to Gus and back to Tony. Meg looked utterly bewildered as if events were developing too fast for her reflexes to respond, like a moving picture projected at a speed that makes it a jerky blur to the human eye. Philippa was staring at Basil as if his question had opened a whole new world of speculation and conjecture. Vera was the only one who answered vocally. For the first time her soft voice became rough and sharp. "What on earth are you getting at, Dr. Willing?"

Basil looked at Tony. "Well?"

Tony's glance flicked Gus—a strategist signaling a staff officer that the time had come to put Plan X into operation, that he wanted whole-hearted support and all flanks protected.

Gus looked at Tony reproachfully. "If only you'd told Willing last night that Amos Cottle was a pen name!"

"How could I tell Amos was going to be murdered?" returned Tony. "If it weren't for that, who'd care whether Amos was a pen name or not? Who ever bothers to check the veracity of a jacket note?"

Gus took a deep breath. "The biographical information on the jacket of Amos's books was furnished by Amos himself and now he's dead so . . ."

Tony sighed. "It's no use, Gus. Sooner or later the police will trace our connection with Dr. Clinton. Basil is our only friend at court. We'd better put all our cards on the table for him while we have the chance."

Gus shrugged. "Roger. Over to you."

"Are we to infer," said Lepton, "that the jacket note was a fabrication of yours, Tony? I had no idea you had such a talent for creative writing!"

"'The wind bloweth where it listeth,'" murmured Philippa. "I hope you kept the TV rights in it."

Tony ignored this flippancy and turned toward Basil, squaring his shoulders as if he were summoning all his agility and address to meet a physical challenge head-on.

"All right, Basil." Tony's curtness lent an air of candor to his words. "We'll tell you everything. The true story of Amos Cottle is known only to Gus and myself, now Amos himself is dead. Not even Phil or Meg know the truth. A secret shared is no longer a secret, especially a secret shared with women, so we made up our minds from the beginning not to let the women in on it. I'm sorry so many people have to know it now. I can only hope that it will go no farther. After all, Amos Cottle is still a valuable property, and all of us present have a stake in him except Basil and Leppy."

"Even Leppy has a sort of stake," interrupted Gus. "He's gambled his critical reputation on Amos's genius. Not that that would ever sway his opinion of Amos's work, but I don't see why anything in Amos's personal history should alter Leppy's appreciation of his writing."

"Of course not," said Lepton. "You may count on my loyalty to Amos."

"And you, Basil?" demanded Tony.

"I can't promise anything," answered Basil. "I can only hope that when Amos Cottle's murderer is arrested, the story of Cottle's past will not be so germane to the prosecution's case that it has to be mentioned in court."

Tony took a deep breath. "Amos Cottle was a man without a past. We haven't the slightest idea who he was or where he came from."

"How is that possible?"

"To explain, I must go back to 1952. Meg, would you like to tell Basil how you discovered Amos's first book?"

"It was quite simple." Meg's voice was strained thin, almost transparent. "Before the war, Gus was a radio writer. When peace came, he used his severance pay to establish the agency. We were living on Long Island then, in a crowded little development. Gus rented desk space in the office of a friend who was already an established agent and tried to keep things going by free-lance radio writing until his own agency should show a profit. He realized that TV was going to kill radio in a few years and he wasn't at all sure he could adapt himself to TV technique, or compete with the movie writers who were pouring into TV because there was so much money involved while Gus was still in the Marines.

"The agency seemed our only hope, but Gus had little time to read all the scripts that came to him as an agent. Most of them were incredibly bad, things by rank amateurs like Mrs. Pusey or things by professionals that had already been rejected by every editor in town. So, while Gus worked on his radio plays, I read the agency scripts in the evening, after the babies were asleep and the dishes washed.

"One night, long after Gus had gone to bed, I was sitting in the living room plodding through this awful tripe when I came across the script of a book in a shabby old box that had once held a ream of typing paper. On the lid was a pasted label that read: THE BATTLEFIELD BY AMOS COTTLE. I thought, what a funny name for a writer! And I began to read, thinking I'd just skim through the first fifty pages and, unless there was something in them that caught my interest, I'd tell Gus to send the whole thing back to this Mr. Cottle in the morning. After all, as the critics say, you don't have to eat all of an egg to know if it's rotten.

"Well, Dr. Willing, I sat up till nearly four in the morning reading every word of that book. I forgot I was tired. I forgot that Polly would wake promptly at six. I forgot that we were nearly broke and wholly discouraged. As I turned the last page down on its face, I heard a skylark sing. At least I think it was a skylark. I don't know much about birds—I'm a city person really—but this song was high and clear and pure, the essence of a blithe spirit, so it must have been a lark. And when I lifted my eyes, I saw that the sky beyond the unshaded windows had turned the purest azure I ever saw and I knew it was about half an hour before dawn. The bird's song and the strange blue sky seemed to be saying the same thing, one in light and one in music. It was one of those moments when it really is a joy to be alive and they are rare after twelve or thirteen.

"You see I knew right then that Amos's book was something unusual and that this was a turning point in our lives."

"She told me at breakfast," Gus took up the story. "I read the first fifty pages going in on the train. I wasn't quite as enthusiastic as Meg, but I did realize that this was the first script we had received that was anywhere near professional standards. It was a bit long. I thought about a hundred pages could be cut to advantage. And I didn't like the title. What could be more pedestrian than *The Battlefield?* Even *Field of Battle* would be better.

"I sent a rather guarded letter to the author saying I liked it and I was going to try it on one or two publishers to see if they shared my opinion. I knew that a beginning author would never cut a hundred pages on an agent's say-so, but he might if a publisher got interested and dangled a contract in front of him."

"Gus brought it to me two days after Meg read it," said Tony. "I was then senior editor at Daniel Sutton and Company, and Dan Sutton was still alive. I'd known Gus and Meg for years, but I hadn't much faith in Gus's agency. I didn't think he had enough capital to hold out long enough to get a foothold in the business."

"Enough capital? No capital at all!" muttered Gus.

"The only other thing he'd brought me was an anthology of short stories that were so bad they were almost funny, but not quite funny enough to publish as a burlesque on the short story, so—naturally I turned this Cottle script over to a girl I was training to be one of our 'first readers.' She was a pert little thing just out of Sarah Lawrence, the daughter of one of Philippa's well-heeled Wall Street friends. Her report, in about two weeks, was cool and neutral. She'd done very well in her English literature courses and her one idea with all scripts was to correct grammar, punctuation, and delete any idiosyncrasies or individual variations in prose style. She was the only literate person we could get for a token salary—she didn't need money—and I gambled on the hope that she had enough common sense not to turn down anything that was actually publishable before I got her trained."

"The way Gide turned down Proust," mused Lepton. "Was Gide a reader for Hachette or Gallimard?"

"Unfortunately," went on Tony, "this girl was much better educated than the reading public we were trying to reach, so I had to watch her reports pretty carefully.

"Her word for Amos's first book was 'readable.' She had an itching pencil. She wanted us to cut out all the 'verys,' straighten out the 'shoulds' and 'woulds,' and change words like 'jeopardize' to 'put in jeopardy.' Her English professor would have been proud of her, but —there never was a bunch of marines who spoke such impeccable English as Amos's would have if Susan had had her way. And in her report she demurely questioned each four-letter word.

"When she said 'readable' that meant I had to read it myself. Her unreadables I rejected without more than a glance at the first page to make sure she hadn't pulled a boner. So I took Amos's book up to the apartment where Phil and I were living then, intending to read it that night, but Phil had a party on and what with one thing or another I forgot all about it for three weeks. Then Gus gave me a ring at the office. I really felt guilty because he was an old friend. I swore I'd read it that very night and I did. I shooed Phil out of my study after dinner, mixed a stiff brandy and soda and sat down, wondering what I could say to poor old Gus if the stuff was as rotten bad as I expected.

"Well . . ." Tony sighed again. "We don't have skylarks in Manhattan and there's too much smog for an azure sky even at dawn, but I was still reading when the milk delivery trucks were rattling through the streets and I think I can honestly say that I knew right then and there we had a potential best seller. I agreed with Gus that it was too long and that he needed a better title. I told Phil all about it at breakfast. She was glad, because she had always liked Meg and Gus and she knew they needed a break for the agency. She was pouring coffee when she said, quite casually, "If it's a war book, why not *Never Call Retreat? Grapes of Wrath* is a pretty good title, but it's been used."

"For a moment I didn't get it. Then I remembered."

Lepton hummed under his breath: "He hath sounded forth a trumpet that shall never call retreat. . . ."

"I had a sort of shiver down my spine," resumed Tony. "I said: 'Phil, that's it! *Never Call Retreat.*' At the office, I phoned Gus and told him to see if he could fix an appointment with the author in my office that afternoon about three."

"Gus called back in fifteen minutes and said he'd run into a little difficulty he'd like to talk to me about if he could come up to the office that morning. I said okay, I could squeeze him in between two other appointments, and he came in looking like the wreck of the Hesperus."

"And no wonder!" said Gus fervently. "You see the script had come into the agency by mail. The return address was in Westchester and it sounded like somebody's country estate: The Willows, Stratfield, New York. I got the phone number from Information. A smooth, female voice answered: 'The Willows, good morning!' I said I wanted to speak to Mr. Cottle. The smooth voice said, 'Patients are not allowed to use the telephone. You may see Mr. Cottle if you come here during visiting hours in the afternoon between two and four.' I said, 'What is this? A hospital?' She answered: 'A clinic. Are you a relative or friend of Mr. Cottle's?' I told her I was a literary agent and he had sent me a script. Then she said I had better talk to Dr. Clinton.

"I did. Dr. Clinton had a calm, lofty, controlled voice—God addressing a black beetle. He said that The Willows was a clinic for neurotics—not psychotics. Most of his patients were alcoholics of good family but he had a few charity patients he had taken in because their cases presented features of interest he wanted to study. Writing and painting were both useful occupational therapy. He had encouraged Amos Cottle to write a book, but he did not know that Amos had sent the book to an agent. He must have bribed one of the attendants to mail it for him."

Tony continued the story.

"It ended with Gus and me going out to Stratfield that afternoon. I knew one publisher who had printed some stuff written by a guy in the time. But Amos Cottle's kind of amnesia is what we call *fugue*—a man's flight from his own past because it has become unbearable to him.'

"At that point I began to wonder if there were anything criminal in Amos's past. Clinton pooh-poohed the idea when I mentioned it, but now Amos has been murdered, I'm not so sure. Maybe he was running away from something pretty horrible and maybe it caught up with him last night."

"He didn't look like a criminal type," said Gus. "That was my first thought when Clinton took us up to Amos's room that afternoon. Amos didn't have the beard then. You could see the frailty of his chin and the sick look around his mouth. He was slender, almost emaciated, with dazed, wondering eyes. There was something quite childlike about him in those days, only he was more quiet and self-effacing than most children."

"In short," resumed Tony, "Amos looked exactly what he was—an incomplete man, a mind that was only half there, a personality without the rich, rounded volume that is added to a man's presence by his long personal memory of the past, his extension in the dimension called time."

"Two-thirds of a ghost," said Gus. "That's what Amos was."

"Or one-third," suggested Tony. "He must have been at least thirty, perhaps thirty-five, when we first met him four years ago, and he'd been in the clinic two years then. The greater part of his life was lost. Intellectually and physically a man, emotionally he must have been about six years old."

"Was there no way of tracing him through his military record?" suggested Basil. "After all, his first book was a war book."

"Kipling wrote a lot about the British Army but he never served in it," retorted Tony. "Clinton was of the opinion that, if Amos had been in the Pacific at all, it was in some civilian capacity, USO or YMCA or something. He could not have passed a physical examination to get into the Army even in war time. X-rays showed a weakness of the spine that must have been a defect of long duration. Something about the cartilage, or whatever it is that connects the vertebrae and cushions one against another, being almost entirely worn away. That was why he tired so easily. Even a draft board doctor would know that Amos couldn't survive an Army training course.

But Amos could have had some canteen job that gave him a chance to overhear the casual talk of soldiers."

Tony smiled a little cynically. "Damn few authors have experienced personally the things they write about. That's one difference between a pro and an amateur. An amateur can't write about something that isn't direct experience. A real writer can write about anything—that's his job. No one really cares if he's technically accurate in every petty detail. The only thing that matters is making it real to the average reader who doesn't know any more about technicalities than the average author. Emotions are what concern a fiction writer. Not facts, but the way people respond to facts inside themselves. That takes imagination—something a lot more rare than factual knowledge."

"Writing about things he hasn't experienced directly probably gives the writer perspective," put in Lepton. "Like those East Indian painters who would paint only from memory, never from direct visual experience."

"So . . ." Tony picked up his story again. "I bought a pig in a poke. I told Amos and Clinton that Daniel Sutton would publish Amos's book, but we couldn't possibly predict whether it would be a real success or not. What publisher can? I gave Amos a decent advance against royalties and he turned part of it over to Clinton to pay for his maintenance at the clinic until we saw how the book went. He also agreed to start another book now he no longer had to earn his keep as a janitor."

"The rest is history," said Gus. "Amos's first book was what we in the trade call the hat trick—best seller, first serial sale, Book-of-the-Week Club and movie. By six months after publication day the money was really rolling in."

"We had a last consultation with Clinton," added Tony. "He said Amos was quite ready to leave the clinic and advised us to forget all about Amos's past. The chances were it would never be recovered. The one thing to watch was the alcoholism, but Amos seemed as nearly cured as any alcoholic could be. Clinton said that Amos would be better off in the country than in the city—fewer temptations —and it was his suggestion that I should live near Amos where I could keep a fatherly eye on him. I'd been wanting to move to Connecticut and this seemed the time to do it. I gave up my New York apartment and bought this house for a song. It was only a run-down farm house then and we've been remodeling it ever since. I arranged for Amos to buy another house nearby and he seemed perfectly happy about the whole deal."

"He wasn't!" Vera's voice was bitter. "Who would be? He was—what did you call him? A valuable piece of property. He was like a zombie working for his masters. He had no life of his own at all."

"Did he ever tell you he couldn't remember his past?" asked Basil.

"No," admitted Vera. "But now I do know it explains so many things about Amos I never understood before. When I urged him to leave Tony and get another publisher he wouldn't. He said Tony had done so much for him, no one else could do as much. He was emotionally, as well as economically, dependent on Tony. How could any man be happy that way? He was just a thing Tony used—a sort of sleepwalker. As Tony says, 'Two-thirds of a ghost.'" She looked at Tony resentfully. "You didn't like his marrying me, did you? You got me that job in Hollywood to get me away from him. You knew I was just fool enough to take it, even though we'd only been married three months."

"You would have driven him back to drinking, Vera," said Tony levely. "You would have killed him."

"He would have had fun being killed that way, wouldn't he?" snapped Vera. "He didn't have much fun with you, living alone and working like hell and drinking iced tea when everybody else was drinking Scotch. I don't believe you even liked Amos. You just used him for your own purposes."

There was enough truth in this to abash Tony, but Philippa was not so easily cowed. "You didn't like him either, did you?" she murmured sweetly. "You just used him for your own purposes, too. Or tried to."

Vera was ashen with anger. "How dare you speak to me like that! Of course I loved Amos. I was his wife, wasn't I?"

"So you say." Philippa was still the smiler with the knife.

Vera started to speak, then closed her mouth.

"I see you're getting the idea," said Philippa. "If Amos was married before he lost his memory and if that wife is still alive, you were never his wife at all."

Gus turned to Basil defensively. "I don't think we did Amos any harm. I think we even did him some good. It wasn't our fault he was in deep amnesia. We certainly gave him a better life than he would have had mopping floors in Clinton's main building. I don't pretend I had any warm personal friendship for Amos. It's hard to feel quite normally toward a man who doesn't know his own past."

"I liked him," said Meg. "I didn't know about the amnesia of course. Perhaps that was why. I always thought of him as a perfectly normal human being—just a little more subdued and reticent than most people. He always looked so—so lost. I felt sorry for him. It seemed too bad for him to have so much vitality in his writing and so little in his own personality. He lived vicariously, didn't he? Perhaps that was one secret of his success. Everything went into his books because he had no life of his own, and he wrote with a detachment impossible to a man with personal memories of the immediate past."

"You all took a mean advantage of his weakness," said Vera. "You couldn't have taken such a big slice of his picture and TV rights if he'd been a normal man."

"There were reasons for that," said Tony quickly. "Take the TV program. I set it up with the advertising agency and the network. I got the sponsor for the agency. Actually I planned the format of the whole show. I even roughed out treatments for each broadcast which the script writers followed. I earned my share of that TV money."

"But not the movie money!" retorted Vera. "Or did you rough out treatments for Catamount?"

"No, but we both did a lot more for Amos than we would have done for a writer in a more normal situation," insisted Gus. "We were always afraid he'd relapse into alcoholism. If anything, we deserved a larger cut of his profits for the amount of time we had to take from other work in order to keep an eye on him. And he didn't seem to mind anything we did."

"Well, I do!" said Vera. "What you did for him was your own choice. He didn't ask you to do it. Either way he should have been paid at exactly the same rates as every other author. Why Sam Karp says Amos's royalty rate was ridiculous. You skinned him all along the line, Tony Kane!"

"Did he ever relapse into alcoholism before last night?" asked Basil.

"Once," answered Tony. "During the three months he was married to Vera. She's right. I did get her the job in Hollywood. That was why."

"There was another time he wanted to and didn't," said Meg. Tony looked at her in surprise. "I never knew that."

"It was nearly two years ago," said Meg. "One spring evening when Amos was in town and we were walking down 57th Street together, we stopped at Madison to wait for a traffic light. The light changed to green but Amos didn't move. He stood perfectly still for three or four seconds and then he said, 'I'm thirsty,' and headed for Schrafft's. I thought he wanted a soft drink, iced tea or lemonade, because it was a warm evening. But when we sat down at a table, he asked the waitress for Scotch on the rocks. While she was getting the drink, I talked fast. He carried Antabuse in his pocket in those days. I got him to take a pill before the drink came and he was saved. So far as I know he never tried to break training again until last night."

"What was he looking at when he stood so perfectly still?" asked Basil.

"I don't believe he was looking at anything," answered Meg. "He was sort of lost in thought."

"But the direction of his gaze?"

"Well, he was looking, in that sense, directly across the street to the opposite corner. There was a drug store there then."

"Was he looking toward the drug store window?"

"No. He was looking up, higher than that."

"At the sky?"

"Not so high as that. He was looking toward the upper floors of the building on the corner opposite us. But I don't believe he was seeing them. His eyes were sort of unfocused like—well, like a man trying to remember something."

"Or like a man who had remembered something?"

Silence made Basil suddenly aware that he and Meg had an audience, listening more and more intently to every word. Before she could answer his last question, he turned back to Tony, as if Meg's story were quite unimportant.

"Was there ever any indication that Amos Cottle had been recognized by someone out of his past?"

"Not that I know of," said Tony. "You, Gus?"

"No."

"Even when he appeared regularly on TV?" persisted Basil.

"Oh." Tony's brow wrinkled. "That did worry us a bit. The offer was too good to turn down, but we realized it was risky. That was when I suggested to Amos that he grow a beard. It did change his appearance quite a lot. And of course the alcoholism must have changed him a good deal from what he was say ten or twelve years ago."

"Is it conceivable that someone recognized another man in Amos Cottle without your knowing anything about it? That perhaps he was even murdered by someone who came out of his past, and for some reason that had nothing to do with his being Amos Cottle?"

"It's conceivable, I suppose, but what motive for murder could last so long?"

"There's always property," said Basil. "In his other incarnation he was someone who had disappeared for at least the six years he was known as Cottle. Suppose he was presumed dead and someone inherited his property because of that. Or suppose a former wife of his remarried. Once he was on TV, this person who had profited by his presumed death or remarried because of it might see him and recognize him and live in daily dread that someone else would recognize him, too, and ruin everything. That situation provides a strong motive for murder. Such a murderer would be hard to unmask, for nothing in Amos Cottle's life would connect him with Cottle in any way."

"It's possible," admitted Tony. "But after all, Amos was killed by someone who was here last night. This hypothetical person out of Amos's forgotten past would have to be one of the Puseys or Emmett Avery."

"Or me." Lepton smiled wickedly. "The rest of you were all a part of his life as Amos Cottle, but we four were meeting him in person for the first time."

"And came to the meeting provided with cyanide?" objected Tony.

"The murderer might have recognized him first on TV," retorted Lepton. "I don't have a set myself but I'm sure Emmett and the Puseys have."

Basil returned Lepton's smile. "I shall keep all these interesting possibilities in mind."

Lepton bowed to the challenge. "I'm not a psychiatrist nor the son of a psychiatrist, but another thought occurs to me: is it possible that Amos did recover his real memory without telling anyone about it? Even his guardian angels, Gus and Tony?"

Gus looked astonished. "Why wouldn't he tell us?"

Lepton shrugged. "Perhaps he wanted a little private life of his own. Perhaps he enjoyed remaining a mystery to you and Tony—the walking enigma without a memory. Or perhaps his past was so shameful he didn't want anyone to know about it."

Basil was interested. "Are you suggesting that he recovered his memory without informing his new associates and then sought out some of his old associates, thereby, consciously or unconsciously, giving one of them a motive and an opportunity to kill him anonymously, as it were?"

"Why not?" Lepton found this possibility diverting. "A man without an official past is pretty vulnerable, isn't he?"

Basil looked at Vera. "How did you meet him?"

"On a TV show. I was an assistant director for the network, assigned to an interview program, and it was Amos's second interview. His second book was just out. He usually came to the studio with Gus, but that night, after the show had been going on about five months, Amos came alone. Gus's little girl was having her tonsils out and he couldn't make it."

"My mistake," murmured Gus.

"So," Vera smiled with self-satisfaction. "I really got to know Amos for the first time. After the show we went out to supper together. He didn't drink anything himself that night, but he bought me a bottle of champagne and he told me how lonely he was. The rest was easy."

"Poor Amos!" Tony looked at Vera malevolently, then turned to Basil. "You can imagine how Gus and I felt when we got Amos's telegram from Asheville. They had been married at City Hall two days before. I flew down and sobered up Amos in time for the next show. I didn't know what to do with Vera until I thought of the Hollywood caper. For three months she lived with Amos and he didn't do a stroke of work all that time. Too drunk."

"I kept telling him to write!" cried Vera indignantly. "I didn't want him to stop. I just couldn't understand why he couldn't be more reasonable about his drinking."

"You got on his nerves," said Philippa. "He told me so after you left."

"I don't believe it!" Vera's retort was hot, but there was self-doubt in her eyes. "Amos never liked you! He wouldn't confide in you!"

Lepton tried to create a diversion. "All artists of any talent are vain and touchy and hard to live with. It's no reflection on you, Vera, that you got on Amos's nerves. Anyone else would have had the same effect on him. He was the type who has to live alone. You probably maddened him. After all, he was a man of some intellect and the only services he needed from you were—shall we say, unintellectual? As his mistress, you would have had a great success and it might even have become a permanent relation. As his wife, you were doomed to failure from the beginning. He couldn't stand any woman in daily doses. Why should a man have to pay such a price for a few minutes' pleasure?"

"There speaks the true-born bachelor," remarked Philippa.

Vera rose regally. "Dr. Willing, all these people hate me. How much longer do I have to remain in this house and be insulted?"

"Hate is a rather strong word," protested Gus. "We weren't happy about your marriage to Amos, but you have no right to suggest . . ."

"I have a perfect right to suggest anything I please!" returned Vera. "Do you know what your wife thinks of me? She thinks I'm an incompetent actress and a vicious woman! She said so."

"That doesn't sound like Meg. . . ." Gus half turned in his chair.

Meg flushed a beautiful pink. "It's true. I—I don't suppose it will do any good if I say I'm sorry."

"No, it won't." Vera glared at Meg like an angry child. She was completely out of control now. Her voice had lost all its sweet artifice. "I'm going to pay you back for that if it's the last thing I ever do!"

"When did you say this, Meg?" demanded Gus.

"I wrote Amos a letter the night I heard Vera was coming back," Meg explained in a stifled voice. "I wrote Vera at the same time suggesting she stay with us. I was confused and—well, I put the letter to Amos in the envelope to Vera and airmailed it to the Coast before she left."

"You see?" Vera turned to Basil triumphantly. "When can I go back to New York, Dr. Willing?"

"Any time you like," returned Basil. "Captain Drew asked me to tell you that any of you are free to return to New York now, if you wish to do so, but the police would like you to remain in either New York or Connecticut for the next few days."

"Hallelujah!" Vera was jubilant. "I'm going upstairs and pack my things right now." Her gaze swept the circle. "Would you people like to know what I think about you?"

"No," said Philippa quickly.

Vera allowed her glance to stray from face to face in a calculated theatrical pause. "I think there is something damned queer about this whole setup. All you parasitic leeches living on Amos's life blood! I think one of you murdered him and I'm going to find out which one. Meg Vesey, I may be an incompetent actress, but you're going to find out now just how vicious I can be as a woman." Her eyes shifted to Tony and Gus. "Sam Karp will call you two literary executors in the morning and give you a choice of changing the terms of Amos's contract or being sued."

"You have no grounds for suit!" cried Tony furiously.

"Sam has a mighty cute lawyer." Vera turned abruptly with a swish of satin and marched out of the room. No one made an effort to detain her. No one spoke until the clatter of her heels on the stairs had died away.

"Typical Hollywood exit," remarked Philippa. "In fact, the whole scene was pure Hollywood. Cinderella in blue satin and mink—the lovely, warm-blooded, impetuous daughter of the common people—denouncing the parasitic, supercilious rich with more decibels than manners."

"I always wondered if Vera could raise her voice," murmured Meg.

"And now you know."

Meg smiled at Gus ruefully. "I'm sorry about that letter."

He squeezed her hand. "It doesn't matter now. It never mattered really."

She shook her head. "Vera would be easier to handle now if it wasn't for my letter. I'm afraid she's going to make trouble about those contracts."

"She would have done that anyway," said Tony. "But legally she's stuck. I have some pretty cute lawyers of my own and they went all over those contracts with a fine-toothed comb before they were signed."

Meg rose, looking happier than she had for the last two days. "I want to get back to Polly as soon as I can. Dr. Willing, if you don't need me for anything further, I'll go up and change."

"Want to borrow a suit?" asked Philippa.

"Thanks, but the velvet dress won't matter in the car and we're going straight home."

Basil said good-bye to Philippa. Tony and Gus trailed him to the front door.

"I suppose we'll be seeing you again in town?" said Tony without enthusiasm.

"Most likely you will." Basil's measured glance considered Tony thoughtfully. "I doubt if this case can be solved until we find out more about Cottle's real identity. What became of the clothing he wore when he was found six years ago?"

"I don't know," said Tony.

"Maybe the Stratfield Police Department kept it," suggested Gus.

"By this time, it's probably vanished," said Basil. "Like the muddy track of the car that skidded into Amos. There never was a case where the physical trail was colder. But there are other clues besides tire prints and personal effects. Less tangible things that don't change with time."

"Such as?" probed Tony.

"The things that Amos wrote," returned Basil. "And he wrote so much. There ought to be a thousand clues to his birthplace and his former occupation, his family, his friends, his hobbies, in those four books he wrote in four years, to say nothing of his unpublished scripts. A man can't write novels without putting a great deal of his own past into them."

"But he'd lost all memory of his past!" cried Gus in amazement.

"When you say his memory was lost, you don't mean it was annihilated—not as long as he was still alive. You mean simply that it was lost to conscious recall, buried in the subconscious. Every fiction writer draws heavily on his subconscious. Such clues are all the more eloquent because they are unconscious and therefore completely candid. 'Oh, that mine enemy would write a book!'"

"I see what you mean." The idea seemed to make Tony uncomfortable. "The author portrays himself in every line he writes and portrayal is always betrayal. The lie is the man."

Basil nodded. "Even a small, everyday lie is a clue to the personality and preoccupations of the liar, like a dream or any other confection of the mind, that is half-conscious and half-unconscious, as all creative acts must be. How much more revealing are four long novels which are, psychologically speaking, four long lies."

"Wouldn't it be kinder to say that a lie is a short work of fiction?" suggested Gus. " 'A story' as my daughter says?"

Basil laughed. "Let's say that fiction and lies are both works of creative art, and creation always reveals the creator. As Cottle's literary executors, will you give me permission to go through every scrap of unpublished work he left behind him?"

Gus and Tony exchanged an uneasy glance. "We can hardly say no," remarked Tony at last. "I'm sure you could get a search warrant or a writ of habeas corpus or something if we did. All the stuff is in Amos's house now and the police have the keys. But I hope you don't find out anything about Amos that will hurt the sales of his posthumous books."

Basil's glance probed Tony's poker face. "You don't have much faith in Amos Cottle, do you?"

"I don't have much faith in anybody," returned Tony.

When Basil's car had gone, Gus said, "Should I offer to drive Vera to New York?"

"No." Tony was emphatic. "You'd be sure to have an accident with Meg and Vera in the same car. I'll drive Vera to the station. If there's no train within the next hour from Westport or Norwalk, I'll take her to Stamford. Come into the study and we'll look up the timetable."

In the breakfast room, Philippa was putting out a cigarette she had just lighted. "What a morning!" She sighed deeply. "All the skeletons are out of the cupboard now!"

"Are they?" said Lepton quietly.

She had risen as she spoke. Now he rose, too, and came around the table to her side. His dark gaze held hers, fascinated. He spoke in a low, almost uninterested voice. "You were intimate with him, weren't you?"

Philippa was unused to shock tactics. She made a mistake. "How did you know?"

"The look in your eyes when you learned he was only—" Lepton's gaze grew speculative, "Two-thirds of a ghost?"

Philippa shuddered uncontrollably and covered her face with her hands.

His voice sank to a whisper. "I'm not a ghost."

He pulled her hands away from her face. His embrace was so hard and urgent she thought she would faint with a pleasure as keen as pain itself. His lips found every nerve end.

"Maurice . . ." she whispered with a kind of awe and drew back.

Movement caught her eye. Her gaze went beyond his shoulder and it was then that she saw Vera, dressed for the street, watching them from the doorway, her face flushed with exultant malice.

Before either of them could speak, Vera was gone.

nine

It was two o'clock when Basil's car turned into the driveway of the house where Amos Cottle had led his lonely life. Basil had invited Emmett Avery to meet him here at three. That gave Basil an hour alone to commune with Amos Cottle's enigmatic ghost.

As soon as he unlocked the door with the key he had picked up at the police station, he was impressed by the stillness within. Tony had said that every wall was soundproof. Basil had a theory of his own that many flaws and failings in contemporary writing can be traced to the hubbub of industrial society. Shelley would never have written his lyrical salute to the skylark quite so felicitously if there had been a pneumatic drill just outside his window and a radio going full blast on the other side of a matchboard partition. But Amos had achieved what so few modern writers can afford—the luxury of silence. And Amos had lived entirely alone. In this vacuum he had invoked the voice of stillness that must speak to writers as well as mystics if they are to attain ecstasy.

Yet, in this perfect setting, Amos had been unhappy enough to long for the numbing effect of alcohol and the writing he had produced was of such uncertain quality that it had provoked a public wrangle between two prominent critics. Now he was dead the hush seemed haunted with echoes, a jostling throng at the very edge of the threshold of human hearing. If only there were some supersensitive sonic device that could break through the time barrier and pick up the dying fall of yesterday's voices. Basil had a curious feeling that the house was trying to tell him something that should have been quite obvious.

The great windows made the outdoors part of the living room. The day had not yet lost its della Robbia clarity. The snowy world was still an innocent white against the tender blue of the sky, sparkling clean in the winter sunshine. Basil's glance moved slowly around the room and paused at the bizarre window above the fireplace. Its calculated illogic struck him as decadent and almost sinister, a contrived effect of deliberate madness. Of course, the house was Tony's choice and the furniture came with the house. These were just layers in the elaborately built up façade of an artificial personality. So were the clothes, all of the finest quality, that filled the closet in the bedroom. There was no clue to the character of the real man.

In the scrapbasket beside the bureau he saw a crumpled piece of tissue stained with something brownish red. Dried blood? Closer examination revealed lipstick of a peculiar russet shade that would be difficult for most complexions. But not for Philippa Kane's. It was the same shade of lipstick she had worn this morning. It proved nothing and suggested a great deal. Evidently Amos had not been quite so lonely as most of his friends assumed.

Basil inspected the kitchen briefly. Amos was no epicure. There were no exotic foods, frozen or fresh. This was a man who ate eggs and bacon for breakfast and meat or fish without sauce or condiment for dinner. An indifference to quality in food showed clearly in the choice of bread and coffee. There could be no question of Amos's true nationality. Only an American would drink coffee that was largely Brazilian and eat bread that was largely air, when even supermarkets now offered tastier alternatives.

The house was proving even more barren of obvious physical clues than Basil had expected. There were only two possibilities left —the papers in the desk and the books on the shelves.

The most prominent shelves in the living room were packed with the four books Amos had written in the last four years. First came the trade editions in gaudy paper jackets, then the book-club and reprint editions. Finally scrapbooks in which a few letters and many clippings of reviews and advertisements had been pasted in chronological order.

The first drawer of the desk was immaculate and sterile—typing paper, carbon, envelopes, great and small, pens, pencils, and erasers, bills, paid and unpaid, bank statements, income tax records, checkbooks. In the second drawer he found cardboard folders, some labeled CONTRACTS, others labeled LETTERS. The third drawer yielded 421 pages of carbon typescript stapled inside a blue cardboard folder, marked in Amos's own neat handwriting:

THE ENDS OF THE EARTH
A Novel
by Amos Cottle

This must be the unpublished book Gus and Tony had mentioned. There were no corrections in ink or pencil. Apparently it had not been styled for the printer or even proofread. It was virgin as it had come from the typist. Or did Amos do his own typing?

Other folders in the third drawer were filled with carbons of books already published, carbons of TV scripts each bearing its own date. The first was scheduled for next January. The sequence ran for thirty-nine weeks, skipping July and August, the season of summer replacements.

But where was the rough draft of the book Amos had just started? And his notebooks and his unpublished short stories?

Basil skimmed through the letters first. In a few moments he realized they were all business letters from Gus or Tony or the advertising agency that ran the TV show. If Amos had received personal letters, he must have destroyed them as soon as he answered them. A man without a memory could hardly be expected to be sentimental. Such emotions were largely a product of memory, increasing as the years accumulated and the pattern of *lacrimae rerum* became more obvious. Amos must have been almost as detached as a child or an animal from the world of adult feeling.

Basil was returning the letter folders to the bottom drawer when he made his first real discovery.

The drawer stuck a little as he tried to pull it out farther. Something had caught in the grooved ledge where it was supposed to slide back and forth. His fingers found the obstruction he could not see until he dislodged it. A small coin purse in limp, cracked reptile skin, faded to a dull mottled tan. He unlatched it and saw something wrapped in yellowed tissue paper. Carefully he unrolled the paper. There was a broad, plain gold wedding ring with an inscription on the inner side A.S. to G.M., 6-10-48. There was a strand of fine, straight, brown hair, tied with a white cotton thread. It was the bright shade of pale brown that catches the light with an almost iridescent tone of bronze, a shade no dye can duplicate, and it was very fine in texture, probably the hair of a young girl or a child. There was one other thing in the little purse—a worn, gold thimble. Its border was embossed with tiny forget-me-nots enameled in pink and blue. The gold part of the border was engraved in fancy script with a single letter "G." Gertrude? Grace? Gloria? Greta? Gretchen? Griselda? Georgiana? Gilda? Garnet? Or even the name that was so resonant with memories for him, Gisela?

Basil stood for a long time looking at the three objects. A woman's ring, a woman's thimble and most probably a woman's hair. When did a woman give up her wedding ring? Only when she was dead or divorced. But would a divorced woman's wedding ring be treasured with a lock of her hair?

Could these things have belonged to a former owner of the house? It seemed unlikely. Anyone who kept things like this would hardly forget them when the house was sold. They must have belonged to Amos. Did he himself know what they signified? Sentiment without memory was psychologically absurd, but it was not necessarily sentiment that might have induced Amos to preserve these trinkets. They might have been kept as the only clues he had to his lost identity. Things the police had discovered in his clothing when they found him wandering and incoherent by the roadside with a wounded head. Things they returned to him when they gave up all hope of tracing him. Things Amos and Dr. Clinton had never mentioned to Tony or Gus, perhaps because they dramatized Amos's lost identity so vividly. After seeing these, Tony might have been more hesitant to publish a book by a man who was so obviously a walking mystery—a man with a past buried like a time bomb that might explode at any moment.

A tap on the glass door dispersed Basil's reflections. He dropped the purse and the trinkets in his pocket.

Emmett Avery stood on the other side of the glass, silhouetted against the fading daylight. Basil crossed the room to let him in.

"So this is the enemy's stronghold!" Emmett's cold, gray eyes surveyed the living room with frank curiosity and lingered on the carbon of Amos's unpublished book. "A posthumous Cottle?"

Basil nodded. "There's a book in rough draft and a notebook and some short stories, too, but I haven't come across those yet."

"*De mortuis* . . ." Emmett sighed. "We'll all have to be sickeningly polite about them, I suppose. There are certain advantages to an author in being dead. . . . Tony and Leppy were very much interested when I ran into them at the station and told them I was coming here to meet you. They wanted to know why and, of course, I couldn't tell them because you hadn't told me. Why am I here, Dr. Willing? As a suspect? Or the devil's advocate?"

"Neither. As an expert witness. Tony Kane says that your father was a publisher's accountant who knew more about contracts than anyone in the business and that you worked for several years in his office before you became a critic. I want you to read these letters and then tell me just how they strike you. Won't you sit down?"

Emmett settled himself in another easy chair and glanced at the first page of the scrapbook Basil handed him. Uninvited he began to read aloud as if this were a jest so rich it must be shared. He had a good reading voice that relished every shade of meaning in the words he uttered.

    Daniel Sutton and Company,
    256A Fourth Avenue, New York 16, New York.

                                 January 14, 1952

Amos Cottle, Esq.
The Willows
Stratfield
New York

Dear Mr. Cottle,

All of us here at Daniel Sutton are quite impressed with the publishable qualities of THE BATTLEFIELD. As it stands, the script is a little too long, and I agree with my first reader, Susan Grey, who insists that the title is not a good selling title. There are a number of other minor revisions I should like to suggest as follows:

Chapter Ten should be eliminated altogether Chapter Eight, now told from the point of view of the Japanese sergeant, should be rewritten from the point of view of the

American soldier who dies in Chapter Two. It will, I am sure, be a simple matter to postpone his death to Chapter Fourteen and write his part, as a living participant, into the intervening chapters. I should also like to see another character introduced halfway through the book—someone from the deep South. All your American soldiers are from the North, East and West. I am sure we would get better sales south of the Mason-Dixon line if we had one Southern character. It would be a relatively easy task to introduce another character and bring the number of soldiers involved up to a round dozen. And one other thing: I think it would be more unusual if the American combatants in this story were marines instead of infantrymen. There have been a number of war books about the infantry lately, but none about the marines. Have you any objection to making this change? The final decision must, of course, rest with the author, but here at Daniel Sutton we all feel that the time is ripe for a book about marines.

If you could do all this acceptably in about six days, the book would be in time for the one spot still vacant on our fall list. If not we would have to postpone publication for another year, and I fear the story would have lost some of its timeliness by then.

Yours very sincerely,
Anthony Kane
Editor

Carbon copy to Augustus Vesey Inc.

January 20, 1952

Dear Mr. Cottle,

We're still holding that spot on the list for you, but we can only do so for another day or so. When will the revision be ready?

Sincerely,
Anthony Kane

REVISION MAGNIFICENT JOB AM DISCUSSING CONTRACT WITH VESEY REGARDS TONY KANE

February 2, 1952

Amos Cottle, Esq.
The Willows
Stratfield, New York

Dear Amos,

Enclosed are three copies of the contract I negotiated with Tony Kane of Daniel Sutton yesterday for your book now entitled NEVER CALL RETREAT. Will you please sign all three and return two, keeping one for your own files.

I am not entirely happy about Clause 6B which gives Daniel Sutton fifty percent of all your subsidiary rights. I argued with Tony Kane about this at considerable length, but he was adamant. He said that a first novel is always a gamble, that they are planning a large advertising appropriation for this book, that the costs of production have risen so high since the war that they are operating at a loss anyway and probably won't be able to stay in business much longer unless they get a larger share of subsidiary money. He also pointed out that if publishers don't make a good profit on books like yours that do sell, they can't afford to print really artistic books that don't sell and the high standards of American literature would suffer in consequence. In short, Tony feels that the popular best sellers should carry the financial burden for the more recondite type of prestige book on a publisher's list. When I pointed out that this was a bit rough on the best-selling author, Tony made a nice gesture and yielded a point. He said that if we would agree to the fifty percent subsidiary rights clause as it stands, he would write in another clause saying that you could have *all* your rights in Italy and Finland! I thought this was quite a handsome concession on Tony's part. I trust you will agree and forward the signed contracts to me immediately.

With all good wishes from Meg and myself,
Yours as ever,
Gus

P.S. You will note that the last clause is an agency clause appointing me your representative in all matters arising out of this contract at a commission of twenty-five percent. This is a little higher than the commission some agents get but will cover the typing charges you are not able to meet at the present time. Also, the cost of long-distance phone calls to the West Coast, cables to Europe and the commissions I shall have to pay other agents in Hollywood, London and Paris. I could send you an itemized bill for these incidentals, but I believe that a straight twenty-five percent commission will prove more advantageous in the long run and facilitate bookkeeping for both of us.

G.V.

Emmett put down the scrapbook with a wolfish grin. "Oh, boy!" he said with malicious delight. "And I always thought Sutton, Kane was a reputable publisher!"

"But you don't now?"

Emmett's face sobered.

"If there were no libel laws, I'd say they were the biggest bunch of crooks that ever lived. Tony Kane is a smart operator. But Gus Vesey is even smarter. That twenty-five percent that 'facilitates bookkeeping.' What a phrase! 'More advantageous in the long run'—to whom? Must have been a powerful lot of long-distance phone calls to Hollywood to justify that for a period of four years. May I see the contracts?"

Basil handed them over. Emmett chuckled indulgently from time to time as if he were reading a rather naughty humorous magazine. "Didn't Cottle ever hear of the Authors' Guild contract? . . . No termination clause—option on the next two books on the same terms. This is the sort of thing that was done fifty years ago before there were any movie or TV rights: one of those self-perpetuating, slave contracts, just like marriage. . . . Royalty, ten percent of the retail price of the trade edition with no increase on copies sold . . . Fifty percent of first serial, reprints, condensations, second serial, movies and TV to Tony, also foreign sales and translations, excepting only Italy and Finland . . . What a gold mine! Whoever killed Amos Cottle, it was not Tony Vane or Gus Vesey!"

"Then you would say this was an unusual contract? Not representative of established trade practice today?"

"Representative? For Pete's sake! Of course there was a time when the author of a first book would accept any terms to get in print and some publishers took advantage of that. But not today. And, even in the old days, ten percent commission was always established trade practice for agents. There must be some reason for Gus Vesey taking more than twice that, but what the dickens can it be? Certainly not the reason he gives in this letter. In a year or so, that twenty-five percent would amount to a lot more than the incidentals he lists. Something peculiar was going on here. Take another point: after Amos was a commercial success, Gus should have tried to negotiate a better contract for Amos with Tony. But apparently he didn't. He just let the old, slave contract roll along on its options-on-the-same-terms clause, like perpetual motion. . . . The only reason I can see is that Tony himself suggested this extra fifteen percent to Gus as a cut-back, if Gus would persuade Amos to sign Tony's fifty percent cut of motion picture and TV rights. That's monstrous! It puts Gus in the same category as agents who pocket their clients' money and it makes Tony a crook, too."

"Suppose Amos had come to realize that he was being gypped and had tried to rebel? Would that be a motive for murdering him?"

Emmett considered this carefully. "No, I think not. You see, I don't believe anyone could prove that Gus or Tony had done anything illegal. There's no law that fixes a literary agent's commission at ten percent. Amos couldn't prosecute Gus. How could Amos prove in court that Tony was bribing Gus to betray a client's interests? If word of what they had done got around in the trade, Gus and Tony might have lost a lot of business in the long run. That's about the worst that could happen. I don't believe either of them would risk their necks committing murder to prevent that. They both have enough to live on now. They don't have to be in business. Of course, if Amos woke up to the facts of life he'd try to get another agent and another publisher. Even then he might need a smart lawyer to break a contract without a termination clause, unless Tony decided to be decent about technicalities, provided Amos kept mum about the sort of deal he'd had from both of them. Losing Amos's future books would cost Gus and Tony money, but they couldn't save that future money by killing the goose that laid the golden eggs."

"Was he really a goose? Personal prejudice aside, how is Amos Cottle really regarded as a writer?"

"Why don't you ask Leppy?"

"I want another opinion. From the devil's advocate."

Avery lit a cigarette. "I'll try to be honest with you. I'll even admit that I was a bit heavy-handed in my review in the *Trib* yesterday. But I still do not think Amos Cottle was a great writer or even a good one."

"What made him so successful?"

Emmett shrugged. "If you could answer that question about any author, you could make a fortune in publishing. Few publishers make really great fortunes, simply because no one knows just what makes a book sell. For one thing it's a quality that probably varies enormously with time and place. *Dr. Jekyll and Mr. Hyde* was a complete flop when it was issued around Christmas. Reissued a few months later, it was an instant success and made Stevenson's reputation.

"In other business enterprises, there is some yardstick for quality. When you produce steel ingots or toothpaste you know that they are marketable if they meet certain standards of quality and if there's a demand for steel or toothpaste. You're sure to make a profit if your costs aren't too high. A publisher has no such assurance. From the very beginning, his acceptance of a script for publication depends largely on the personal tastes and caprices of the publisher and his readers. Even intelligibility is no longer a criterion. It is stylish to be unintelligible. You can almost insure artistic success that way, though commercial success is still much more subtle and unpredictable. Highbrows have literary fashions to go by, lowbrows don't."

Avery exhaled a long plume of smoke and Basil said, "I'd like very much to hear an analysis of Cottle's success from someone as hostile to him as you were."

The wolfish grin came back to Avery's face. "The popular writer is always a pale carbon copy of the artistically fashionable writer of the previous generation. It's sort of like Third Avenue copying a Paris model two years later at a price of fourteen ninety-five. But in books there's a cultural lag of almost thirty years.

"Amos came along at a time when the popular writer was taking over the technique of the artistic writers of the Twenties. Style confused and subjective, but not absolutely enigmatic. Mood sensual and emotional, but the more common sensualities and emotions, nothing recondite. The popular writer never needs to worry about intellectual content anyway, so its absence from the new look suits him to a T. Freudian symbolism he wisely leaves to the literary aristocracy whenever he can, but he's just as much at home with violence, poverty, vulgarity and sex as the highest brow, and his dialogue is just as colloquial if a little less ungrammatical. For the popular writer, the real innovation is the gradual abandoning of plot which must have cost him and his readers quite a psychological wrench, for plot has always been the backbone of popular writing until now. But they made the adjustment, as the psychologists would say. Even TV and slick magazines are abandoning plot for mood, as the high priests of literature did in 1925. Today a plot is indecent anywhere outside a mystery, the last refuge of the conservative writer.

"Amos was typical of the popular writer of his generation, with nothing great or enduring about him. The curious question is this: why did Amos's books have such a great success when a dozen or more of exactly the same type are dropped out each year with a dull thud and forgotten in six months?"

"Advertising?" suggested Basil.

"Not exactly. Advertising doesn't sell books, but it does sell Hollywood and then movies sell books. The tail wags the dog. *Retreat* was sold to Hollywood before publication on the strength of the proposed advertising campaign. From then on the commercial success of that one book was insured, and the thing was bound to snowball, provided that Amos produced enough books of the same type regularly. That was the real secret of Amos Cottle's great success. Productivity. He kept right on, doggedly doing the same thing on the same scale at the same level once a year for four years. That was the thing Amos had that other writers at his level didn't have—an enormous, almost superhuman fertility in the writing of bad books. The sheer weight and number of his books was overwhelming in volume. He was bound to end with a TV program and the Bookbinders' Award. With that fatal facility and Tony and Gus to guide him, he just couldn't lose.

"That's why I hated his books. I hate fads and I hate frauds. Amos was perhaps unconsciously both a fad and a fraud who built a great reputation on one thing—sheer volume of production. And he made a hell of a lot of money out of it, while my own budget runs around a hundred and fifty a week and always will because I don't have the knack of writing pastiches of all the popular novels of the last thirty years and doing it regularly once a year. If I could, I would!"

"Why does Lepton take Amos so much more seriously? **Lepton seems intelligent.**"

Avery grinned again. "Put it down to professional jealousy, but I think Leppy is the same kind of critic that Amos was a novelist. Leppy's criticism is a pastiche of all the fashionable criticism of the last thirty years and I don't think his fraud is unconscious. I think Leppy is completely cynical. He pans most books, because he can be very amusing when he does and that's what sells his articles. But he's shrewd enough to know he can't pan every book that comes out, so—I suspect Leppy gets hold of a copy of *Publishers' Weekly* when it prints advance spring lists, takes a pin, closes his eyes and sticks the pin blindly in the page. The first work of fiction he hits with the pin becomes the one book Leppy praises for that season. If the author grows in popularity, as Amos did, Leppy feels he's committed and sticks with the guy. But if the author is lazy about producing books or loses his popularity, Leppy drops him with a little review saying that Mr. Inkblot has not fulfilled his early promise. . . ."

"Gosh, this scrapbook is fascinating!" Avery began turning pages. "To think of Amos solemnly pasting up all his reviews, good or bad. Listen to this, from Gus to Amos:

Dear Amos,
  This review will appear in next week's *Chicago Tribune*. It should make you very happy.
                                                    Regards,
                                                    Gus

NEVER CALL RETREAT. A novel by Amos Cottle. Daniel Sutton and Co., $3.75. Reviewed by Mark Kitteridge

Here, believe me, is a book by a new writer that is not entirely without interest. Mr. Cottle has a sharp sense of the futility of the human predicament especially in time of war. Indeed it seemed to me that the war scenes were handled with vivid flashes of an almost intuitive perception of the causal relationship between bullets and fear.

On the other hand the book is far too long and extremely

dull. (Typical Kitteridge: This book is brilliant, on the other hand it is damned dull. That boy never goes out on a limb!) The flashbacks that give us a glimpse of each marine's life in peacetime are not up to the standard of the battle scenes. We suspect that Mr. Cottle, like so many authors today, had one eye on Hollywood when he wrote these glimpses of civilian life introducing several mawkish and irrelevant love scenes and one really pornographic episode, that seriously damage the unity and integrity of his tale.

Each marine involved is from a different part of the country and this obvious appeal to regional sentiment smacks of calculated commercialism. The title *Never Call Retreat* is inappropriate, since each man is quite ready to retreat at the end and only refrains from doing so because there is nothing to retreat to but the Pacific Ocean. The book should have had some stark, simple title like *The Battlefield* and it would have had far more general interest if it had concerned the infantry instead of a small, élite corps like the marines. It would have been more in keeping with the fact that the Japanese are now our allies against communism if at least one of the scenes had been told from the point of view of a Japanese soldier. The scene where the sergeant is shot in the belly is in questionable taste. War really does not have to be made quite so gruesomely unappetizing in fiction. The fighting man's use of profane and obscene language is grossly exaggerated in the opinion of a reviewer whose memories of the Army go back to 1917. (Gosh, I didn't know Kit was that old!)

Basil was beginning to feel as if he had strayed into a world as queerly inverted as anything Alice found on the other side of the looking glass. "Why on earth did Gus Vesey expect such a review to make Amos happy?"

"Oh, an agent always seems to think a writer will be pleased if a critic devotes a lot of space to him," said Avery, "no matter how inimical the criticism contained in that space. And it's not really a bad review for a first book. Look what good use Tony's publicity department made of it."

Avery held up the scrapbook so Basil could see the next page.

It was entirely covered with a half-page ad cut from a newspaper. A picture of a giant bugler in marine's uniform with a bugle at his lips towered above a vague suggestion of shadowy palm trees and the minute figure of a bearded man in rags holding his stomach in both hands while blood trickled through his fingers.

Below came the big, bold letters:

>NEVER CALL RETREAT
>By AMOS COTTLE
>Daniel Sutton and Co., $3.75
>MARK KITTERIDGE in the *Chicago Tribune:*
>"Here, believe me, is a book. . . ."

Avery turned a page and Basil read the next ad.

>Catamount Pictures Proudly Presents
>The Picture That Has Everything
>STUPENDOUS, COLOSSAL, FABULOUS!
>SPENCER TRACY AND RITA HAYWORTH
>on the widest screen in the world
>in
>NEVER CALL RETREAT
>Scenario by Len Gumroot
>(from a novel by Amos Cottle)

See the beautiful Japanese geisha dying for love of an American marine!
See the luscious siren of the San Diego waterfront stealing the marine's last dollar before he sails into the fiery hell of war!
See the flame-throwers! The tanks! The napalm bombs!
A picture that will inspire a whole generation of Americans!
Mark Kitteridge in the *Chicago Tribune:* "One really pornographic episode . . ."
Opening tonight at 8:00 P.M. Continuous performance tomorrow from 1:00 P.M. Tickets $2.95, $2.45, $1.90, $1.50 at the Pinchbeck Theatre . . .

"I believe we didn't have napalm until Korea," said Avery. "But who in Hollywood cares?"

Painted flames encircled the text of the advertisement like an inky inferno, with a glimpse of a writhing body here and there.

Basil turned his head suddenly. "It may be suggestion but—do you smell something burning?"

Avery put down the scrapbook. "I believe I do."

Both men looked around the room. The sky had darkened. It was not quite a night sky yet, but it was too dark to see anything but their own reflections in the great sheets of glass on the garden side of the house.

"You must have been mistaken," said Avery.

"I think not." Basil was on his feet. "Look."

Avery looked toward the open door into the bedroom. A thin coil of smoke was rising from the crack between two floorboards.

"Where would the door to the cellar be in a house like this?" demanded Basil.

"Kitchen probably."

Basil led the way. There were two doors in the kitchen. Avery jerked at one and it opened on the fresh, cold, winter night. Basil snatched at the other door. Avery had a second's glimpse of towering black smoke shot with scarlet flame before Basil slammed it shut again.

"Call the Fire Department. Then help me get Amos Cottle's papers out of here."

Avery ran to the phone in the bedroom as Basil began pulling drawers out of the filing cabinet. Carbons—all carbons of books already published.

When Avery came back he looked frightened. "Do Cottle's papers really matter now? The bedroom floor's on fire and there's smoke even in here."

"Get out if you want to," said Basil. "I'm going to save what I can."

"You're nuts!" protested Avery. "Tony or Gus will have another carbon of that unpublished book and copies of all the contracts."

"What about the rough drafts and short stories and notebooks Tony and Gus want to publish posthumously?"

"Why should you care? You're not a stockholder in Sutton, Kane and this room is going up in flames in another moment!"

It was true. Basil could feel the heat of the floor through the soles of his shoes. Smoke pervaded the room, not in sudden gusts or coils, but invisibly. It had seeped slowly from every crack until it became a part of the air in the room, bringing water to the eyes, rasping nose and throat and lungs with the threat of suffocation.

Basil took one last look around the room. He had searched the desk and the filing cabinet—in vain. Where did a writer keep his rough drafts? He had a vague recollection of Meg Vesey having said something about Gus keeping TV scripts in the kitchen salad bowl.

Suddenly, silently a wicked tongue of fire shot up from the floor and licked the edge of a nylon net curtain. With a flash and a sigh, the curtain became a sheet of flame.

Avery was running for the glass door. Basil followed him.

They were just in time. Outside, on the lawn, every window was a red blaze. They drew the pure, outdoor air into their tortured lungs, thankful even for its coldness.

Avery looked at Basil shrewdly. "Was this an accident?"

"I wonder . . ." murmured Basil. "I told Gus and Tony that I was coming to this house this afternoon to look over Amos's unpublished work."

"And I told Tony and Leppy that I was going to meet you here," added Avery. "What was the big idea? To kill two birds with one stone?"

"No. Whoever did it must have known we would probably get out in time."

"What then?"

"Somebody didn't want us to find something that was there and could not be removed."

"Such as . . . ?"

"Perhaps Amos Cottle's rough drafts and notebooks. Or perhaps these." Basil put his hand in his pocket and drew out the pathetic trinkets he had found in Amos's desk. The incised and pocked gold of the thimble glittered brightly in the red glare of the fire.

"They could have been removed," said Avery. "So could the rough drafts."

"Not if they couldn't be found," retorted Basil. "These trinkets were in a little purse stuck in the groove of a desk drawer. A hasty search might not have discovered them. And I wasn't able to find the rough drafts myself. Did someone know they were in the house and, failing to find them, leave an incendiary device in the cellar so that they would be consumed along with the house and no one else would ever read them?"

"Why would anyone care if you found Amos's rough drafts or somebody's old thimble and ring?"

Basil seemed to be thinking aloud as he went on: "It's possible that the house was burned for an entirely opposite and even more surprising reason."

"Opposite? Am I supposed to understand that?" asked Avery.

"No. Though something you said this afternoon gave me the idea."

"What did I say?"

Basil was spared the necessity of answering as the fire truck roared up the driveway with its siren at full blast.

ten

When Vera woke Tuesday morning, the sky was gray again. She had no inner strength to resist the impact of a gloomy day. She looked at the bleak scene outside the window as if the weather was a personal insult designed especially to annoy her by malignant nature. She had no eyes at all for the luxury of the hotel bedroom. For the last three years she had taken luxury for granted and she had no intention of losing it now.

She slipped her narrow, corded, old-looking feet into satin mules with frivolous frills of ostrich feather. She covered her lacy nightdress with the furred gown of polished, ice-blue satin and called room service for orange juice and coffee.

In the sitting room of her suite, she turned on the TV set and caught the eleven o'clock news on Channel 5.

". . . the latest development in the Amos Cottle case was the burning of Cottle's palatial house at Weston, Connecticut early yesterday evening. Everything in the house was destroyed, except a few documents rescued by Dr. Basil Willing, psychiatric assistant to the District Attorney of New York County, and Emmett Avery, the well-known critic. Connecticut State Police have evidence that the fire may have been of incendiary origin, but they are unable to identify the arsonist. And now for the stock market. It opened with . . ."

Vera switched off the set and sat plunged in thought. The house must have been worth at least fifty thousand. No doubt there was adequate insurance, but would it cover a fire of incendiary origin? And could she . . .

The telephone rang.

"Sam? About time you called me! Come right on up. I'm just having coffee."

Sam and the waiter arrived at the same time. Sam stood aside as the waiter wheeled a table on castors into the sitting room. Like so many modern waiters, his manner was compounded of insolence overlaid with tongue-in-cheek civility. His cynical eyes took in every detail of Vera's appearance and Sam's as if he were cataloguing their ages, their financial and social standing and their hidden vices. The coating of civility wore transparently thin when Vera gave him a niggardly tip and told him to bring another cup for Sam. Poor Sam, who liked to be liked by everyone, even waiters, was so embarrassed that he slipped a folded dollar bill into the man's hand surreptitiously.

Vera sat down at the table and poured coffee. It was characteristic that she appropriated the single cup for herself. Sam would have to wait until the waiter came back and the waiter would probably never have come back at all if Sam had not augmented his tip. It was one of those rare cases where a disinterested impulse paid off immediately. Sam was quite impressed with the moral lesson.

But the waiter didn't hurry and by the time he came back the coffee was lukewarm. Sam sipped it without relish while Vera continued to unburden herself of all her many grievances. Sam was plump and bald and swarthy and his hooded, deep-set eyes had a look of ancient, immutable sadness. They were eyes steeped in wisdom, but it was not the kind of wisdom that brings happiness. Even Vera had a strange feeling that Sam's eyes had looked at too many unspeakable things.

"So there it is." Vera finished her coffee and lit a cigarette with a toss of her brassy hair. "Tony and Gus are sitting in the driver's seat. 'Literary executors,' they call themselves. All I know is this. If I can't get another agent and another publisher to handle Amos's posthumous work, I want my rightful share of the money from Tony and Gus. I want Gus to take only ten percent as his commission and I want Tony's share cut to only fifteen percent of subsidiary rights. I'd rather it was ten. And I want to see Amos's will."

Sam sighed. "What you need is a lawyer, baby, not an agent."

Vera was furious. "But you said . . ."

"Look, baby. The situation has changed. Amos is dead. If he were still alive, I could steer him to another agent and another publisher. Even then Gus would still have been the agent for all the old books and Tony, the publisher. Leaving an agent and a publisher is like getting a divorce. It changes the future, but it doesn't change the past. See? As things are—well, the minute a guy's dead all his assets are frozen anyway until his estate is settled."

Vera fumed. "You mean I'm stuck with this?"

"Looks like it. Tony and Gus will pay you what they would have paid Amos if he were still alive and that's that. You can't change their contract with Amos now Amos is dead. A corpse can't sign a contract."

"Damn!" Vera looked like a thwarted tigress. "Is there no way I could sue them and get more money?"

"Well, you can sue anybody for anything, but it's another thing to win your case. What grounds you got for suing?"

"You said it was monstrous that Gus should get twenty-five percent and Tony fifty. Couldn't you call it extortion?"

"Darned hard to prove." Sam shook his head dubiously.

"Then why did Tony and Gus get so much more than is usual? If it isn't extortion, what is it?"

Sam shrugged. "Amos was no businessman. What author is? Most authors like to think of themselves as being pretty dumb about business. That's a sign that they're artists or gentlemen or something quite above anything as sordid as business. Naturally some publishers take advantage of this. And then most authors are so darn glad to get a first book published in real, honest-to-God print that they'll sign anything. This was seduction, not rape. Amos had reached the age of consent. You know," went on Sam, pleased with his own felicitous metaphor, "an author with a first book is awfully like a virgin and a publisher is awfully like an old rake. He knows what he's doing and he knows the author doesn't know, but that's not his business—that's the author's business. Is he responsible for the author? Certainly not. He doesn't force the author into anything, he just woos him a little. All publishers have printed contracts. That's what they try on first. If the author, or his agent, knows his way around, he takes a pen and scratches out half the print and writes in something that gives the author what the traffic will bear. Some publishers don't really mind this too much. On the contrary I think they have more respect for an author who knows what he's worth, just as a rake has more respect for a woman who knows her way around. But if the author is new and dumb or innocent, and falls into the hands of an unscrupulous publisher, then said publisher just takes him, quite without any personal malice or hostility but quite without respect or consideration either. I guess that's what happened to Amos, only he had worse luck than usual because his agent was crooked, too."

"Crooked?" Vera snatched at the word. "Then . . ."

"Well, in this case," amended Sam hastily. "Look at it from the agent's point of view. He's a middleman. He's got to live on good terms with authors and publishers both. But, of the two, publishers are more important to him. They'll be around a lot longer than most authors. As a rule an author has only one book to sell at a time, but an agent has a dozen or more. He may want to offer the same publisher a book tomorrow, so . . ."

"But the author pays his commission!" protested Vera.

"Sure." Sam shrugged. "But he'd be no good to the author if he hadn't an in with publishers, would he? And he's only human, so he's bound to make package deals, holding out for good terms with a best seller and letting his new authors go cheap. Or sometimes refusing to sell a best seller unless the same publisher will take on some new guy who isn't worth beans."

"Why didn't Gus demand better terms when Amos became so successful?"

"Don't ask me. Ask Gus."

"He wouldn't tell me anything. He hates me and so does his wife."

Sam brooded over this a moment. "I wouldn't advise suing. I can't see how you could prove anything. But I'll admit it seems to me like a queer setup. As my old man used to say, 'There is more in this than meets the eye.' "

"What, Sam? What could it be?"

"I don't know. But this whole deal, as you tell it, strikes me as peculiar. These two guys running Amos's career for him as if he were a sort of robot. But I suppose that's explained by his having lost his memory. He really wasn't all there and somebody had to run things for him. What a hell of a note! To be in your thirties or forties or whatever Amos was, and have a memory that went back only six years as far as personal things were concerned. The way you tell it, this wasn't complete amnesia. He remembered all the things he'd learned as a child—to walk and talk and eat and read and write—only he didn't know who he was. Funny they were never able to trace him."

"Maybe they didn't try very hard. Maybe Gus and Tony liked it that way."

"Could be."

"Maybe the police will do it now Amos has been murdered."

"That might not be so good for you, baby. Suppose Amos already had a wife?"

Vera winced as all the possibilities inherent in that situation unfolded before her once again. "Sam, you'd better get all the money you can for me out of Gus and Tony right now, before anything like that happens."

"I'll try." Sam wasn't very hopeful. "But it may take some time to settle the estate and collect insurance on that house that burned down. The lawyers may want to find Amos's true identity first and make sure there are no other heirs. I suppose it's the police who are keeping that amnesia stuff out of the papers now, but they can't do so forever. If they don't find Amos's murderer pretty soon, the lawyers will make them publish the whole story in the hope of identifying Amos. . . . Funny thing is, I can't figure out who killed him."

"What do you mean?"

"Well, obviously, it wasn't you."

"Sam! How dare you . . ."

"You don't gain a thing," went on Sam imperturbably. "It's the same way with the Kanes and Veseys and those two critics and the Puseys. Nobody gained anything and most of you lost something."

"There are other motives for murder besides gain."

"Such as . . . ?"

"Hate, fear, blackmail . . ." Vera paused. "Sam, do you suppose Gus or Tony did dig up something about Amos's past and it was so bad they were in a position to blackmail him? Instead of asking for cash, they might try to make everything look legal and aboveboard by writing contracts with him that gave both of them a big hunk of his dough, much bigger than most agents and publishers get."

"Sounds reasonable enough, but—why kill him in the end?"

"Maybe he got tired of being blackmailed. Maybe he told them to go to hell, no matter what the consequences."

Sam considered the idea thoughtfully. "You may have something there. As literary executors, they're still in the saddle for the next two books. But if Amos had lived and quit them, they would have had no control over those books. On the other hand, since Amos's production of future books stops wth his death, they . . ."

"But if he was going to quit them, his production was going to stop anyway as far as they were concerned. They had no interest in keeping him alive."

"Was he going to quit them?"

"He didn't want to, but I started trying to persuade him the moment we met at the airport."

"Did they know that?"

"I told Meg Vesey at the Kanes' supper party. She could have told Gus or Tony."

"But whoever poisoned Amos must have planned to kill him before the supper party." Sam rose slowly. "Well, baby, it's a tangle all right. We'll probably never know what really happened between Amos and Gus and Tony now Amos is dead." He smiled suddenly. "You know that old gag about the guy who, just for a bet, sent five anonymous telegrams to the five most prominent citizens in his town? 'Fly at once—all is discovered!' The gag is that the joker didn't know a thing about any of them but next morning all five had left town. I wonder what would happen if someone sent telegrams like that to Gus and Tony now?"

Vera brushed this aside. "Are you going to see them this morning?"

"What good would that do, baby? We got to wait till the will's probated. Nothing I can do now." Sam spread his hands apart helplessly.

"Well, what about a part for me in a Broadway play?"

"I'm working on that, baby. Matter of fact, I've got a one-shot for you on a TV show. The National Pig Iron Hour. Audition this afternoon at three P.M. Joe Grimalkin is the producer, so you'd better be prompt."

"Okay but a one-shot . . ." Vera sighed. "That's just peanuts."

"May lead to other things. TV is a showcase for talent. Give you a bit of spare cash anyway. Be seeing you . . ."

Sam shuffled out of the room and Vera was alone again.

Being alone affected her as adversely as bad weather. The solitude that is so essential to the artist or thinker who lives in the depths of the mind is torture to the active person who lives on the surface of the mind as Vera did. She liked bustle, crowds, company and hated the loneliness that brought her face to face with herself.

The moment Sam had gone, she took a long, warm, scented bath and dressed with care in her most becoming dress of Dior blue with everything to match including the sapphire brooch. If Sam wouldn't walk into the lion's den for her, she would go herself.

The offices of Sutton, Kane and Company were still in the old publishing district on Fourth Avenue. They had been expanded in the last few years to take in two whole floors, but the general dinginess of every office in the building was not improved by this. Tony didn't care. He had nothing but contempt for small publishers who established themselves in Radio City and then went broke.

Vera looked at the grimy elevator with distaste. She was even more contemptuous of the reception room. Plain gray walls, one sofa, one table, one lamp—all looking as if they had come from Macy's basement. A lot of shelves with books on them. No other decoration but a framed picture that wasn't a real picture—just a painting that was reproduced on the jacket of one of the books. How differently Hollywood did that scene in a New York publisher's office! Catamount's decorator had been paid well for his gorgeous marble and glass interior, all in rose and white with even the carefree young publisher, Jay Millard, wearing a white suit and a pink carnation in his lapel and singing in a tuneful baritone as he performed a subeditor's duties correcting galley proofs.

There was no doubt about it in her mind—the Hollywood idea of life was much more satisfactory than life itself. For years Vera had been trying to remold reality in the shape of a Hollywood film. In all that she herself said and wore and thought she had come quite close to what she wanted, but the life outside her personal control still proved stubbornly resistant to the imposed ideal and, just as the plush décor so often eluded her, so did the happy ending.

She had felt more at home in some of the magazine offices she had seen in New York than she did here. These book publishers were an inexcusably shabby lot and their offices were dowdy. Look at that little windowed cubicle where a tired, untidy receptionist was trying to type and answer the phone at the same time. Jay Millard had had three girls in his outer office—one typist, one receptionist and one telephone operator, all three fresh and smiling with beautifully painted lips and almond nails lacquered rose-red.

Vera primmed her mouth and brought out her voice at its silkiest. "Mrs. Cottle to see Mr. Kane."

"Oh . . ." The girl's eyes were round with something between sympathy and curiosity. It suddenly occurred to Vera that perhaps she ought to have worn black, but Dior blue was so much more becoming. . . .

She pretended to study the silly picture on the wall while the girl mumbled inaudibly at the telephone. Vera had very nice manners. Didn't she always behave as if she couldn't hear a thing when she was listening to one side of another person's telephone conversation? Annoyingly enough she really couldn't hear anything this time.

The girl raised her voice. "Mr. Kane will see you now, Mrs. Cottle. Shall I show you the way?"

"Thank you." Vera's voice was a creamy blend of butter and sugar. Her pointed face looked almost innocent.

Tony's office was a corner room with windows on two sides. No producer in Hollywood would have put up with the scuffed, leather chairs, the threadbare Persian rug, the clutter of books and typescripts on the wide, plain desk. The only personal touches here were a framed photograph of Philippa on the desk and several of Amos on the walls. The one that showed Amos with a pipe in one hand and a shaggy dog at his feet was signed with a neat, small autograph: "To Tony, best of friends and wisest of editors, Amos Cottle."

Tony himself rose from behind the desk. Gus, lounging against a window sill, came to attention and pushed out an armchair for Vera.

She sat daintily, her ankles crossed, not her knees. She threw back her furs and displayed the curves of her wrists on the arms of her chair.

"You're looking much better, Vera," said Tony kindly.

"I feel better, thank you," said the schooled, gentle voice. But how differently Hollywood would have written the dialogue for this scene! *Baby, you look like a million dollars!* Still Tony had tried to be nice in his stuffy way and he deserved a smile—one of the timid, shy, melancholy variety that suited the occasion.

"Tony, I've come to talk to you about money. Just what is my situation?" She was the little woman now, helpless and sweet, just asking the great big man to help her.

Tony was as susceptible to this approach as any male. He shuffled some papers on his desk and cleared his throat. "Well, until Amos's will is probated, everything is pretty confused. Gus and I have just been looking at his account as of last Saturday. There are a few thousands in accrued royalties from the trade edition of *Passionate Pilgrim*. There'll be more in a few weeks when the second printing is out. Then there's some reprint money from the last run of *The Rudderless Ship*—about seven thousand. And in another six months we should have the book club money on *Pilgrim,* which is a tidy sum. Amos was paid on a six months' royalty schedule so none of these payments are due his estate until May, but in view of the special circumstances I can advance you the cash already paid into his account as of today, which runs to—well, something over nine thousand dollars. And I'll pass along the book club money as soon as it comes in. But I'll have to hold the second printing money until we see about bookstore returns.

"You see, Vera, I'm willing to gamble nine thousand cash that no other heirs of the estate will turn up. If they do, and if you've spent the money by that time, I'll have to make up the difference out of my own pocket."

Gus added, "I was holding about three thousand of the TV money in Amos's account with me when he died. That income will stop now of course, but of the three thousand I'm holding, one thousand, one hundred and twenty-five is Amos's and you can have that now in addition to the nine thousand Tony is advancing you."

These terms were far more generous than Sam had thought possible before probate of the will. If he had been there, he would have been curious to know the reason for such unexpected generosity. But Vera's greedy little mind fastened on only one detail of all that had been said.

"One thousand, one hundred and twenty-five out of three thousand!" She looked at Gus with venom. "Amos didn't get much of his TV money, did he? Fifteen hundred to Tony and three hundred and seventy-five to you!"

"That was the agreement," said Gus firmly.

Tony's handsome face hardened. He turned bleak blue eyes on Vera. "You may take it or leave it. Ten thousand should be enough to see any woman through the first few months of widowhood, especially one who has other sources of income from her own earnings. I shan't keep my offer open after today. I'm taking a real chance, for if Amos has other legal heirs, only part of this money is rightfully yours, if that."

"Then why are you willing to give me any of it?" Vera's voice was still soft. There was even a hint of a sob in it.

"Because I suspect you're broke," said Tony brutally. "And I'm willing to take a chance on Amos not having any other heirs that the police can discover. If he has and if I have to make up the difference out of my own pocket, I shall deduct that nine thousand from your share of payments on his posthumous books."

There was no question that Tony meant what he said. Vera felt as if she had bumped into a stone wall. It didn't occur to her that Tony had shown any generosity. In Hollywood any sum in only four figures was known as "peanuts" or "chickenfeed"—one week's salary. And this was what Tony and Gus were offering her for several months' living! She couldn't stay at her luxury hotel on this income. She couldn't buy the spring wardrobe at Saks and Hattie Carnegie that she had been counting on to help launch her Broadway career. It was a bitter moment. Her trained face stayed smooth. Her eyelids hid her eyes. Only her lips quivered. In her heart she hated Tony Kane and Gus Vesey as she had never hated anyone else before, even Amos.

She knew enough not to argue. This was no time to fight. This was a time to scheme. She turned to Gus impulsively. "You know I've been thinking about the future of Amos's work. I've just remembered that Sam Karp told me once about another best-selling author who died at the height of his career. His name, I think, was Frank Ames and he wrote the Captain Donovan series. Sam said that when Frank died, his widow and his publisher and agent got together and hired a hack writer to produce more Captain Donovan books under the Frank Ames' name. They went on for years and years and made lots of money for everyone. Why can't we hire some hack to write more books signed Amos Cottle?"

Tony sighed as he balanced a pencil between his fingers—the old-fashioned kind of pencil you have to sharpen, not the automatic, gold-mounted pencil of a publisher in a movie. "Because Amos himself was never a hack writer like Frank Ames."

"But Frank Ames was very successful!"

"Oh, yes, but he was still a hack writer. Captain Donovan was a police captain and the stories were mysteries that just happened to catch on, largely because the character, Donovan, had appeared in some B-movies. A mystery is not a book, Vera. Anyone can write a mystery. It's just a job like carpentering or plumbing. I've always maintained that a mystery writer should not be paid in royalties at all, any more than you would pay a carpenter or a plumber royalties. He should be paid a modest lump sum, and any money that comes in from subsidiary rights should go to to his publisher who has been put to a great deal of expense to publish his book and who can only just break even on the trade edition with costs what they are today and mystery sales so low in hard covers. When Frank Ames died, any one of twenty other mystery writers could have written his Donovan stories. But Amos was a serious artist, Vera, and his art dies with him. He was unique. No one else could write like Amos, any more than anyone else could write like Tolstoy or Proust. You can't duplicate style once an author is dead."

"I don't know what you mean." protested Vera in sincere bewilderment. "In Hollywood we look on *all* writers as if they were plumbers or carpenters. When anything goes wrong with a script on location, the director calls the studio and says, 'Send me a writer.' He doesn't care which writer it is."

"Well, it's a little different in the world of books," said Gus with a slight smile. "We do care which writer we get. I don't think Tony has ever called my office and said, 'I've got a vacant spot on the fall list. Send me a writer.'"

"We're old-fashioned," said Tony.

"You certainly are!" There was acid in the sweetness of Vera's voice, like lemon candy. She gave a last scornful look around the threadbare office as she rose.

"Will you please send the check for nine thousand right away to my hotel? I'm staying at the Waldorf."

"I'll see it gets in the mail this afternoon." Tony moved forward to open the door for her.

"Good-bye, Gus." Vera cast a long, peculiar side glance back at him over her shoulder. "Be sure and give my love to your sweet wife!"

Gus flushed uncomfortably.

Tony's sense of the fitness of things compelled him to walk to the elevator with Vera. They deplored the weather and wondered whether the H-bomb explosions were at fault. It was an armed truce. When the elevator came and Vera smiled a sweet good-bye, Tony stood for some moments looking at the door that had closed after her. He had an unpleasant premonition that he had not seen the last of Vera by any means.

Vera herself had a curious feeling that she had been cast adrift without rudder or sail. *The Rudderless Ship*—that was the book of Amos's that was supposed to be in reprints now. She looked for it on the rack beside the newsstand, but there wasn't a copy in view and she didn't care enough to ask for it. She had nothing to do until three o'clock, when she must report for that piddling, little audition that wouldn't bring in more than fifteen hundred at the most.

Aimlessly she strolled up Fourth Avenue to Park and then crossed to Fifth where the shop windows were more interesting. California women dreamed of vacations in Manhattan, yet, here she was, in one of the world's greatest luxury markets, without a penny to buy any of these lovely things!

That cape of ginger chinchilla in Revillon's window. She had never had chinchilla—only mink—and ginger chinchilla was so much more distinguished than that old commonplace silver chinchilla. As she came to Cartier's window she was almost faint with desire. That gorgeous diamond and sapphire necklace—just the thing for her coloring, but there wasn't one chance in a million that she would ever possess it now. And oh, dear, here was Plummer's with those adorable Royal Worcester coffee cups!

The shop windows lured her farther uptown than she had intended. She had gone several blocks beyond the Waldorf when she turned to retrace her steps. Even the little shops on the cross streets proved enticing. Tweed and leather, linen and lace, and rich, gaudy Siamese silks . . .

There on one corner of 57th and Madison stood a tall man looking up at a building across the street from him. There was something vaguely familiar about the noticeable profile under the shadowing hat brim. Suddenly she realized who it was. That psychiatrist who worked with the police. Basil Willing.

She thought he didn't see her. He was standing quite still on the street corner, his intent brown eyes raised to the sky now as if he were trying to read a riddle in the clouds. A dreamer, she decided. Lazy, too. Just loafing on street corners, not working at all. He would never solve the mystery of Amos's death or even the lesser mystery of Amos's identity. In movies murder cases were solved either by blunt, brutal policemen or by gay young amateurs who danced and drank their way through their cases exchanging merry quips with the prettier among the female suspects. Basil Willing didn't fit either stereotype.

She watched him covertly as he finally turned and began to walk uptown. It seemed to her that there was indolence in every one of his slow, controlled movements. He wasn't hustling. He wasn't even walking. He was just strolling, as if he had all the time in the world. Vera's lips contracted away from her white, rodent teeth in a sly smile. She reflected, "It's later than you think . . . much later."

She went on down Park Avenue, her own step brisker, as if the very sight of Basil's leisurely progress had made all thought of sauntering distasteful to her. She walked through the modern version of the old Peacock Alley remembering the ancient jest about the first Waldorf—"exclusiveness for the masses." There used to be another gag too—something about putting your boots outside the door at night and finding them gilded instead of blacked the next morning. Well, she wouldn't be here long enough to test that one. . . .

She was on her way to the desk to give up her rooms when an inspiration came to her, full-fledged and complete at its birth. A daring idea, but—nothing venture, nothing have, and she did want to stay at the Waldorf.

She changed direction and hurried toward the elevators.

The maids had been in her rooms. Everything was in order. A lesser hotel wouldn't have service as prompt and thorough as this. She sat down at the writing desk and drew a sheet of hotel notepaper toward her. She smiled a little as she remembered Sam Karp. "Fly at once—all is discovered." Pretty crude that, but the same thing could be done with more subtlety. You didn't have to wait for exact information when you knew something queer was going on. You could just bluff. And wouldn't it be amusing to blackmail the blackmailers who had taken so much from Amos?

She began to write.

Dear Tony,
Since I saw you this morning, I have learned the whole truth about Amos and everything else. Thank you for your promise of nine thousand dollars. I shall expect an additional check for the same amount when you receive this note.

Sincerely,
Vera

Even the police could hardly call that a blackmail letter if ever it came to their attention. It didn't say a word about the additional check being the first of many payments for her silence about what she had discovered, did it? But Tony wasn't stupid. He would get the idea. And he wouldn't dare show the letter to the police anyway.

She wrote a similar note to Gus anticipating an additional check of eighteen hundred and seventy-five from him. She addressed both envelopes to the homes of the recipients—there were so many nosey secretaries in offices.

She was so pleased with herself that she sat still for a few moments savoring her self-satisfaction, and it was then that a further inspiration came to her. She drew another sheet of paper onto the blotter.

Dear Philippa,
You had better come here to see me sometime tomorrow afternoon. I am sending the same invitation to Maurice Lepton.

That was really subtle. No district attorney could do a thing in court with a letter worded that way and yet—the meaning would be perfectly clear to Philippa. She could get hold of some money without appealing to Tony. Didn't she have those marvelous emeralds?

Dear Mr. Lepton,
You had better come here to see me sometime tomorrow afternoon. I am sending the same invitation to Philippa Kane.

There was none of the literary artist in Vera. When she found a useful phrase she would use it over and over again in the same letter and she would have worded the same invitation in exactly the same way to a dozen or more people without bothering to vary each letter with little personal touches.

Down in the lobby again, she bought stamps for her four letters and dropped them in the mail chute. Then she drifted toward the Sert Room, her heart lighter than it had been for days while she tried to decide whether she would have a martini or a daiquiri before luncheon.

Basil Willing was perfectly well aware of Vera's covert observation as he stood at the corner of 57th Street and Madison Avenue. At the moment he was not particularly interested in Vera. He could only hope that she would not come nearer and force an exchange of insincere civilities which would distract him from the subject of his thoughts.

This was the street corner where Amos had stood with Meg that spring evening two years ago when something had stirred him so deeply that he had nearly relapsed into alcoholism. Such relapses were always a sign of psychic disturbance. What was there about this busy, commonplace street corner that had affected Amos so powerfully at that moment?

A passing pedestrian he recognized? No, Meg had said he was looking up at the building directly across the street. A face at a window? You'd wave and smile if it were someone you knew well. You'd turn away hastily if it were someone you didn't like. Amos had done neither. He had just stood and stared in a kind of trance. What could it have been? Something that was still here on this winter afternoon two years later?

The building on the opposite corner of Madison was an ordinary-looking structure with a drug store at street level and several floors of small shops and offices above. It was neither old nor new, low nor high, shabby nor luxurious. It might have stood for the prototype of the usual building in this section of New York. But once, at least, there had been one thing about it unusual enough to catch the eye of a casual passer-by. Was it something that had significance only for Amos himself or something that anyone might notice?

Perhaps it was a mistake to study the façade of the building with such scrupulous attention to every detail. Perhaps it would be better to glance at it suddenly, as Amos himself must have done. Then perhaps the little oddity or discrepancy would stand out from the mass of irrelevant detail.

Basil allowed his eyes a moment's rest by gazing at the mottled cloud patterns. Then he cast a single, swift glance at the building and saw it at once—the little, off-beat detail seemed to leap out at him.

On the fourth floor there was a sign with two lines of print annoyingly off-center:

>   HORTENSE
> HAUTE COUTURE

It was bothersome as a picture hung crookedly on a wall. The Western eye, trained to read from left to right, started with the lower line, which was really the second line, and then had to move up in an unaccustomed diagonal for the next line which should have been the first. *Haute Couture Hortense*. It was confusing and stupid. It must have been bad for business.

There was a great deal of arty affectation in advertising typography—proper names without capital letters, script that should have been print, type face of such fancy design it was almost illegible, trade names that were misspellings of real words, since you couldn't copyright a real word. But there was always some purpose in all this, either aesthetic or commercial. Basil could see no purpose at all in this asymmetry. There seemed only one explanation. Hortense had had a partner. The sign had originally read: *Blank and Hortense*. The other name had been just long enough with the addition of an "and" to fill in the blank space before "Hortense" and make the two lines even. The partner had died or resigned. Hortense hadn't had enough money to order a new sign. She had just had the partner's name with its "and" removed from the old sign and left the thing clumsy and off-center.

Suppose it was the asymmetry of the sign that had caught Amos's eye? Why would he stand still and stare at it? Did the name Hortense have some special associations for him? Or had he seen the sign before, when it was intact, and was it the missing name which he remembered that had significance? That seemed more likely. Your eye would slide over a familiar name without pausing, even if that name was important to you. But you would pause to stare and think, if you were trying to recall the name no longer there, if you were vaguely aware that you had seen the sign before when it meant something more to you than it did now.

There was no reason to believe that Amos had recovered his memory that evening two years ago. So, if the missing name had something to do with his unknown past, he might not have remembered the missing name consciously when he saw the sign. He might not have had the slightest idea then why the sign disturbed him. But because the memory was there, buried in the darkness of the subconscious mind, that memory had stirred in its sleep. The impact of that unconscious recognition would reach his conscious mind as a feeling of distress and malaise apparently without source or reason, yet poignant enough to make him long once more for the narcotic of alcohol.

Musing on these possibilities, Basil crossed the street at a leisurely pace. Like many men with quick minds, he hated physical haste—scramble and bustle and rush. He strolled along the sidewalk past the drug store until he came to the entrance of the building. A self-service elevator took him to the fourth floor and there, directly opposite the elevator, was a door painted jade green with a sign exactly like the one outside:

HORTENSE
HAUTE COUTURE

He opened the door and found himself in a shabby waiting room. Manhattan's black dust had taken its toll of the once-white paint and a pathway was worn down the center of the green carpet. The presumption of *haute couture* became a little pathetic. This was a struggling seamstress who must have a hard time competing with the miracles of mass production.

She came through the curtains before he could ring the bell on the reception desk. She was little and old and poor, in a tight black dress with shears and pincushion dangling from her belt. She was surprised when she saw her visitor was a man.

"I'm sorry to disturb you," said Basil. "But I'll only take a minute of your time. Didn't you have a partner a few years ago?"

"Yes." Her manner was curt now she realized there was not going to be any profit in this transaction.

"How long ago?"

"Six years."

"What happened to her?"

He could see the words forming in her mind: *What business is it of yours?* But she didn't say them. She wanted to get this unprofitable interview over quickly as possible and get back to her work. Argument would only prolong it, so she answered quickly, "She married and went back to Scotland." She turned toward the curtains again as she said it, but Basil's voice halted her.

"What was this partner's name?"

Suspicion dawned. "Why do you want to know?"

"I'm looking for a man who lost his memory. I have reason to believe he may have known her." Basil wondered if this would be enough, or if he would have to go into a long explanation and produce credentials.

It was enough. After one shrewd, comprehensive glance at his face and his clothes, she decided to take him on faith. "The firm name was Girzel and Hortense. That was her real name: Girzel Stuart. I took Hortense as a trade name because my real name is Hannah and Hannah don't sound much like *haute couture*. Of course Girzel don't either but it's kind of classy because it's different. Scotch."

Basil unfolded a clipping from last Sunday's book review section of the *Times*. It was a really clear picture of Amos and it had reproduced well. The caption folded over so it didn't show.

"Did you ever see this man before?"

She looked at it steadily for a few seconds. "No. Never."

"Without the beard?" Basil laid a finger over the lower part of the face.

"Wait a minute. Is he an actor? I think I seen him on TV."

"That's quite possible. But I want to know if you ever saw him in person."

"No. What makes you think I did?"

"I had an idea he might have known your partner, Girzel Stuart."

"If he did, I never saw them together. Girzel wasn't much of a girl for the men. She had this boy back in Scotland she'd promised to marry before she came over here. They wrote letters every week."

"One more thing: was there any great shock or tragedy in her life when you knew her?"

"Only tragedy was we weren't making enough money here, but that was no shock. We both knew dressmaking on a small scale is a dead duck these days, but we didn't know any other trade and we hoped that maybe in this neighborhood we'd pick up enough customers who liked everything done by hand without having to pay too much for it. Our mistake. I'm down to mending and altering now."

Basil took his leave and went down to the street again, turning the puzzle over in his mind. Had it been another "Girzel" that Amos had known? Had he noticed the sign in its original form, *Girzel and Hortense*, some time before he lost his memory, just because Girzel was a name that already meant something to him? And because it was an uncommon name he wouldn't expect to see anywhere? Then after he lost his memory and became Amos Cottle the imbalance of the lettering on the sign caught his eye and disturbed him deeply but inexplicably because far below the conscious level he recalled the missing name which reminded him of another Girzel who was part of the life he was trying to escape when he lost his memory, a Girzel who was the "G" of the wedding ring and the thimble. Perhaps that other Girzel was at the very heart of the shock or tragedy that had driven him into escape through amnesia in the first place. That would explain why the mere subconscious suggestion of her name had so much emotional impact that it drove him into the nearest bar after two years of rigid abstinence.

In his own office on lower Park Avenue, Basil telephoned the officer in charge of the Missing Persons Bureau at the Police Department whom he had known for many years.

"I understand you've been going through your files, looking for a record of some unsolved disappearance that would fit Amos Cottle's previous identity."

"Right, but there doesn't seem to be a thing. I think that guy came here from Mars in a flying saucer six years ago."

"I've been piecing together a few small clues and I'm beginning to get a picture of the sort of man Cottle was originally. I'd like you to try a little experiment. Forget all about Amos Cottle and look for this other man just as you would if it were a routine disappearance."

"Okay. Let's have your picture of him."

"The man you're looking for was probably in his thirties. He had a weakness of the spine that made him inactive physically. You can safely assume that his initials were A.S., that he came from the Middle West originally, that he became an alcoholic about seven years ago, that he was a doctor or a medical student, that on June 10, 1948 he married a woman of Scots origin whose first name was Girzel and whose maiden name began with the letter M, who liked to sew, who had pale brown hair, straight and shining with bronze highlights, and who died about seven years ago, probably under shocking circumstances—accident, suicide or even homicide."

"Did you say 'small clues'? Hell's bells, we're going to crack this case in a few hours! Doctors and medical students can't live anywhere without leaving all sorts of records and no one can die without leaving a record. We'll get onto it right away—hospitals, medical schools, medical societies. If he were a full-fledged doctor, he'd have to have a license to practice in New York and if his wife died here there must be a death certificate made out for some woman named Girzel. Maybe there are hospital records of a patient with that name or motor vehicle records of an accident. Wonder if either of them had a car? And what about income tax and social security? Thank God, it's an uncommon name like Girzel, but even if it were Mary we have enough clues with the initials and the fact that he was a doctor or a medical student. You're sure of that?"

"I'm sure."

"Are you sure this man's disappearance was reported six years ago?"

"That's when he disappeared, but I'm not sure that it was reported."

"Why wasn't it?"

"You're looking for a man who either had no close friends or who lost them when he became an alcoholic. A man who was both consciously and unconsciously running away from something, probably something pretty horrible."

At home that evening Basil reread Lepton's now famous review of Amos Cottle's last book. There was one passage that held his attention for some time.

> . . . Edgar Wharne, the principal protagonist in *Passionate Pilgrim,* is a young undergraduate at the University of Chicago who is expelled for assaulting and nearly strangling a young Hawaiian girl student. This difficult subject is handled with the most sensitive delicacy and a compassionate awareness of the stark tragedy inherent in human compulsions which leaves the reader breathless. Wharne doesn't resent being expelled from the University. He even

accepts his jail sentence with a noble resignation. But he is troubled by the subtle change in the attitude of his former friends toward him when he comes out of jail. There is a pathetic little scene where he invites them all to a cocktail party in his shabby rooming house and nobody comes, except one eccentric reporter who arrives drunk. Wharne is bitterly aware that he has been rejected by the smug hypocrisy of his snobbish, middle-class friends, but even then his spirit is valiant enough to turn resolutely to the future. Wharne gets a job as a bartender in a South Side dive and this gives Cottle an opportunity to show us fascinating vignettes of the tramps and prostitutes who frequent the bar— all warm, earthy, salty characters filled with sly humor and the grace of an infinite compassion, unlike the middle-class hypocrites who have deserted Wharne.

But Wharne is not content with this easy path to social acceptance. His disturbed spirit wants to know the answers to all the great questions man has been asking himself for the last six thousand years, so Wharne sets forth on a pilgrimage to the sources of our thinking. He reads every book he can lay his hands on. He works his way through Harvard and enters a divinity school. Just as he is about to be ordained, the dean discovers the story of Wharne's past. Once again he is expelled in an acidly etched scene that excoriates the professions of conventional morality.

For the first time Wharne is assailed by doubts of his own innocence and the goodness of God. He sets off on a journey that takes him to London, to Rome, and finally to the Far East—seeking, always seeking, the great answer and never finding it. In the end, Wharne dies in a night club in Singapore. In a splendid, moving passage he describes the old Chicago days to a Eurasian girl. 'I want to tell you good-bye,' he says simply. But she is not even listening. She is not interested in anything but herself. And so this great fugue ends in a cry that has a dying fall of futility. Even Wharne's last words break against an inattentive ear and he sinks to dissolution, unremembered and unloved for all his striving. . . .

Basil's eyes were musing as he laid the review aside. Was Wharne a self-portrait with eroticism substituted for alcoholism as the consuming vice and the church for medicine as a profession? With a sigh, Basil realized he ought to read the whole book, but it was too late in the evening to tackle its four hundred and fifty pages. He went to sleep with the question still unresolved in his mind.

eleven

On Wednesday the cold spell broke. It was one of those sudden caprices of the New York climate when the thermometer shoots up twenty-five degrees, the snow melts to muddy slush, the sun shines with warmth as well as brilliance and the more literate citizens begin quoting: "Fairest hour of unborn spring, through the winter wandering."

Breakfast at the Veseys' on school mornings was always a mad scramble, particularly on those winter mornings when the weather was unseasonably mild. The period from seven-thirty to eight-forty was a long symphonic variation on one simple, recurrent theme: "Mommy, it's so warm! and none of the other girls wear leggings. Only babies, who go to nursery school, wear leggings. Jane Smith doesn't wear leggings. She wears slacks. Sally Stevens doesn't wear leggings. She wears knee socks. Why do I have to wear leggings? The sun is shining and I don't like leggings!"

Hugh was old enough to dress himself sensibly with some dispatch and eat his breakfast with a normally standardized appetite. Polly was old enough to dress herself, but not sensibly. And not with dispatch, and her appetite was still as capricious as an April day. There was no time for Meg to eat her own breakfast, if Polly was to leave the house properly washed and brushed and clad by eight-forty.

This morning as usual, Meg listened with dismay to her own voice growing sharper and more cackling every moment and realized that she probably looked and sounded very much like a mother hen rounding up a recalcitrant chick with pecks and raucous cries. Gus quietly drank his coffee and glanced at his mail as if he were a thousand miles away. Hugh was allowed to go down to the lobby and board his school bus by himself, but Meg always slipped a coat over her housedress and went down in the elevator with Polly to make sure that Polly didn't wander into the middle of the street.

The "bus," run by a very progressive kindergarten, was actually a station wagon. Polly crossed the sidewalk with the slow and stately step of a princess entering a coronation coach. She had kissed her mother before the bus came. Now it was here, she didn't wave to Meg or throw her a backward glance or acknowledge her relationship in any way. That would have been babyish, the sort of thing you did when you were little and went to nursery school. The door of the station wagon shut with a bang and it swung into the stream of traffic. Meg could see Polly's hat and braids through the car window, her gaze fixed sternly, looking straight ahead of her.

Meg sighed. These kindergarten departures were the beginning of many farewells that would take Polly farther and farther away from her, to school and then to a job, to marriage and motherhood, to war —or whatever the dark womb of the future was gestating for Polly's generation in this most unpredictable of all historical periods. When she tried to peer into Polly's future like this, Meg felt as if she were watching a tiny figure of Polly dwindle as it receded down a corridor as infinitely long as the queer, inverted vista seen from the wrong end of a telescope. It was the corridor leading to the unimaginable time when there would be no mommy to insist on warm clothes in winter or anything else, and Polly would be a grown woman with children of her own, repeating the same cycle again. For an instant, Meg longed to run after Polly and take the child in her arms and cling to her just as she was now, holding time back by sheer force of desire for one little, stolen moment, one unfated kiss.

Meg came back into the dining room where Gus was still opening his always abundant mail. He handed her a large, thick manila envelope. "Please read this today if you get a chance. God knows what we're going to do with it!"

"What is it?"

"Short story. Hard-hitting, well-written, fascinating background material, vivid characters."

"What's wrong with it?"

Gus groaned aloud. "It has a plot."

"Then why should I bother to read it?" cried Meg indignantly. "Send it back at once."

"I know." Gus shook his head. "I've told that guy again and again that there is no market anywhere now for a story with a plot. But he seems to have some sort of neurotic compulsion—he just can't write a story without putting a plot in it."

Gus buried his nose in another typescript.

"Better open your letters before you start on scripts," said Meg.

"You open them," murmured Gus.

Meg made three neat piles of bills and appeals for charity and advertisements. There was only one personal letter. It was on Hotel Waldorf stationery, and the return address was a room number.

She opened it and began to read.

"Oh . . ."

The weakness in her voice startled Gus. He put down the typescript, rose and came around to her side of the table. She gave him the brief handwritten note. "It's from Vera."

He frowned as he read.

"What on earth does she mean, Gus?"

He hesitated, then: "Damned if I know!"

Meg forced herself to go on. "It sounds like—blackmail."

"It is blackmail," agreed Gus promptly. "But I'm not going to buy a pig in a poke. She'll have to be a little more explicit than that. I think she's bluffing."

"It doesn't make sense," said Meg slowly. "What could make her think she has any knowledge that you would pay her to keep quiet about?"

"That's the bluff," said Gus. "Vera is angry because I am getting twenty-five percent commission on Amos's posthumous earnings. She wants me to get ten. She's implying that there's something shady about my deal with Amos. Something she'll expose if I don't go down to ten percent."

"That's ridiculous!" cried Meg. "You did everything for Amos! You and Tony. Where would he have been without you two?"

"I wonder if Tony got one of these?"

"Why should he?"

"Vera didn't like his fifty percent of subsidiary rights either."

"The woman's mad!" Though Meg spoke vehemently, her very vehemence showed a lack of conviction.

Gus began stuffing papers into his dispatch case. "I think I'll drop in at Tony's on my way to the office." He put on his overcoat and gloves and picked up his hat. Meg brought him the dispatch case and lifted her mouth for a kiss. "Gus." She caught the lapels of his coat in either hand. "There wasn't anything shady about your deal with Amos, was there?"

"Of course not," Gus said stoutly and smiled. "Don't worry."

One advantage of the central neighborhood where they lived was that Gus could not only walk to his own office but to most of the other offices he had occasion to visit as well. He went down Park to Fourth, detouring around Grand Central, enjoying the sun and the relaxed look the weather brought to faces of other pedestrians. The ancient elevator creaked up to the floor occupied by the editorial offices of Sutton, Kane, and the receptionist gave Gus a welcoming smile. "Mr. Kane just got in, Mr. Vesey. Go right ahead."

Even for Tony's easy-going office this was a little surprising. She elaborated. "He just told me to get you on the phone. He wants to see you at once."

Gus passed down a corridor. Through open doors on either side he could see the men and women who worked as assistant editors busy at their desks. They were all young, fresh from college, for Tony paid the lowest salaries in the business. As soon as you had any experience or reputation, you went to another firm where subeditors got a living wage, and Tony culled the finest flower of the graduating classes once again. He had trained more editors than any other publisher in New York.

"Hi, Gus!" Tony stood by the window, looking down at Fourth Avenue, a cigarette in his mouth, his hands in his pockets. "You can't have got my call yet. Telepathy?"

"Coincidence." Gus tossed Vera's letter on the desk.

"Oh—you got one, too. Our little Vera is thorough. She doesn't miss any bets."

Gus stood looking at Tony's face, wreathed in smoke, and thought, He's much harder than I am. Running a publishing house single-handed takes a lot more gall and grit than being an agent. When Tony's hackles are up, he really looks like a very tough customer. I couldn't look as ruthless as that if I practiced every morning before breakfast. . . .

The people who knew Tony as a genial, apparently carefree host at Philippa's parties would hardly have recognized him now. Neither would the authors to whom he showed such charming camaraderie and patient editorial help as long as they didn't ink out too many of the clauses in the printed contract.

Tony was comparing the two letters. "Carbon copy to Mr. Vesey," he said grimly. "You'd think she'd address me in slightly different terms, but Vera hasn't any literary imagination even when it comes to writing blackmail letters."

"What are you going to do?" asked Gus.

"There's only one answer to blackmail," said Tony quietly. "The classic answer: Publish and be damned!"

"Millions for defense but not one cent for tribute?" murmured Gus.

"Exactly. What have we got to lose?" Tony looked directly at Gus. "We have done nothing illegal."

"Thank God," whispered Gus half to himself.

"If Vera wants to make a scandal and wreck the sales of Amos's posthumous books, that's her business. She'll lose as much as we do."

"You're going to tell her that?"

"I shan't bother." Tony tore his letter across once and again and tossed the scraps into the wastebasket. "I shall pay no attention to that impertinent communication whatever, and I advise you to do the same. If we ignore it, she'll know we're not scared."

"And we aren't?"

"You may be. I'm not. What on earth is there to be afraid of, Gus? Even financially it doesn't matter now. I'll admit that Amos was damned useful when I put the pressure on Dan Sutton to make me a partner. I laid it on the line with Dan. I said, 'I'm tired of being on a salary. I want a full partnership and a piece of the firm.' Dan knew I hadn't enough money to buy into the firm, but he also knew I'd got our best-selling author in my pocket; and, if he didn't make me a partner and let me take half my salary in stock for the next five years, I'd go elsewhere and take Amos Cottle with me. Dan was licked. He died two years later. I've been running Sutton, Kane ever since.

"Now Amos is no longer our only best-selling author. We have Bradstreet and Ellen Gabor and about a dozen top-flight authors who bring in nice money in aggregate, to say nothing of our small, solid mystery list and our textbook line. I can get along very nicely without Amos Cottle, if Vera wants to upset the apple cart."

Gus nodded slowly. It was true. Amos had brought in a great deal of money each year, but Sutton, Kane was now in a position to survive his death without going into bankruptcy or even pinching pennies.

"It's the same way with you, Gus," went on Tony. "You have Giles Simpson for prestige and Irving Crossman and Arthur Agate for dough. You can get along without Amos now."

"It's a little more difficult for me," insisted Gus. "As I told Meg the other evening, a really big best seller like Amos can make or break a small agency like mine."

"You may have to pull in your horns a little, but you'd be better off that way than paying blackmail to Vera," retorted Tony. "Besides, one of these days you'll have a stroke of luck and pick up another Amos."

"You think so?" Gus looked at Tony sharply.

Tony smiled for the first time that morning. "Why not? Tear up Vera's letter and forget it. And now run along. I've got work to do."

"All right." Gus started toward the door, then paused to look back. "I suppose you phoned me to find out if I'd got the same sort of letter from Vera this morning?"

"Right."

"I wonder if anyone else got a letter from her this morning?"

"Could be." Tony shrugged. He had taken his line and he was going to stick with it no matter what Gus did. Gus, going down in the elevator, envied Tony his composure and wondered just how much Vera knew. . . .

There was nothing in Philippa's life that compelled her to rise early. She woke at any time she pleased from nine to noon. When she had no guests, she always rang for breakfast to be served in bed. Most of her youth had been spent at a French school in Switzerland where breakfast was served to all students in bed. This is one habit that is hard to break once acquired. The sensible French never considered it a luxury. The cheapest student hotels in the Sorbonne district of Paris automatically supplied a tray of *café au lait* or chocolate with rolls and butter to their patrons. True, the French breakfast was not the best in the world. There was no fruit or egg and, as you descended the financial scale the coffee might be overloaded with chicory and the bread a little stale. Even then it was more agreeable to Philippa than the best breakfast in the world prepared by herself. She did not really mind cooking a buffet supper for intimate friends. It was rather fun to put a becoming silk organdie apron over a cocktail dress and play around daintily with casserole dishes and salad dressing if you didn't have to wash dishes afterward. But, as she had once remarked quite seriously to Tony, the really bad thing about poverty was having to get your own breakfast while you were still sleepy.

As life usually gives us the things we really want most, Philippa had achieved the certainty that when she woke and rang a bell long after Tony had driven to the station, some Katie or Amanda or Simonetta would appear a few minutes later carrying a big tray with little legs to stand on, a pretty embroidered cloth and napkin, a single flower in a small vase, Bavarian china ornamented with forget-me-nots, a silver coffeepot and fruit, eggs and toast, all just as hot or cold as they should be. And with it, of course, came the morning mail to be perused leisurely over the second cup of coffee.

Her maid always weeded out the bills, advertisements and charity appeals and set them aside for Tony the following evening. Philippa never got anything but personal notes and invitations, and breakfast time was usually rather like a pleasant hour's gossip with old friends. This morning the letter from the Waldorf was the last one she slit neatly with the pearl-and-silver paper knife. As she read it her knees jerked and the coffee in her cup sloshed over into the saucer, spattering the fine linen napkin. Philippa couldn't bear to eat or drink from a soiled tray. She put it on the bedside table without finishing her coffee and leaned back against the lacy pillows.

In her whole life she had never received anything like a threatening letter. She had never so much as dreamed that such a thing as blackmail could happen to her. In this first moment of shock she was not so much aware of danger as of an atrocious breach of taste. Truly Vera was a creature out of the gutters and sewers of New York, a dirt-and-disease-carrying insect to be destroyed without compunction.

But Philippa had a shrewd mind, and as she calmed herself she began to realize that it would be difficult to destroy Vera. It would be like a boxing match with someone who had never heard of Queensberry rules. Vera was not restricted by any sort of code whatever. The only thing she would respect was superior force.

Philippa bathed and dressed with more haste than usual and then looked at the timetable. If she got the next train she would reach New York shortly after one.

She left her little Austin in the parking lot at the station and caught the train just as it was pulling out. At Grand Central she took a taxi and gave the driver an address in the East Seventies.

It was the first time she had been to Maurice's apartment. She never thought of him as "Leppy." That masculine, hail-fellow-well-met nickname belittled him in her mind.

As she got out of the taxi, she looked with approval at the quiet residential street, the park at one end, the river at the other. The building itself was large but not too large. The doorman was polite, the carpet soft, and the elevator silent, with an attendant almost as well trained as a manservant in a private house.

She asked quite brazenly for "Mr. Lepton's apartment."

It was eloquent of the change in manners in the last generation that the man was still deferential and incurious when he answered, "Ten B, madam. To the right."

Somehow it was reassuring. Today women of her age and the standing her dress and manner indicated often had purely business friendships with men like Maurice, and visited their apartments quite casually without anyone caring enough to suggest scandal. Of course Tony would probably have pointed out that such women were usually unmarried. However the elevator man had no reason to think of her as anything but a perfectly free unmarried woman so it was all right.

She found a small pearl button in the doorjamb and pressed it.

Maurice opened the door himself. He was wearing sandals and slacks and a sport shirt open at the throat. "Phil!" He was greatly surprised.

She smiled. For a moment she was almost grateful to Vera. Without that disgusting letter, she would have had no excuse for coming to Maurice's apartment so soon. She was so much in love with him now that she was eager to see and touch and relish everything in his intimate surroundings. Now she would be able to visualize him more vividly at home when they were separated. She moved into the living room, looking about her eagerly, almost greedily.

It was just the sort of room she had imagined for Maurice. The rug was Chinese, a fascinating design in beige and *sang de boeuf*. There was oxblood porcelain in exactly the same tone of deep rich red. There was mahogany and teak and book cases with glass doors that locked with keys; cases for treasured rare editions, not those awful, open, modern shelves filled with reprints and a few current novels in cheap-looking paper jackets, eked out with reproductions of modern sculpture and little pots of scentless plants.

It was a corner room. One row of windows gave on the Park, the other showed the long vista of Fifth Avenue looking south to the fountains in front of the Plaza Hotel. Far beyond and higher, where the atmosphere thickened even on a day like this, the Empire State Building, veiled in thin layers of otherwise invisible mist, looked like a phantom tower in faint watercolors, a gray mirage towering above the solid reality of buildings closer to the ground where the air was clearer.

Philippa noticed a typewriter on the table in the corner. "This is where you work!" she cried sentimentally.

"Yes." Smiling, Leppy ripped a sheet of paper from the roller and laid it on a pile of typescript face down.

"You don't have to be sensitive about your writing with me!" cried Philippa.

"I'm sensitive about my writing with everyone when it's still in first draft," said Maurice. "I don't want anyone to see it before it's been revised."

"Not even me?" She came close to him.

"Not even you." His smile softened the words. He took her in his arms and kissed her adequately, but not with the same passion he had shown on other occasions.

She drew back instantly. "Did you get a letter from Vera this morning?"

"Yes." His face sobered. "I understand she sent you one too?"

Philippa nodded. "Sheer malice, of course. But—what do we do?"

Maurice frowned. "What would Tony do if she went to him with a story about us?"

Philippa smiled a little crookedly. "That's what I've been wondering all morning. She doesn't know about Amos and me, of course. Just about you and me. It would be her word against mine. Tony doesn't like her, but . . ."

"But what?"

"There's a streak of cynicism in him. He's quite ready to believe the worst of anyone. Like all cynics, his one real fear is of being taken in by somebody and made to feel he's been naïve. The cynicism is his armor against that. They can't gull him as long as he never believes in anything or anybody. Until now I've been lucky or maybe just discreet. I think he believes in me. Or maybe he has been looking the other way subconsciously because deep down inside he didn't want to find out that he had been deceived in me. But if it's forced on his attention by someone like Vera, he could be nasty. Even if he pretended to believe me when I denied it, he would certainly be more suspicious of me in future. I'd lose a great deal of the freedom I've enjoyed until now, just because he never did suspect me of anything."

Maurice smiled at her unconscious egoism. "And what would he do to me?"

She looked startled as if she had not considered that aspect of the situation. Even now she did not seem greatly disturbed by it. "Nothing violent. Tony is really quite well brought up. It's always hard to predict how jealousy will affect anyone, but my guess would be that, if we both denied everything, Tony wouldn't even think of getting a divorce. He'd make a great show of still being friends with you, but he wouldn't really be your friend underneath. He'd always be quarreling with you for some other reason that had nothing to do with me and, in the end, he wouldn't see any more of you at all and neither could I unless I took great risks and saw you secretly.

"Of course, I suppose Vera is hoping for something completely Hollywood—Tony shooting you or knocking you down and me weeping and all of us heaving our chests and batting our eyelashes and talking in broken sentences according to the latest fashion in dialogue. Of course it wouldn't be at all like that. It would be worse in a way. We'd all keep up appearances and pretend to believe in each other and, underneath, my marriage would die and your friendship with Tony, to say nothing of our love for each other."

Maurice nodded agreement. "You're an acute psychologist. I think that's just the way it would be."

"Unless . . ." She paused.

"Unless what?" he demanded sharply.

"Unless I asked Tony for a divorce."

Maurice was visibly shaken. "What on earth would you do that for?" He was almost shouting.

But even the most sordid love is blind. Philippa missed the look of utter horror in his eyes, as she said, "Then I could marry you."

Maurice's face congealed and he stood, speechless. As the pause lengthened, color came into Philippa's usually pale face. There was calculation in Maurice's eyes now—the calculation of a surgeon selecting the most effective instrument with care. He chose brutality. His voice was savage as he said, curtly, "Wait till you're asked!"

Philippa was like a man wounded in the heat of battle who cannot feel the pain of his wound in his highly strung condition. She simply rejected the meaning of the words. "Maurice . . ." She came toward him, arms outstretched.

He caught her wrists in his hands and held off her embrace by force. "Philippa, be your age. I'm not a callow boy and you're not a dewy-eyed young girl. We know these things don't last. We've been there before. We've had fun, but we're not going to mess up our lives for something like this. You haven't a penny but what Tony gives you, and I haven't anything like the kind of money you're used to."

"I don't care."

"But I do. Why do you think I have never married all these years? I don't want a wife. I want to be free. I want to live alone with my work and my ideas. I want to come and go as I please and not be answerable to anyone. I'm not an emotional parasite on other people. I don't need wife or child or even dog or cat or canary. I'm me— Maurice Lepton—and all I ask of the rest of the human race is that they leave me alone. You used the word *love* just now. I've never loved anyone in my life and I never will. Don't you know what it is to lead a really intellectual life? One is always alone. One has to be. If you married me, I couldn't stand it. I'd go mad!"

She stepped back and he let her wrists go. Her face was pale now. "I never loved anyone till I met you."

"More fool you to pick me, of all people! You should have had more sense. I'm the male version of a born old maid. I can't bear to share a room or an apartment with anybody even for a few days. And another thing: I don't want my relations with Tony messed up. He's a very useful friend to a critic."

"You should have thought of that before," said Philippa.

"I had more respect for your common sense. I thought you had been around a lot of men a long time. I didn't think you'd go overboard for any one man. Look, Philippa! There's just one thing to do. Our association ends right here and now. Then it doesn't matter what Vera tells Tony. He'll never really believe it."

"Suppose I told him that what Vera said was true."

Maurice looked at her with something close to hatred. He spoke quietly. "I'd kill you. I really believe I would."

Before she could respond, the doorbell rang.

Philippa's face underwent a subtle change. A moment before it had seemed as if it were broken down into its component parts, ravaged and chaotic. But now her many years of presenting an enameled façade to the world came to her rescue. It was a composed and integrated mask once more, beautiful, impenetrable. Even her voice was quite colorless again as she said, "Expecting someone?"

"No." Maurice walked down the room and threw open the door. On the threshold stood Basil Willing.

"I . . ." He saw Phillippa and paused.

"I was just leaving." Philippa began to draw on her gloves with studied langour.

"Do come in!" Maurice's self-control was as magnificent as hers. "This is a most unexpected pleasure. Let me take your coat."

By the time Basil was seated, both Philippa's hands were gloved, but she made no move to go. She called Basil's attention to the charming view of the city beyond the windows and the sparkle of glass and chromium on the toy cars far below. "Manhattan at its best. Don't you think so?"

Basil took his cue from her. "Perhaps you can spare me a few minutes, Mrs. Kane. . . ."

"Philippa, please." She smiled.

"You can both help me." His glance included Maurice. "I've come because I need informed opinions of Amos Cottle's ability as a writer. I've already listened to the prosecution—Emmett Avery. Now I'd like to hear the case for the defense."

"Leppy can be more help to you than I." It was the first time she had ever called him "Leppy." "It's his job to assay the gold in the nugget. I'm merely the wife of a publisher."

"I think he was a very great man," said Maurice simply. "It was perhaps the utter detachment of his point of view that gave his writing its peculiar distinction. That quality in his work intrigued and puzzled me from the first. Now I believe it is explained by his amnesia. Here was a mature man, obviously a well-educated man, whose brain had retained all the intellectual fruits of his training, but the emotional memory, the conditioning, the prejudice and bias that infects all of us was wiped clean from Amos's mind. It was like a lens of flawless white crystal perfectly cut and polished and through it he saw things as they really are down to the minutest detail. The rest of us have minds of variously curved and tinted glass that color and distort everything we see. Avery once called Amos inhuman but it would be nearer the truth to say he was superhuman."

"Then why did critics like Avery and Kitteridge treat him so much less kindly than you did?"

Maurice grinned. "It's a compulsion with most of them. You see, some men become critics because they're sadistic and others become sadistic because they're critics. It works both ways. Critical sadism is an occupational disease, like miners' silicosis."

"But you're a critic yourself," remarked Basil.

"Should that keep me from being as objective about criticism as I am about other forms of writing?" Lepton laughed.

"You make the psychology of the critic sound like the psychology of the murderer," went on Basil.

The word *murderer* brought a little chill into the pause that followed. Then Lepton smiled, like a chess player who sees several moves ahead of his opponent.

"Psychologically, a critic is more like a vitriol thrower. He doesn't just kill; he disfigures and tortures. And for the same reason—he's a sick man."

"Why, Maurice!" cried Philippa. "You're serious!"

His smile twisted. "Haven't you ever understood the morbidity of criticism, Philippa? A critic is always a sick man, because he is a literary man who lives by destroying literature, a bird that fouls his own nest, and this is perversion. If he's honest, like me, he'll admit he'd much rather create, but—he can't. So he transmutes his frustration into aggression, but in the book world aggression is called criticism and people get paid for it.

"Even when a critic praises a book, he is destroying it, for he must tear it to pieces in order to see what makes it tick. Analysis is always the inversion of synthesis—death against life. Biologists are beginning to study animal tissue under the microscope, while it is kept alive artificially, but a book is such a delicately balanced organism that the critic still has to kill the parts as well as the whole, before he can put a book under his microscope for examination. No nutrient fluids will keep alive a paragraph torn out of context. So, as even the worst critics have a certain love for books, we are like animal lovers forced to practice vivisection in order to earn our living."

"Surely you perform a useful function as literary scavengers?" suggested Basil.

"We laud as many bad books as we condemn good ones," retorted Lepton. "We're too sensitive to literary fashions to escape that. Besides, who loves a vulture? No, Willing, a critic is not a scavenger. A critic is a person who rationalizes his likes and dislikes in such impressive language that the layman thinks he is reasoning instead of rationalizing. Emmett Avery would never admit that, but I'm as sincere in my insincerity as Sainte-Beuve. . . . I wonder if Emmett's review really got under Amos's skin? It would be easier to tell if we knew who Amos really was and now—we never will!"

"Oh, but we shall," answered Basil quietly.

Maurice bent a keen glance on him. "What makes you think so?"

"We already know that he was a doctor and a Westerner, that his initials were A.S., that he was an alcoholic, that he was married to a woman of Scottish descent with light brown hair who died about five years ago, who was fond of sewing, whose initials were G.M. and whose first name was Girzel."

"Emmett told me about the thimble and the hair and the wedding ring," said Maurice. "But how do you know he was a doctor?"

"Several things suggested that from the first. A doctor or a medical student is about the only person likely to identify the Islets of Langerhans as promptly and accurately as he did when we were playing Two-Thirds of a Ghost. When I was introduced to him that evening, he said he had read my book *Psychopathology of Politics* when it came out. I believe that was a true memory because it was intellectual, not personal, and his amnesia was personal. The book was required supplementary reading in several medical schools a few years ago and, as Tony will tell you, it did not have a big sale elsewhere."

"Seems a pretty selective kind of amnesia," said Maurice. "Could he have been faking it all these years because he wanted to hide something shameful in his past?"

"I think not. Amnesia is always selective even when it has a physical cause. Some brain injuries produce muteness—amnesia of speech —and there is one form so selective it discriminates among the various parts of speech, forgetting verbs but remembering nouns and so forth. The Amos Cottle you knew was not a fake. He was just emotionally dead but otherwise entirely normal."

Basil smiled sadly. "How I wish he had been sober the one time I met him. His alcoholism blurs my mental picture of his real personality. It's almost as if I had never met him at all, for all men are pretty much the same when they're drunk. But it's different with you. One of you knew him very well personally."

Philippa's eyes shimmered for a moment as if she suspected a double meaning.

Basil went on: "The other made a careful study of his work as a writer. Between you, it does seem as if you should be able to give me a clearer picture of him as a man and as a writer. Did it ever occur to either of you that he had once been a doctor?"

"Not to me," said Maurice quickly.

Philippa was less positive. "Not at the time but now—you've brought it up I remember several little things. For one, he warned me against the abuse of sleeping pills the way a doctor would. For another, he did seem to know a great deal about the physiological effect of drugs and he had a great contempt for patent medicines. He made a remarkably neat bandage once when Tony cut his hand rather badly. It was just like the picture in the Red Cross book. I couldn't have done it though I have taken first aid. I wonder why a doctor would run away from his past?"

"I can think of a lot of reasons," said Maurice. "But I don't believe we'll ever know which one it was in his case. You've so little to go on, Willing. The wife's first name, the color of her hair, the date of her wedding and her initials. The bridegroom's initials and a guess at his profession. You'll never identify Amos."

"If he was a doctor in New York I shall," insisted Basil. "There cannot be many doctors in New York with wives named Girzel."

"Even if you do find out who he was, you'll never find out what he was running away from!" exclaimed Maurice. "Medical scandals are hushed up very carefully. Just finding out what Amos's real name was won't bring you a step nearer finding out who killed him or why."

The telephone rang. "Excuse me . . ." Maurice went through an archway into the hall. "Hello . . . Lepton speaking . . . Yes, he's here."

Basil rose. "I took the liberty of telling the police I could be reached here this afternoon."

"The police?" said Philippa a trifle breathlessly.

"Yes." Basil cast her a probing side glance. "This is still an unsolved murder."

She watched him uneasily as he moved down the room through the archway.

Maurice came back to the window seat where she was sitting and spoke in an almost inaudible voice. "Don't do anything foolish about Vera, Philippa. The police will be prying into all our lives for some time to come. The less they know about you and me or you and Amos the better."

Philippa looked down at her gloved hands. "You won't consider paying Vera?"

"To keep her quiet? She'd be insatiable. I can't afford it and neither can you. We've got to gamble that she'll hold her tongue when she finds we don't scare easily."

"Will you write her? Or shall I?"

"Nothing in writing. I'll call her on the phone."

They were silent as they heard Basil's voice speaking into the telephone. "Right away. Good-bye."

He came back into the living room with a brisker step and brighter eyes. "That was the Bureau of Missing Persons. You were wrong, Lepton. They've already discovered the identity of the man you knew as Amos Cottle."

Philippa's hand went to her throat as if she felt a choking sensation there. For a moment, Lepton looked as if Basil were threatening him with a loaded revolver.

Basil could guess why Philippa was dismayed. She had known Amos so intimately she could not anticipate learning about the other side of his life and the other women he had known, with complete equanimity. But why was Lepton, who had scarcely known Amos at all, so deeply disturbed?

twelve

Lerner Memorial was one of the newer hospitals. By the time it was founded, the price of real estate in the heart of Manhattan was prohibitive to a hospital maintained by voluntary contributions, so the founders had gone northwest to the very edge of the city limits. The white stone buildings were constructed on a heroic scale with the simple, massive solidity of ancient Egyptian architecture, which for some inexplicable reason was called modern in the thirties. Standing high, it was a perfect counterpoint for the flat face of the New Jersey Palisades across the river. Whenever a slight mist blurred its corners and dimmed the glitter of its many windows, it could easily have been mistaken for a mirror image of the rugged cliff face, transferred by some trick of refraction to the New York shore.

A heavy soundproof door led into the west wing where the administrative offices were housed. The director's private office was a large room facing the river, flooded with light from windows like pillars of glass running from floor to ceiling. It was monastically chaste in its sparing use of furniture. A great flat desk, three plain uncomfortable chairs, a row of filing cabinets, telephones and an interoffice communicator. No rug, no pictures, no books, not even a typewriter. It seemed a thousand years removed from the fancier Wall Street offices with their gentleman's library look—their open fireplaces, TV sets and concealed bars. Here there was nothing unnecessary and nothing comfortable.

After all, thought Basil, the research hospital, like the university, has something of the same relation to the general public that monasteries had in the Middle Ages. Here was an austere tradition sustained by an absolute faith in ideals that happened to be secular. This was the domain of people who thought and lived on another plane from that of their contemporaries, who cheerfully accepted relative poverty, cushioned by minimum security, as the price that must be paid for more leisure to cultivate the inner life than was possible to anyone involved in the fierce competitions of the market place. Set apart from the human harvest, like seed corn, they were able to germinate ideas that would have perished if there had been no such communities withdrawn from the mainstream of modern life. As always, the eternal could only be preserved by those who rejected the contemporary with all its flashing, distracting and deceiving delusions.

George Hansen, the director, was small, fair and effeminate. Put a woman's wig on his sleek, sandy head and you would accept him immediately as a woman schoolteacher or librarian in her late forties. The plain, neatly knotted dark tie, the immaculate linen with a hint of starch, the hands that looked as if they had just been washed—all indicated a man orderly, punctilious, a little rigid, a little petty, but sure to fulfill any administrative job with flawless precision and meticulous attention to detail. He would have made a good abbot, but he would not have survived for one day among the robber barons.

"Dr. Willing? I understand that you are interested in the history of Alan Sewell."

"The Missing Persons Bureau believe that he is the man I am looking for," said Basil, cautiously. "What can you tell me about him?"

There was a folder on the spotless blotter—the only thing besides a pen on the bare desk. Hansen opened the folder and glanced at the papers inside. "Alan Sewell was born in Adamant, Vermont, in 1918."

"Vermont!" Basil was astonished. "Are you sure?"

"I have all the documents here. Why shouldn't he be from Vermont?"

"I had a strong suspicion that he was a Westerner."

"So far as I know, he was never in the West. He was a graduate of Harvard Medical School and he interned in this hospital in 1948. He showed considerable promise as a surgeon. He was married during his internship to a childhood sweetheart, Girzel MacDonald. She had come on here from Vermont about two years earlier, and she and another girl ran a small beauty parlor in this neighborhood."

"The other girl's name?"

"Alice Hawkins."

"Is she still in the neighborhood?"

"No, she has a big place on Fifth Avenue now under the trade name of Alicia Armitage.

"Girzel MacDonald had some savings of her own which made the marriage possible financially while Alan was still an interne. They lived in a small apartment near the hospital and they seemed happy. Then Alan finished his internship and became a staff doctor, which eased the financial situation. Unfortunately Mrs. Sewell died suddenly of acute appendicitis. The operation had been delayed too long."

"Why?"

"My dear Dr. Willing, you can hardly expect me to answer that question. I did not know the Sewells intimately. But we all know that appendicitis is not always easy to diagnose. We've had several cases here where every test was negative and then a purely exploratory operation has revealed infection close to the danger point. Presumably it was one of those cases. Of course it was a most tragic thing to happen to so young a man and it had an unfortunate effect on Sewell's personality. Until then he had been quite gregarious and well liked, but he became so morose and withdrawn that a number of his colleagues complained he was difficult to work with. No one suggested that he neglected his duties in any way, but his manners, or lack of manners, created a bad impression.

"The situation remained stationary for several months. We all hoped he would snap out of it eventually, but then—I began to hear reports that Dr. Sewell was drinking heavily. I questioned him about this. He assured me that he did not drink on duty, only when he was alone at home. I pointed out the dangers of solitary drinking, especially for a doctor, and tried to say a few words of fatherly advice. I admit I was beginning to be troubled about the whole thing. In a job like mine you have to keep the future constantly in mind, and I could foresee the possibility that in a few more months Dr. Sewell would have to be asked to resign, if he didn't pull himself together. I did not relish the prospect, naturally, and then . . . Well, fate intervened and I was spared that unpleasant necessity."

"What happened?"

Hansen leaned back in his chair and looked out the window. Basil had an odd impression that Hansen was relieved, as if he felt he had got over the most difficult part of his story without being asked the one question that he feared. Certainly he was now choosing his words with less care and his whole manner was more relaxed.

"It was a rainy evening in winter very much like this."

"The date?"

"October 14, 1950. Sewell was in the coffee shop downstairs having a sandwich before leaving to go home. One of the nurses was with him, a Miss Linton. She was a sweet little thing and completely devoted to Sewell. This is her story. No one else in the coffee shop was paying any attention to Sewell at the time. She said afterward that he seemed more than usually depressed. She suggested that they go to a movie. Rather to her surprise, he agreed. He paid for his sandwich and hers and they walked to the front entrance together. He stopped on the way to buy a pack of cigarettes in the lobby and they discussed the movie they were about to see. *Hamlet,* I think, with Laurence Olivier. The rain was coming down violently as they came out of the entrance under the porte-cochere. He said, 'You wait here. I'll get a taxi. I won't be a minute.' He pulled down his hat brim, turned up his coat collar and plunged into the rain. She waited for five minutes, for ten, for twenty. No one here ever saw him again.

"After Miss Linton had waited about twenty minutes she put up her umbrella and walked over to the taxi stand nearby. There were two taxis waiting and both drivers were regulars at that stand, familiar with all the hospital personnel. They told her they had been there thirty minutes and they had not seen Dr. Sewell walk down the driveway to the street. She phoned his apartment. No answer. He had vanished into thin air for no apparent reason.

"After twenty-four hours we reported the case to the Missing Persons Bureau. They were never able to trace him. He had no close relatives surviving in Vermont and neither did his wife, so there was not quite the same pressure on the police to find him that there is when anxious relatives are involved."

"What was the state of his finances when he disappeared?"

"About eight hundred in a checking account. No debts. All but the most recent bills paid. No insurance. No car. Just a few personal effects."

"He made no attempt to withdraw the eight hundred?"

"No, he was finally presumed dead and it went to a distant cousin in Oregon."

"What do you think happened?"

Hansen drew a deep breath. "Dr. Sewell had been brooding over his wife's death. He knew we disapproved of his drinking. He may have realized already that he would not be able to control it. I thought of suicide and a body that was never discovered. Washed out to sea, perhaps. Less probable, but perfectly possible, was fugue, amnesia—a sudden blotting out of all personal memory, an unconscious attempt to flee from the past and begin a new life."

"But why at that particular moment?" demanded Basil. "Suicide might be the culmination of weeks of brooding, but wouldn't it take some shock to precipitate fugue so suddenly?"

"That's more your line than mine, though I believe I have heard of cases where fugue set in suddenly for no immediate cause but simply as a final result of accumulated stress. After all, fugue is a psychological suicide."

"Would the death of his wife, for which he was in no way responsible, set up such extreme tension?" persisted Basil.

Hansen shrugged. "Each individual mind has its own breaking point. . . . Dr. Willing, I am really curious to know what did become of Sewell. What is your half of the story? You know it's as if we were trying to match two halves of a broken coin. Do the points of my jagged edge fit the bites in your edge where something has been ripped away?"

"Would you be surprised if I told you that Alan Sewell was found on a Westchester road the next morning in a state of complete personal amnesia with a wound in his head?"

"Westchester? What was he doing there?"

"At that time there was a celebrated clinic for alcoholics there at a place called Stratfield."

"You mean Dr. Clinton's place?"

"Yes. As a doctor, Sewell could have heard about it. He could have been on his way there hoping to arrange for a cure."

"Walking? At night?"

"He could have been walking from the station. On a rainy night the taxis might all be out on the road when he arrived."

"And the head wound?"

"There's some evidence he was struck by a car."

"Did that account for the amnesia?"

"I thought so until today. But how explain his abrupt desertion of Miss Linton unless the amnesia started a moment or so after he left her? Of course we only have Miss Linton's own word for the nature of their parting. If she said or did something to anger him, something she thought it wise to leave out of her story, then I should not conclude the amnesia was caused by the head wound."

"What happened to Sewell afterward?"

"His alcoholism was cured at the clinic. He never recovered his memory. He became the celebrated novelist, Amos Cottle, who was poisoned last Sunday."

Hansen had himself under almost perfect control, but he could not repress a slight start of amazement. "You are on the wrong track, Dr. Willing."

"Why?"

"Writing novels just doesn't fit an inarticulate personality like Sewell's. I'm not a psychiatrist. I could be wrong, but . . ."

"It's easily tested." Basil took the photograph of Amos Cottle out of his pocket and laid it on the desk.

Hansen gasped. "I apologize, Dr. Willing. You understand human nature better than I do. For that is Alan Sewell. No question about it." He laid a finger over the beard. "Yes. I'd know Sewell's brow and eyes and nose anywhere."

"You never saw him on TV?"

"I detest TV."

"What about the others who knew him here?"

"Doctors are pretty busy people—as you know. If this was a daytime program . . ."

"It was a Thursday afternoon program."

"Then that explains why none of us saw it."

"What about the nurses? And the girl who ran the beauty parlor with Girzel Sewell?"

"Working women don't watch TV in the daytime. Only housewives and children."

"I'd like to talk to that one nurse who was the last person to see him as Alan Sewell. Miss Linton did you say?"

Hansen dropped his eyelids. "Unfortunately Miss Linton is no longer with us. She went overseas with the Army when the Korean War broke out, and she's still in Japan."

The interview ended politely, but Basil left the room with an uncomfortable feeling that he had learned less than he had hoped to. This was only the skeleton of Alan Sewell's story. How was it to be clothed in flesh and blood?

Back in his own office he telephoned his friend Lambert of the Medical Examiner's office.

"You had a research project at Lerner Memorial several years ago, didn't you?"

"Yes."

"Was there an interne named Alan Sewell there at the time?"

"No. I left before he came. I've heard about him though. Didn't he disappear about six years ago?"

"Yes. Did you know Hansen, the director?"

"Everybody there knows Prissy!"

"Would he tell the truth about something that might be perfectly legal, but that might also reflect a little on the efficiency of his hospital?"

"Of course not. Would you?"

Basil laughed. Lambert's skepticism was always refreshingly frank.

The atmosphere of Alicia Armitage, Inc. was as different from the atmosphere of Lerner Memorial as it was possible to be. Nothing monastic here. This was a luxury trade built on superstition, a witch cult of the robber barons' wives. Here you plunged with joyous abandon into the main stream of modern culture and all its most cherished myths and foibles. Here was faith, too, but a pagan faith without austerity or dedication.

Here you belived that a mysterious God named Science, whose icon was an image of a handsome young man in a white coat, would make you young and beautiful and desirable no matter what your age or appearance or character, if you gratified him by putting blanched and perfumed mutton fat on your face, dyes of various colors on your hair, lips, eyelids and nails, brought your weight down and spent large sums of money on your clothes.

Here in scented, softly lighted chambers of turquoise and silver with velvet underfoot, Marie Laurencin on the walls and Muzak in the air, there were diet and vitamin bars, cubicles for hairdressing, manicuring, massage and exercise, Turkish baths and a shop that sold clothes and cosmetics. They could mold and tint your hair into any shape or color you wanted, erase your face and replace it with a porcelain mask, carve your body in the proportions of the life-size plastic dolls in dress-shop windows and leave you finally with almost as much individuality.

The ministering acolytes were all clad in white, but the high priestess proclaimed her own distinction by her ceremonial vestments of black crepe and her insignia of three strands of pearls. Her hair was a lovely, unnatural copper, her face white as pipe clay—latest reaction from the suntan cult that had become too common to be fashionable. Her long nails and full lips were exactly the color of fresh blood. Because the rest of the building was turquoise and silver, her sanctum was orchid and gold with touches of black. She was a showcase for her own wares. Little scars at either temple explained the smooth rigidity of her face, but one thing about her had remained alive—the tawny, hazel eyes that looked out of lashes black and sticky with mascara—eyes that were alert and intelligent and responsive.

She offered cigarettes in a malachite box and talked freely.

"Sure I remember Alan. Poor kid! He was all cut up over Girzel's death. Let's see. I met Girzel at the beauty parlor school here in New

York. She told me she was engaged to a young interne at Lerner Memorial. He wasn't making anything, of course, but she was going to save her money so they could get married a little sooner. We became friends and opened that little hairdressing place uptown on a shoestring. We had just enough money for rent. I borrowed money for equipment and we both worked like hell.

"I got to know Alan pretty well. I had a boy friend then and we all went on double dates together. What was Alan like? Easygoing. He hated scenes. He always tried to agree with everything that other people said. Good at his job and ambitious. More so than Girzel. She wanted to go back to New Hampshire or Vermont or wherever it was and settle down in a big house and have a lot of children. No ambition at all. But she was kind and sweet and loving—much too good for Alan. What she saw in him, I never could understand. She kept her job after they were married and things went on that way for about two years.

"Then, one evening, Irving and I were up at their apartment having one of those beef stew suppers when Girzel was taken ill. Violent pain in the abdomen, no other symptoms. Alan's hospital was the nearest, so we rushed her over there. Another staff man examined her and came up with a diagnosis—acute appendicitis, operate at once.

"It was after midnight then—a quiet time even for a hospital. None of the doctors on duty was particularly good at surgery. Alan knew that. And he knew that he was supposed to be tops even among the older men."

Basil looked at her with dawning horror. "You don't mean to say he operated on his wife himself?"

"How did you guess? I know doctors have a thing about operating on members of their own family. After that night I think it's just as well they do. It was a sort of emergency and Alan was supposed to be the best surgeon there, but I could see the other doctors didn't like it much. Alan had one glaring fault. He was vain of his surgery. I believe he honestly thought they couldn't get another surgeon as good as he was without spending quite a lot more money, to say nothing of delaying the operation dangerously.

"Afterward I talked to one of the nurses who'd been in the operating room. She said it was ghastly. She never saw anything like it before or since. It all started off smoothly, teamwork, sterilize this, hand me that—the business, you know. I've seen it in the movies often enough. But the moment Alan took that knife and made the first incision, he—well, he went to pieces. He did everything wrong. The nurse said she and the others didn't quite realize it the first few minutes. It was just too monstrous to realize. And when they did—it was too late. She died an hour after they wheeled her back to her room."

"And I never thought of asking Hansen who had operated!" Basil reproached himself. "That was the question Hansen feared all the time he was talking to me. But how could I, a doctor myself, have dreamed . . ."

"I know. It's one of those rare things that do happen sometimes. Things that hospitals just have to hush up. What would happen to public confidence if they didn't? Surgeons mustn't be fallible. They must be gods. Ninety-nine percent of the time nothing goes wrong. But this was the hundredth time. The hell of it was that Alan loved Girzel. I suppose that was why it happened. He was in a state of shock when he started to operate. His nerve crumbled. He lost his head and cut her up so she could never be put together again."

Basil wondered. Alan must have wondered, too. That must have been his own peculiar, lonely hell. He would know some medical psychology. Enough to know that even under stress you do nothing that some part of your mind does not want to do. Had there been some ambivalence in his feeling for Girzel? Some disillusion buried deep in the subconscious that came to the surface when he made that first incision that had seemed to this woman and all the other witnesses purely an accident?

Freud's theory of unconscious purpose in every slip of the hand was only a theory. There was a formidable mass of evidence to support it, but some day a later psychologist might prove that it was not the whole truth about the working of brain and nervous system. That very uncertainty would make Alan's doubt of himself all the more torturing. He could never know the truth. Did I kill her because deep in the undermind I always wanted to kill her? The childhood sweetheart pursuing her first love to New York. His horizons changing, hers remaining provincial. An interne's poverty and the strain on both of her keeping her job after their marriage. No children. Had it been one of those adolescent "understandings" with a girl who was sweetly determined and wholly faithful, an understanding that was really a misunderstanding because he wanted to break it and couldn't without despising himself? One of those troths that is more binding than marriage itself because it is a debt of honor. One that had condemned Alan Sewell to a dreary, uncongenial marriage because he "hated scenes. He always tried to agree with everything that other people said. . . ."

So he became a murderer. An unpunishable murderer who would never know himself whether he had really killed or not. A strong man would hardly have survived the shock of such a self-revelation. Alan didn't sound like a strong man. Vain of his surgery and fatally weak in keeping the letter of his promise to Girzel after the spirit had died, afraid to hurt her or let her hurt him with her reproaches. In every glimpse of him he was a man who followed the line of least resistance.

"What happened afterward?"

"He never operated again. They kept him on as staff physician but I think they were just waiting until the talk had died down a little and then they'd have got rid of him quietly. He started to drink. He even drank on duty sometimes, but Prissy never new that. The nurses covered up for Alan. They knew he was headed for skid row and then —he just disappeared. I always thought he killed himself. I'm sure that's what the hospital people thought. They must have been glad the body was never found."

"It's all logical. It all fits," said Basil. "First he tried to escape through the artificial amnesia of alcohol. Then, the night the young nurse wanted him to go to the movies with her . . ."

"Linton? Oh yes, I remember her. Nasty, scheming little thing. She made a play for Alan after his wife's death. I don't think he liked her much. He wouldn't have liked any woman then. It was too soon. Especially a woman who had been in the operating room when it happened, as Linton had. But she was too stupid and greedy to realize that. She was always pestering him to go to the movies with her. So he wouldn't spend the evening drinking, she said. Her real object was matrimony, of course."

"You say she was pestering him," mused Basil. "And she was particularly distasteful to him because she had been one of the nurses in the operating room when it happened. She was a constant reminder of something he wanted desperately to forget. Let's see if we can reconstruct his last evening at the hospital.

"He didn't want to go to the movies with her that night, but he was weak and suggestible and he had agreed to go without thinking because it was the line of least resistance. Once outside in the fresh air, away from her, he dreaded the very thought of an evening with her. We have only her version of the story. She may have said something to him that was the last straw."

"She probably did. Something like: 'You've got to stop drinking. They're going to fire you if you don't.'"

"He didn't go near the taxi stand," went on Basil. "He must have found a taxi cruising and it suddenly came to him that he didn't have to go back to her. He didn't have to let her force this unpleasant evening on him. In a way this was the line of least resistance again. Instead of going back and excusing himself to her on grounds of a headache or something, he just went off and left her without a word, thus sparing himself an unpleasant scene. It's all quite in character. He didn't mind hurting her as long as he wasn't there to see her being hurt. People without imagination are often like that."

"But why didn't he just go home?"

"He knew Linton would phone his apartment. She did, too. He probably went to a bar and got fairly drunk. That was one thing he couldn't do as long as she was with him—not without a scene."

"Why didn't he go home afterward?"

"I think he sat in the bar and remembered all she had said to him and realized what his future would be like if he kept on as he was. And then—I think he made one last effort to escape from the horror that enclosed him. He took a taxi to Grand Central and bought a ticket to Stratfield, New York."

"Why Stratfield?"

"There was a famous clinic for alcoholics there in those days. Dr. Clinton's. Alan could know about it because he was a doctor in a city hospital where there are always some alcoholic cases. He went that night, late as it was, because he wanted help then without waiting another moment. He was afraid to wait. Afraid his resolution might wilt. And he was far too drunk to worry about gaining admission in the middle of the night.

"He walked from the station in the driving rain in the dark. A car hit him and sped on. That blow on the head gave him what he had been seeking ever since he killed his wife—Nirvana. How thankfully his conscious mind must have let those unbearable memories sink into the subconscious, never to be recovered.

"The clinic was the nearest hospital. They took him there, where his alcoholism was recognized immediately as well as his concussion and amnesia. He stayed there as a charity patient and—eventually he became someone else."

"Who?"

"Amos Cottle, the novelist, who was murdered last Sunday."

"Alan became Amos Cottle? Well! You never can tell, can you? Was he murdered as Sewell or Cottle?"

"That's what we'd all like to know now. Did Girzel have any devoted brothers?"

"You mean someone who recognized Cottle as Sewell might have killed him because he had killed Girzel and gone unpunished?"

"It's one possibility."

"Her parents were dead. She had a married sister in Deerfield, Massachusetts. No brothers. Somehow I can't see a married sister . . . Not one in Deerfield."

"Another childhood sweetheart besides Sewell?"

"I wouldn't know about that, but . . . Sounds a bit Corsican, doesn't it? Killing a man years later because he made a mistake when he was a surgeon operating on your childhood sweetheart and killed her inadvertently?"

"Perhaps he didn't think it was inadvertent. Or perhaps he had always felt a jealous hatred for the more successful suitor."

"But after so many years . . . It still sounds too Corsican to me."

"Premeditated murders are always hard for the normal person to understand," Basil reminded her. "None of us is incapable of unpremeditated murder, but the other thing is—well, across the borderline. We recognize this when we make the penalty so much heavier. We're expressing revulsion for something we cannot understand or forgive."

Vera was alone in her sitting room at the Waldorf watching TV, when the telephone rang. She was so depressed and lonely that she was almost glad when the operator said that Dr. Willing was in the lobby and wished to see her. She shut off the TV set, refreshed her lipstick and left the door into the corridor open.

He looked more tired and serious than she had ever seen him when he came in. She urged various drinks upon him, but he shook his head. "I can only stay a moment. I really have only one question to ask you. Did you ever know anyone named Alan Sewell?"

She looked at him blankly. "Someone in Hollywood?"

"No, in New York."

"Should I know him?"

"Perhaps not. Does the name Girzel MacDonald mean anything?"

"No."

"Did you ever see these before?" He put the snakeskin purse, the gold thimble and wedding ring, and the lock of hair on the table. Recognition came into her eyes.

"Amos kept those things in his desk. He told me they had belonged to a sister who was dead."

"I have reason to believe they belonged to his wife."

Vera's eyes flared like flame in a draft. "Do you mean . . . Is she going to get the royalties now?"

"She can't hurt you. She died long before you met Amos."

"Then—who was Amos?"

"A young doctor named Alan Sewell."

He told her the whole story.

"It makes sense," she admitted. "Amos knew all the Latin names for bones. And he used to laugh at patent medicines. He could have been a doctor. But what has all this to do with his death?"

"I'm not sure yet. It may be a blind alley. He may have been murdered because he was Amos Cottle for reasons that had nothing to do with his identity as Alan Sewell."

"The Sewell business really doesn't change anything for me, does it?" said Vera complacently. "I was his wife legally and I'm his legal heir now. Nobody can take that away from me."

She was happy and relieved.

Ever since his death she had been dreading the revelations that might follow the discovery of Amos's true identity. Now everything was going to be all right. Nothing in the past affected her status.

When Basil left she called the desk to see if there were any letters or telephone messages for her. There had been none this morning. Not even a call from Sam about the audition. She must have flopped. He never called to tell her bad news, only good news. Then his voice would be bubbling with exuberance and he would shout, "Oh, boy, baby, we're in business!" But when one of his schemes went sour, he never mentioned it again.

When she wrote the four letters yesterday the last thing she had expected was this stunning, unanimous silence. It was unnerving somehow. What were they thinking? What were they doing? Nothing? That was inconceivable. Philippa, Lepton, Tony and Gus—surely at least one of them would be frightened enough to make some move in her direction and what move could any of them make without answering her letter?

Perhaps the answers would come tomorrow. Meanwhile there was an evening to be killed. Call one of the theatrical crowd? She was out of touch after three years in Hollywood. The boys should have called her when they saw her arrival at the airport in the papers, but they weren't quick to call someone whose option had been dropped in Hollywood. She turned on the TV again. A shadowy, gray face mouthed at her silently. Then as she twiddled another dial, the sound came on.

". . . and this evening at eight o'clock we shall take you to the Bookbinders' Award dinner, where an award of ten thousand dollars will be given to the Most American Author of the Decade. . . ."

She switched off the set. The announcement made her feel more forlorn than ever. The award Amos was to have had, and she didn't even have an invitation to the dinner.

The silence of the empty suite became unbearable. She tried calling Sam's office number, and got an answering service. Sam had gone home to New Rochelle and his wife and two little sons. There he led a life quite different from his celebrity-spangled existence in Manhattan, playing tennis, going to PTA meetings and suppers at the Unitarian Church, and in summer sailing his boat on the Sound. To Sam who had been born in a city slum, it was a romantically delightful existence. Vera who had been born in a similar suburb of Cleveland couldn't understand this. To her Sam's home life represented everything she had been trying to get away from all her life. She never even telephoned him when he was at home.

She must kill the evening somehow. Dinner at a restaurant and then a movie.

A taxi took her to a French restaurant on Third Avenue that she chose because someone had told her it was the most expensive in New York. As the menu was in French and handwritten, she told the waiter to select her dinner. It took a long time and when it came she had no idea what she was eating. There was a large bottle of wine with it that made her a little sleepy. Perhaps she shouldn't have had those cocktails first. She asked for black coffee and refused brandy. The bill was so enormous that she was convinced the food had been good.

Outside under the marquee she realized suddenly that this was not the best place in the world to find a taxi on a rainy night. She was so used to having a car or a man to find a taxi for her that she never wore boots or raincoat. Tonight her sandals were cut low, her hat a confection of tulle, and her furs the glossy kind that would be ruined by a real soaking. Gusts of wind driving the rain slantwise had swept the street of pedestrians for the moment. The doorman went off with his big umbrella but returned after a while without a taxi. Madame would have to wait a little longer.

Suddenly Madame no longer cared about her sandals or her hat or her furs. Down the street glimmered a neon sign, "Bengal Lancers." An old, old film. It *would* be on Third Avenue. But anything was better than boredom.

She drew her furs around her chin and bent her head before the rain. She had gone a block when she heard footfalls behind her as rapid as her own. She didn't look back. Only by keeping her head down could she keep the rain out of her face. The insides of her sandals were soaking now, her stockings clammy against her legs. Forget the movie. Walk to the hotel. Have a hot bath and turn on the TV and watch the Bookbinders' Dinner. Gus and Tony were sure to be there. Maybe they would be shown on the screen and she might be able to tell from their faces what they were feeling. Or maybe there would be a telephone message for her now. She turned west and entered a long crosstown street, ill-lit and deserted and slummy in this block between Third and Lexington.

All the lighted windows were closed and shaded except one on the third floor of an old brownstone house across the street. It was wide open and bright like a single eye vigilant in the night.

The footfalls turned with her and now they were closer. For the first time she felt the icy touch of a physical fear. There were all sorts of stories about muggers in New York—gangs of half-grown boys from the slums who snatched your purse if you were well dressed and alone, late at night, boys who sometimes hurt you with homemade weapons—broken glass, razor blades . . .

It couldn't be happening to her. Of course not. There was only one set of footsteps behind her.

She felt better as she entered the circle of light from the one street lamp in the middle of the block. Lexington, always bright and crowded and cheerfully vulgar, beckoned her on. She ventured one glance back over her shoulder. The sudden flood of relief was sweet as fresh air after a stuffy, rancid night club.

Her smile was really cordial. "Oh, it's you!"

She was quite unprepared for the arm that clamped around her neck like a vise and the hand flat against her mouth.

The invalid woman at the open window across the street turned away from it. She had seen the smile, the sudden turn of the head and now she thought she was seeing two lovers embracing. She didn't want to spy on them.

thirteen

When Basil Willing married and moved to Connecticut, he kept his bachelor apartment in the old brownstone house on lower Park Avenue. It was a convenience on a night like this when he planned to attend the Bookbinders' Dinner with his English publisher, Alexander McLean. They had met casually years ago when McLean's Ltd. issued the English edition of Basil's first book. They had become friends when they shared common war experiences in Intelligence during the invasion of Germany.

Basil changed his clothes for the dinner, always a full-dress affair, then settled himself before the fire in the old library with the pith-white paneling and crimson curtains that had so many associations with past cases he had solved. None of them, he thought now, had been quite so puzzling as the deceptively simple murder of the man known as Amos Cottle.

The tangible evidence was spread out on his coffee table, the things that he and Avery had rescued from the burning house—the ring, the purse, the thimble, the lock of hair, the first editions of Amos's four published novels, the carbon of his unpublished novel, the scrapbooks with their clippings of reviews and advertisements and the folder with its letters and contracts.

He had not had time to read all the five long books. While he waited for Alec, he decided to glance at *Passionate Pilgrim* once more.

The fire purred, the wind rattled the window frames, the rain hissed at the panes and he read on, more and more absorbed in the dead man's narrative. Things he had not noticed before began to take on new significance. There was a pencil in his hand. Now and then he marked a passage by drawing a light line along the margin. One paragraph sent him back to Lepton's review of *Passionate Pilgrim* and he marked a paragraph in the review with a double line.

> . . . One of the women characters has a grandmother who was a madam in a Bowery brothel in 1898. This old woman appears only once in the story, at the moment when she is dying. And she utters only one phrase: 'I don't wish him no harm—oh, no—but I wish to God he'd fall down and break his damned neck!' What else do we need to establish the character of this woman? It is all there—the sly, salty humor, the earthy realism, the humane scorn of the sanctimonious hypocrisy of the brief, gaslit period that ended the long reign of Victoria. I can see that old woman as she must have been in her heyday, loaded with Roman pearls and rhinestones, white glacé kid on her fat hands and perfumed violets at her high-corseted bosom and a flowing skirt tarnished with Bowery mud, leering from the balcony at Daly's Theatre. Who but Amos Cottle could have written such a line today?

Gradually Basil's interest became tinged with amazement. The glimmering of an idea that had come to him first the afternoon he spent with Avery in Cottle's house began to glow and swell and take on form and substance. Could this be the answer?

He was so absorbed he forgot all about Alec until the doorbell rang downstairs. He sat up with a jerk and went into the hall to release the spring that unlocked the street door below. He stood at the head of the stair as Alec appeared below, foreshortened against the black and white marble of the vestibule.

"Come on up, Alec. We've time for a drink and I have something here that will interest you."

Alec got rid of his wet coat and hat and approached the fire, rubbing his hands, a tall, fair, impressive person, much more English than Scots, in spite of his name.

Basil mixed two whiskey and sodas and they sat on either side of the hearth, one fair, one dark, the coloring of each set off by the unrelieved blacks and whites of their almost archaic ceremonial dress. Anyone seeing them would have assumed they were two gentlemen of leisure spending a quiet evening together, which was not the truth at all.

Alec had the incurable optimism of a man who has been fortunate all his life. He had inherited McLean's from his father and he knew all the folklore of publishing on both sides of the Atlantic. He was a natural cosmopolite who passed every psychological frontier with ease, just as much at home in New York or Morocco as in London or Paris.

Basil told him all he knew of Amos Cottle, reserving only the things he suspected.

"I never met Cottle," said Alec. "But I know Tony Kane. He was the chap who made all his book sales outright to England in 1940. So afraid Hitler would win, he didn't want any royalties tied up in England. Not that he wanted us to lose. He just didn't want it to cost him anything if we did."

"That sounds like Tony." Basil grinned. "Alec, a most extraordinary idea has come to me. I want to check it with someone like you who knows the literary shop from A to Z. Indeed, that's one reason I suggested we go to this dinner together tonight. Almost everyone involved will be there and I have a feeling that something will break loose—especially if we give it a nudge. I want you to cast an eye over these passages I've marked in reviews, clippings, letters and books and see if—well, if you see what I see."

Alec sipped his drink, lit a cigarette and began to read. The fire sighed softly, the windows rattled again. It wasn't long before Alec put down the books and papers and looked at Basil with a sharp, bright eye. "Fantastic! Impossible! And yet—by Jove, it could be."

"Could it?"

"Why not? Can you think of any good argument against it?"

"Let's make sure we're talking about the same thing. Suppose you tell me the points you think are significant. Or should I say meaningful and richly rewarding? Or perhaps just queer?"

Alec chuckled. "Nothing queer about old Cholmondeley? Hell,

there are at least ten things damned queer about this when you put them all together."

"Ten?" said Basil. "Let's see if I've got that many:

"1. The name Amos Cottle.

"2. Cottle's failure to answer the first question when we played Two-Thirds of a Ghost.

"3. The arm-breaking scene in *Passionate Pilgrim*.

"4. The gap of three months between Tony's first letter to Cottle and the publication date of *Retreat*.

"5. Tony's apple woman story.

"6. Gus's war service.

"7. Lepton's ignorance of anatomy.

"8. The fact that Cottle stopped working when Vera was living with him.

"9. The fact that Avery said Cottle's work was a pastiche of all the bad novels of the last thirty years.

"What's the tenth? You're one up on me."

Alec smiled. "Leppy's love of malicious mischief. All this is fascinating, Basil, but we still don't know who murdered Amos Cottle."

Basil returned the smile. "I can guess. Can't you?"

"Yes." Alec's face sobered. "I'm afraid I can. Poor devil, what a waste!"

"Come to think of it, there's an eleventh point," mused Basil. "Lepton's father was a bookbinder. . . . Another drink?"

"A quick one. Then let's get on to this dinner. I wouldn't miss it for anything now. Quite like the old days in Germany. How are we going to run this show?"

"You can help me cut him out from the crowd. Then meet us outside his place in a taxi. If we don't come down in thirty minutes, you'd better come up."

The Bookbinders' Association had rented a dining hall and reception room in one of the largest hotels. When Basil and Alec arrived, people were just beginning to drift from the bar in the reception room to the reserved tables in the dining hall. At Basil's suggestion, Alec had secured two seats at a mixed table next to the table reserved for Sutton, Kane and Company.

Alec recognized Tony and Lepton and smiled at them. "Who are the others there?" he asked Basil in a low voice.

"Philippa, Tony's wife, beside him. Then Gus Vesey, Cottle's agent, and his wife, Meg. Who is that woman between Lepton and Tony? Oh, I know. One of the Vesey stable of authors, Ellen Gabor."

The diners plowed through a five-course dinner served by a multitude of waiters at an inexorable speed that outdistanced their appetites. As coffee appeared, a man rose at the long, head table facing the room and tapped on his glass with his spoon.

"Coming here this evening, through the drizzling rain, I was reminded of a little story. . . ."

After ten minutes even the weariest anecdote must wind its way to the sea. The audience's relief was expressed in scattered applause.

"And now, ladies and gentlemen . . ." The speaker paused. There was a moment of agonizing suspense. Would there be another little story? Several diners signaled waiters surreptitiously for brandy.

". . . as President of the Bookbinders' Association, it gives me great pleasure to introduce the Chairman of the Awards Committee, Miss Hermione Featherstone, who is also Chairman of the English Department at one of our most distinguished women's colleges. I am sure you all know Miss Featherstone's exquisite little novella, *The Sandpiper and I,* to say nothing of the many delightful essays she has contributed to the *Atlantic Monthly* and *Harper's*. Miss Featherstone."

Loud applause. Miss Featherstone rose and spoke in a high, clear voice with a cutting edge. Gray-haired, her hard face reddened by the rigor of New England winters and her lean body dressed in the fashions of twenty years ago, she was known as one of those careerists who claw their way to the top of the academic world, which is almost as jealously competitive as the theatrical world, especially among women. Obviously this was one of the high moments of her career. It brought her out of the cloisters, where the higher the marks she gave her students, the more certain their stories were to be rejected by editors, into the heady, exotic world of real publishers and real authors who got things printed and paid for.

Yet for a few moments they were all looking up to her and deferring to her critical judgment. Something they would never have done if the issue at stake had been risking money on publishing a first book by an unknown writer instead of the bestowal of an honorary award that didn't cost them anything since it was financed by endowment.

True, there had been others on the committe with her—Maurice

Lepton, the critic, and Tony Kane, the publisher, and Ellen Gabor, the novelist, and Sloan Severing, President of the Bookbinders' Association. But she had been the chairman and it was her name that had been most widely blazoned in the press. "Prestige stuff," as Tony's publicity man had explained to her.

The trade in postprandial brandy grew rather brisk as Hermione Featherstone, who was used to a captive audience, took her listeners through a comprehensive survey of the literature of the English-speaking peoples starting with the Venerable Bede. Most of the guests were on their third brandy when the chairman whispered that it was later than she thought. She shot by Thomas Hardy with a side glance at Henry James and plunged into her dramatic peroration.

"Your committee felt that there was only one author in the contemporary literary scene who had the sure artist's touch in portraying humane compassion for people as people, the noble gift of wringing music from the plainer, simpler words of our language, and the lofty feeling for man's grandeur as well as his pathos, which we expect of our foremost novelists. It is a tragic disappointment to the committee that, owing to an unforeseen catastrophe, he cannot be here with us tonight to receive his award in person. But, in his absence, I shall ask his publisher, Mr. Anthony Kane, to step forward and accept the award for the inspired and dedicated chronicler of our times—Amos Cottle."

This time brandy and thankfulness that the long ordeal was over at last lent real enthusiasm to the applause. Miss Featherstone smiled and bowed and sat down trembling visibly with gratification.

"Mr. Chairman, ladies and gentlemen." Tony's voice seemed unusually rich and resonant after her thin, cutting tones. "It is a great honor for me to accept this award in the distinguished name of Amos Cottle. I will not dwell on the tragic circumstances of his sudden death. I will only say that if Mos Cottle could have been here with us tonight, I know it would have been the proudest moment of his life."

Tony's voice shook and thinned on the last sentence, as if there were tears in his eyes. There was real sympathy in the warmth of the applause. Only Basil and Alec suspected that Tony's perturbation had another cause than grief for the death of Amos Cottle.

The moment for last drinks and table-hopping had come. As guests began to circulate from table to table, a whisper ran through the crowd, like wind through a field of wheat. Alec, who had gone to another table to greet old friends, came back to Basil with the news.

"Some reporter heard it on TV just before he came in to cover the speeches after dinner. Cottle's wife, Vera Vane, was found dead in the street a little while ago. Apparently someone had choked her and forced cyanide into her mouth. Who could have foreseen that?"

"She must have tried blackmail," said Basil. "There's a vacant seat at Tony's table now. Gabor's gone home. We'd better get over there before they break up."

Tony received them exuberantly. "Basil! And Alec McLean! You must join us for a last drink. Take this seat, Alec, and I'll grab another chair for Basil. What will you have?"

"Nothing at the moment, thank you." Basil looked around the table. Apparently the rumor hadn't reached this side of the room yet, but one of these five knew that Vera was dead—the one who had killed her.

"Alec, I've got a book on my spring list you'll want to publish in England, if I know you as well as I think I do. It's a French book we're doing in translation but the English rights are still open. My translator couldn't think of a selling title and then I had an inspiration —we'll use a French title *Bonsoir, Maîtresse*. Get it? It's a combination of *Goodbye, Mr. Chips, Good Morning, Miss Dove* and *Bonjour, Tristesse*—just like *Lincoln's Doctor's Dog*—only it has sex appeal, too. And snob appeal. People who don't know enough French to read it in French are going to be awfully flattered by having a simple French title on an edition printed in English. Like cartoons with French captions in American papers. Why just going into a bookstore and asking for a book called *Bonsoir, Maîtresse* will bring a thrill into a lot of drab lives."

"Somebody really should write a book called *Lincoln's Doctor's Dog*," remarked Leppy. "Or maybe they did."

Basil looked around the table. "There's a question I'd like to ask you."

"Yes?" Tony was still smiling and self-confident, but the others looked wary.

"A quite simple question," Basil went on quietly. "Who really wrote the books that were signed Amos Cottle?"

fourteen

Tony's face darkened. "I don't know what you mean. I . . ."

"Don't deny it." Basil spoke wearily. "There's far too much evidence for you to deny it now. The letter you are supposed to have written Amos, accepting his first book, was dated January, 1952. The book was published March, 1952. Three months between acceptance and publication. Improbable before 1939, but quite impossible today. It takes six months or more to produce a book since the last war. The rare exceptions are books of especial timeliness commissioned from known writers. Amos's was a first novel by an unknown.

"I suspected that Cottle had medical training when he identified the Islands of Langerhans correctly while we were playing Two-Thirds of a Ghost. Now I know that before he lost his memory the man you knew as Amos Cottle was a young doctor named Alan Sewell. His identification of the Islands of Langerhans proves that he had retained his intellectual memories. His amnesia was personal and emotional as amnesia usually is. Yet in *Passionate Pilgrim* this passage occurs: "As I bent his arm behind his back with all my strength, I heard the dry crack of his tibia." No doctor, however inexperienced or incompetent, would ever write a passage in which the arm bone is described as the tibia. That happens to be a leg bone.

"Cottle was from New England, but passages in his last novel suggest a Middle Western origin. Certain turns of phrase like the hero's last words: 'I want to tell you good-bye.' On the eastern seaboard we say, 'I want to give you good-bye,' or 'I want to say good-bye.'

"During that same game of Two-Thirds of a Ghost, Cottle failed to identify Byron as the author of *English Bards and Scotch Reviewers*. Whoever adopted the name Amos Cottle as a pen name must have known that poem and its author very well for there are two lines in it:

> *'Oh, Amos Cottle! Phoebus! What a name*
> *'To fill the speaking trump of future fame!'*

"The first Amos Cottle, Byron's contemporary, was a writer now forgotten who pandered to the reading public of his day with a mishmash of all the commonplaces of the era, just as the later Amos Cottle did in our day, according to Emmett Avery. Someone with a sense of mischief was gambling on the idea that a generation brought up in progressive schools, both public and private, where, thanks largely to Billy Phelps, more contemporary novels are studied than classics, would never recognize a name taken from one of the great classics of English letters. And how right this gambler was, for no one—not even Avery—recognized the name Amos Cottle. Today *English Bards and Scotch Reviewers* is one of those things students hear about and never read.

"No wonder Avery felt Cottle's work was a fad and a fraud, a pastiche of every bad novel of the last thirty years. The whole Amos Cottle personality was a pastiche and a fraud, one of the great literary hoaxes of all time, and heaven knows literature has produced more colossal hoaxes than any other art or profession—Ossian, Chatterton, Sainte-Beuve. The very device of the pen name incites such trickeries as *Moll Flanders* and *The Young Visiters,* and the girl writer who more recently pretended to have been a sailor before the mast and the man writer who claimed he'd been an Intelligence officer in Germany when he hadn't. The literary mind has a flair for plots and deceptions that is hard to keep within the boards of a book. The psychological similarity of the lie and the tale are acknowledged by children who call a fib a story.

"No wonder Cottle-Sewell didn't do any writing during the three months when Vera lived with him. He had never written anything in his life but a few letters and school exercises. No wonder Tony had to get Vera a job in Hollywood to break up that marriage. No wonder her return threw you all into such a state of dismay. If she lived with Cottle-Sewell for any length of time, she was sure to discover that he was not writing at all and she was the kind of woman who would have blackmailed Cottle-Sewell and the man who was running the racket as soon as she discovered who he was. You had to keep her from finding out the truth.

"No wonder there were no rough drafts or notebooks in Cottle's house as there would have been in the house of a real writer. Just books and carbon scripts and clippings and contracts. No wonder the house was burned down before I had time to search it thoroughly and make sure that Cottle had left no notes at all, not even ideas scribbled on the backs of old envelopes. I would have known then that no writer had lived in that house.

"Which one of you three men wrote those books? The first book was about the Marines. Unlike Cottle-Sewell, Gus did serve in the Marines during the war. On the other hand Lepton quoted with approval the passage that referred to an arm bone as a leg bone in one of his reviews. Obviously his anatomy is weak enough for him to have been the author of the books. Was he praising his own work when he lauded Cottle so extravagantly? Lepton once told me that creative writing was a greater art than criticism which he compared psychologically to vitriol throwing. Would a critic say a thing like that? It sounds more like a creative writer who has been subjected to criticism.

"Whoever wrote the books used certain Western turns of phrase like 'tell him good-bye.' Cottle, an Easterner from Vermont, would have written 'give him good-bye.' So would Gus, a product of New Orleans and New York. But either Tony or Lepton might have written 'tell him good-bye.' Tony hailed from the West Coast originally and Lepton from Chicago, the principal scene of Cottle's last book. On the other hand, the apple woman story is a favorite of Tony's. It also appears in one of the Cottle books and it was singled out for praise in one of Lepton's reviews.

"Why did you need a physical stand-in for the Amos Cottle personality? Because of the TV program? Was it a modern version of Dr. Hale's story, 'My Double And How He Undid Me'? The story where an Irishman who substitutes for a literary clergyman on lecture programs gives the whole show away by getting drunk?

"There's still another possibility. Can it be that all three of you were in this together? Tony and Gus and Lepton? That you were three-thirds of one 'ghost,' as a writer is called when he signs another, more famous name to his work?

"That would explain the peculiar financial arrangement. It was always so hard to believe that a decent agent like Gus Vesey would take twenty-five percent commission instead of ten. But suppose Gus was writing one third of the Amos Cottle books and this was the only way he could get a quarter of the profits openly and legally without any bothersome questions from auditors or income tax people? A quarter because, of course, Cottle-Sewell had to have his quarter, even if he wasn't doing any writing at all. That was paid to him openly and aboveboard as royalties. But Tony Kane got fifty percent of the subsidiary rights because Tony had to be rewarded for his share in writing as well as publishing the books, and Tony had to pay Lepton for his share in the writing. Lepton's payment was the only sub rosa payment in cash, because you just couldn't figure out a way to pay Lepton openly and legally for writing his share of the books he praised as a critic.

"Another odd detail: You were a triumvirate, and what is the most famous triumvirate in history? Octavius Caesar, later Augustus, Mark Antony, and a little man named Lepidus who might have been called Leppy if the Latins had gone in for that sort of diminutive. Gus, Tony and Leppy—three-thirds of a ghost. Like the name Amos Cottle, it was oddly suggestive of a poltergeist sense of humor, a spirit of malicious mischief pervading the whole situation."

Lepton cocked his head to one side. His long, slender fingers played with his coffee spoon. "We'll have to tell him, Tony."

"Leppy's right," said Gus. "We'll have to tell him. Maybe he won't make it public."

"All right," said Tony. "But I want to make one thing clear first. It isn't fraud. Not legally. Even this ten thousand award is being paid to the men who actually wrote the Cottle books. Pen names aren't fraud. You can even sign a contract with a pen name and it's still legal."

"Then you were all three in it?"

"I'll have to go back to 1951," said Tony. "It seems a long time ago. We three were old friends, our parents, friends before us, all brought up in the book trade. I was a salaried editor at a small struggling publishing house run by a nitwit old dreamer, Dan Sutton. Leppy was even worse off—a free-lance critic trying to live on casual book reviews in magazines and newspapers. He'd spilled his guts writing one book he hoped would make his fortune. It didn't. High praise from the critics and a sale in the trade edition of about six thousand copies. Leppy was broke and discouraged. Gus was just out of the Marines with a wife and two small children. He was having trouble getting back into radio. TV was going to kill radio anyway and he didn't think he could adapt his writing to the TV technique. He'd started a literary agency on a shoestring and he was trying to support himself and his family with radio writing, hoping the agency would catch on before radio pegged out altogether. Unfortunately most of the scripts he was getting as an agent were duds.

"We three all met one night in a Third Avenue bar. We didn't see any future we liked. We felt thwarted and bitter. It was Gus who said,

'The hell of it is, each one of the three of us has a pretty good brain and knows everything there is to know about the writing and selling of books. But none of us can find an outlet—a way to use our brains profitably. If only there were some way we three could pool our wits and our knowledge . . .'"

Lepton took up the tale. "It was then that Amos Cottle was born. I got the idea from our names—Gus, Tony and Leppy—the triumvirate. We'd all been trying to write fiction on the side—to pick up a little extra money, even Tony. Now and then one of us would get an acceptance. Just often enough to keep hope alive. The torture of hope. More often we got rejections, and we all three knew that freelance writing is the most heartbreaking trade in the world.

"So, that night I said, 'Volume of production is damned important in writing. If you produce enough stuff regularly you're going to wear down opposition sooner or later. That's where most writers fail. They don't produce enough, often enough for their names to be remembered first by editors and later by critics and public. But there's one way we could get around that. We could pool everything that we three write and sign it all with one fictitious name. Then that name would be producing just three times what an ordinary writer could produce in the same time, and the sheer massive weight of that volume of production would force recognition sooner or later.'

"We were just tight enough and desperate enough to think that such a cockeyed scheme would work. And it did.

"We planned every detail as carefully as if we were plotting the grand strategy of a major war. Tony was in a position where he could, with any luck at all, induce Dan Sutton to publish the first book. I had enough prestige as a critic to launch it with a really enthusiastic review. In order to cover our tracks, in case anyone for any reason ever investigated the history and origin of Amos Cottle, Gus should act as his agent. If Cottle ever became really famous, we'd better have a complete record of how he first came to our attention as a writer. The sort of thing you could show to some nosey scholar like Hermione Featherstone or some naïve student who wanted to write a Ph.D. thesis on the *Oeuvre* of Amos Cottle. Hell, someone might even want to write his biography if he really clicked.

"So we decided that Gus should slip the script into the pile of junk Meg was reading for the agency and let her discover Cottle. We'd decided from the beginning that no woman was to be in on the secret.

A secret shared with a woman is no longer a secret. Besides, Meg would make such an honest witness about the way Cottle was discovered, if ever the thing were questioned. The other scripts Meg was reading that night were so bad she was bound to think Cottle pretty good. She just couldn't help discovering him. After all, we are three pretty good writers.

"Of course Tony picked the girl he was training as a first reader to give Amos's script a preliminary reading before he tackled it himself. Her detailed report would be helpful. If ever Cottle's relation to Tony was questioned, that girl's written comments were documentary evidence that Tony didn't know or care anything about the script until he read it himself, that it was just another unsolicited typescript of a first novel by an unknown writer."

Philippa looked at Tony, furiously angry. Meg looked at Gus, hurt and reproachful. Each woman was thinking of the thousands of little daily lies that had kept the myth of Amos Cottle afloat for the last four years.

"I'm sorry." Gus laid a hand on Meg's hand. "We were so damned broke, I had to do something."

"You might have told me," said Meg. "You should have known you could trust me. How can I trust you now, after all the lies you have told me?"

"Not lies. Stories," said Basil. "You must make allowances for the literary mind."

Tony met Philippa's anger with a rancor that equaled hers. "I've always suspected that you rather admired the man you thought of as Amos Cottle, didn't you, Phil? You were so careful to pretend to me that you didn't like him or his books. That amused me. For I'm sure the only reason you admired him was that you thought you'd found a great mind at last and—the poor devil had only half a mind, if that."

"How did you manage the collaboration?" asked Basil.

"Gus wrote a rough draft of one book each year and Tony revised it," explained Lepton. "That's how we got our four books in four years. Both drafts were pretty rough—hardly more than extended plot outlines, but both Gus and Tony are quite fertile in inventing incidents that follow a story line. I'm not. I'm not really a fiction writer. I'm a critic. And—excuse me, Gus and Tony—but any fool can plot. The plots of *Anna Karenina* and *Vanity Fair* are just nothing when summarized in one paragraph. They might both be stories from pulp magazines. It's all in the writing whether or not a thing becomes literature. That's where I came in.

"Tony dictated his stuff to a tape recorder when he was alone in his office. Gus banged his out on an old typewriter in his office. I took these pulpy melodramas and rewrote them in the fashionable style of the moment, with all the tricks of the trade I had learned as a critic. I made them literary. You see, I was saved the effort of inventing incidents, just as Shakespeare was when he rewrote the *Ur-Hamlet* and bits from Plutarch's *Lives* and the Holinshed Chronicles for the stage. Like Shakespeare, I could concentrate all my attention and effort on the manner of the writing."

"Modest fellow, aren't you?" muttered Tony. "I thought the stuff was dreadful. Never could understand why it sold."

Leppy ignored this.

"And where did you ever get Sewell to play the role of Cottle?" interposed Meg.

"I'm coming to that," said Leppy. He continued. "As Cottle's agent and publisher, Gus and Tony could associate freely with Sewell-Cottle and with each other. But as the critic who praised Cottle, I had to keep away from all of them in public, even though we were old friends. I met Gus and Tony secretly, when there was anything to discuss, and I never did meet Sewell-Cottle in person until the evening of the party at Tony's house. It was an especially effective piece of misdirection to be able to say truthfully that Maurice Lepton had never met Amos Cottle. Made me sound unbiased as hell.

"Sewell-Cottle knew all about what we were doing. Gus and Tony had explained everything to him. He seemed perfectly happy about the arrangement. He was getting a far better income than a man without a past could hope to earn on his own and he didn't have to work. Of course he knew less than nothing about writing and the book trade. That's why it never occurred to him that he was in a position to blackmail Gus and Tony by threatening to expose the whole thing unless he got a larger share of the profits."

"I don't see how he could have done that without ruining himself," said Tony. "Amos Cottle, the celebrated novelist, announces that he never wrote a line, that all his books have been written by his agent, his publisher and his most laudatory critic? He would have been exposing himself as a fraud and his income would have stopped right then and there. He couldn't have bluffed us into believing he'd do that—not Amos!"

"One thing I don't understand," said Alec McLean to Lepton. "If your style made these books successful, why didn't you use the same time and energy to write novels under your own name? You wouldn't have had the volume of production and made so much money, but you would have had recognition as a novelist. That means a lot to most writers."

"Dear Alec!" Lepton laughed. "You sound just like a publisher. If you were a writer you would understand. I am one of those unfortunates born at the wrong time and place. I've written novels by myself. They've all been rejected, because with stories of my own invention I cannot enter into the spirit of the twentieth century enough to please its reading public. With the plots and incidents of Tony and Gus it was different. I despise the folk myths of our era and I can't fake faith in them. That sort of faking is almost impossible. Any reader can detect real insincerity, and real sincerity will make even bad writing acceptable. But the Cottle books were perfectly sincere. You know why?

"My very hostility to the literary stereotypes of this age stimulates my critical sense, and therefore I can write parodies of contemporary novels with real relish and sincerity. That's what the Amos Cottle novels were—parodies so subtly wrought that a bonehead like Emmett Avery missed the cryptic humor and took them for honest pastiches while the asinine public thought they were great novels."

Lepton sighed. "Of course the whole thing succeeded far beyond our wildest dreams. We never expected anything like this Bookbinders' Award tonight. We ran into our first snag three months before publication. Someone in TV had heard a rumor there was a pretty hot advertising campaign being planned for a book at Sutton, Kane. He came to Tony and offered five hundred bucks for the author to be interviewed on TV on publication day. Tony stalled him and called a conference.

"The five hundred didn't matter much, but there might be other occasions when Amos Cottle would be asked to appear on TV. There's a lot of money in lecturing and of course a regular weekly TV program is a gold mine. It seemed a pity to miss all that, especially as the TV man said he was interested in a regular weekly program run by a popular author. It couldn't be one of us who would appear as Amos Cottle. We were too well known in the trade. Leppy couldn't admit he was Amos Cottle if he was going to praise the Cottle books in print. Dan Sutton would have got stuffy if he'd found out Tony was writing a book they were publishing under another name. Dan wouldn't have let Tony have terms as good as those Gus was going to demand for Amos through Tony. Dan was a dreamer but he was also a publisher and he didn't get dreamy about contracts.

"Gus didn't want to combine the roles of agent and author. As Amos's agent he could demand better terms for Amos in TV than he could possibly hope to get for himself when everyone in TV knew how broke he was. But if he were acting for Amos, he could easily hold out for good terms, saying that Amos didn't need money and wouldn't settle for less. Besides we all thought our triumvirate should be based on equality among the three of us. If any one personality became the TV Amos Cottle that the public knew, he'd have the whiphand over the other two. He could demand more than a third of the profits and get it. The other two couldn't get rid of the man who was known to the public as Amos Cottle just as networks can't get rid of an actor who has played one character in a series of programs so long he's become that character in the public mind.

"Obviously it would be better if we could get a fourth man who for a fourth share of profits would play the role of Amos Cottle on TV. If he were someone who couldn't write a line himself, he'd never be in a position to take over the property and put the other three out. After all, the writing was just as necessary as the Cottle personality to keep the thing going. The question was how could we find a man without a past who could step into the role of Amos Cottle publicly without dragging any of his own personality behind him?"

"That's where I came in," said Tony. "Mrs. Pusey's husband was a patient in that alcoholic clinic before he died and through the Puseys I got to know Dr. Clinton and heard the weird Caspar Hauser story of the sudden appearance of a man without a memory who had been found on the road and never identified. I asked Clinton to let me see him. The moment I did I thought he was made for the job. He was small and quiet and meek and utterly passive. As long as he never recovered his memory he was perfect for it, and Clinton didn't think there was much chance of his relapsing into alcoholism as long as he was watched carefully.

"He was beaten, resigned, half a man—just what we needed for the robot Amos Cottle.

"I didn't want Clinton to know the truth. So I fixed the deal with Alan Sewell himself. When he was offered a choice of writing or painting as occupational therapy, he was to choose writing. He was to make a certain amount of noise with a typewriter every day in his room copying out the telephone book or anything he liked. Of course he must refuse to show Clinton his work. If after a while Clinton got insistent, Sewell was to tell Clinton that he had bribed an attendant to mail the script to the Vesey literary agency in New York. Even if Clinton didn't get insistent he was to tell him that after about thirty days. He didn't really have to mail anything, of course. We took care of that."

"I did," said Gus. "I went all the way out to Stratfield Post Office and mailed the script to my own office in New York and then planted it in the slush pile for Meg to find and read. Tony insisted on writing letters to Cottle-Sewell about the revisions and contracts just as he would if he were a real author. The carbons he kept in his office and the letters were kept by Cottle-Sewell in a file so there would be a complete record that looked open and aboveboard."

"It was fun writing those letters," put in Leppy. "I could indulge my taste for parody again as I did when I wrote the biographical note for the jacket of Amos's first book.

"After a few years we began to feel we had a tiger by the tail," Leppy continued. "We couldn't let go and of course we didn't want to with so much money rolling in, but the thing had snowballed so it was a little frightening. Tony used Cottle to become a partner at Daniel Sutton, and made the firm Sutton, Kane when Dan Sutton died. Gus, as Cottle's agent, attracted a bunch of other authors, successful but not quite so successful as Amos. Still they made the agency a going concern. I wasn't able to launch a business on the basis of Cottle, as Gus and Tony did, but I did get my share of the profits and began living in a style to which I had never been accustomed before. Vera was a headache but we got rid of her by sending her to Hollywood. Naturally we were upset when she came back, but we'd have found some way to deal with her."

"Someone did," said Basil. "Vera was killed tonight with cyanide. I can only suppose she found out something or pretended to find out something and tried blackmail. She was just naïve enough to blackmail a murderer if he were someone she knew well."

Tony looked at Basil with narrowed eyes. "Now you know the whole truth, you must realize more than ever that none of us three had a motive for killing Cottle-Sewell. Even now he's dead we'd rather all this didn't come out. We still have that posthumous book on the spring list, and for fall there's the rough draft of another book to which Leppy can give the inimitable Cottle touch."

Basil exchanged a glance with Alec McLean. As if it were a signal, Alan murmured something about its getting late and rose.

Outside on the sidewalk a little unobtrusive maneuvering got Alec into Tony's car with Phil and the Veseys. There was no room for Basil or Lepton. They called out cheerful good nights and Lepton hailed a taxi. He gave the driver his address and made no comment when Basil slid into the seat beside him.

Ten minutes later Basil was standing before Leppy's bookcase, looking at the handsome gold-tooled volumes that came long ago from the elder Lepton's bindery.

"Drink?" said Leppy.

"No, thanks."

"I believe I need one." Leppy mixed himself a long drink and came back to the bookcase. "Like to see them?" He turned the key in the lock. "This *Green Willow* illustrated by Warwick Gobel, this *Arabian Nights* with illustrations by Edmond Dulac. They don't print books like this today. Too expensive, and who cares for illustrative art now all representation is unfashionable?"

The paper was thick and white and heavy, the type face clear and decorative. The color prints used many tones of every color, and each picture was mounted on heavy brown paper with a cover of tissue paper to protect it, the title engraved there. "These fairy tales are nice, too," said Leppy. "George MacDonald . . . This Chisholm . . ."

"Yes." Basil's fingertips touched the intricate gold-leaf scrolls embossed on the cloth binding.

Leppy said quietly, "How did you know?"

"Gus and Tony each launched a business through Amos Cottle. Going concerns that will pay for themselves whether Cottle is alive or dead. You're still a free-lance critic. Without Amos Cottle's royalties you have nothing. You knew when Vera came back that she meant to stick with Cottle since she'd lost out in Hollywood. You knew that if she lived with Sewell-Cottle for any length of time she would find that he was not a writer. She'd soon realize he didn't do any writing when she was around and she'd worm the truth out of him when she got him drunk. Then she'd blackmail all three of you, bleed you white. But with Amos himself dead she might never find out the truth and the thing could have gone on for years with his literary executors 'discovering' more and more masses of new, unpublished material. The unpublished Cottleana, notebooks and so forth, would be good for five or ten years, and then there would be all sorts of reprints and library editions. Posthumous writers can be very profitable to their publishers and agents. You were better off with Sewell-Cottle dead."

"But why me? It profited Gus and Tony, too."

"You yourself said the critical mind is the most sadistic of the literary temperaments. You even compared the critic's morbid psychology to that of the vitriol thrower. Murder is a sadistic business so —the murderer had to be a critic, not a hack fiction writer like Gus or a businessman like Tony."

"How did I do it?"

"The poison wasn't in the whiskey or the soda, or the glass that had only a slight trace. What remained? Only one thing. The ice and it was you who served the ice. The delayed action of the poison made us think of a capsule. We wondered about a capsule that would dissolve in either water or alcohol. But there's one thing we all know that dissolves or rather melts in both—ice. It was you who served the ice for the second round of drinks. The poison was in a capsule of ice you brought with you."

"How could I make a capsule of ice?"

"Poison poured into that little hollow on top of an ice cube that appears when the cube is half frozen in the refrigerator. Then water poured over the cube to the level of the compartment in the ice tray, and the whole thing refrozen in the refrigerator. You could have done it at the Shadbolts after they were all asleep that night you spent at their house before the party. You could have brought the poisoned ice cube with you to the Kanes in that insulating paper grocers give their customers for transporting frozen food. You could have put it on top of the ice in Tony's bucket when you picked up the bucket and served ice to Amos with Tony's tongs."

"And where would I get cyanide?"

Again Basil looked at the gold tooling on the book in his hand. "Do they still use cyanide for polishing gold leaf? They certainly did in your father's day. You must have inherited his effects. There'd be some cyanide. And you still carry on bookbinding as a hobby. Did Vera blackmail you?"

Lepton nodded. "Not about Cottle. About my making love to Philippa. That's why I had to follow her this afternoon and force her to take poison—my first act of real violence, something that was repugnant to me but necessary to my own safety, I thought. Phil always sought literary qualities in her lovers. Her intuition was quite sensitive. She had been very friendly with Cottle but she'd begun to doubt his literary taste. The moment she met me she was drawn to me because she realized unconsciously that mine was the mind she had met in the Cottle books, that I was the real thing she had been seeking. I was flattered. It was a kind of recognition and I'd had no other recognition as a novelist from anyone. But—it would have broken up the whole conspiracy if Tony had found out. He couldn't have forgiven me. I was a fool to get entangled with Phil, but . . ." Lepton shrugged. "We all make mistakes. To think that my last words should be a cliché!"

Basil knocked the glass from his hand before it reached his lips.

"You're coming downtown with me now to see Inspector Foyle of the Police Department. By this time I think Alec McLean will be waiting for us in a taxi downstairs. I told him we'd be down in about thirty minutes."

Lepton looked at the spreading stain on the Chinese rug. There was a faint, rank odor of poison in the air familiar to criminologists. "I suppose *I* can plead insanity."

"And probably get away with it," returned Basil. "No one totally outside the literary world is ever going to believe that any literary person is sane."

THE END

>>> If you've enjoyed this book and would like to discover more great vintage crime and thriller titles, as well as the most exciting crime and thriller authors writing today, visit: >>>

The Murder Room
Where Criminal Minds Meet

themurderroom.com

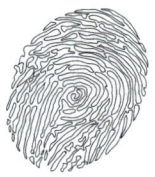